CURVY GIRLS CAN'T DATE SOLDIERS

KELSIE STELTING

Copy Edited by Tricia Harden

Cover concept by Angsty G

Cover design by Najla Qamber Designs.

Sensitivity reading by Darcy Von

 Created with Vellum

To Erin, Dakota, and long distance love that turns into happily ever after.

CONTENTS

ONE

NADIRA

NOTHING LIKE GOING BACK to school after winter break. I couldn't wait for all the body shaming in the hallways, school dances I wouldn't get invited to, and—you guessed it—subpar school lunches I would be embarrassed to eat in front of anyone because of my size.

By ten, I usually had my homework finished and was sliding under the covers. Tonight, at eleven, I was still wide awake. If I stayed up, that meant tomorrow wouldn't come, right? Maybe I could somehow magically fast forward to graduation a few months from now and be done with the horrible social experiment people referred to as "high school."

And since everyone knows anxiety-induced

insomnia calls for extra food, I walked down the stairs in search of a midnight snack. Luckily, the light was already on—Mom must have forgotten it. Then I saw her at the table, hunched over her computer.

I stopped in the hallway, half-surprised, half-worried to get scolded for being up too late. "You're still working?" I asked.

She looked at me from the screen, took off her reading glasses, and rubbed her eyes. "What time is it?"

I glanced at the clock over the stove. "Eleven. I woke up and couldn't get back to sleep, so I thought I'd get a snack." Lies.

But she bought it. Nodding, she closed her laptop. "Could you get me one too?"

"Of what?" I asked, stepping into the kitchen and opening the pantry door.

She waved her hand before going back to rubbing her temples. "Whatever you're getting."

Scanning the scant shelves, my eyes landed on a box of chocolate cereal. I reached for it, but the box was empty. Silently, I cursed my brothers. Were guys seriously incapable of throwing away empty boxes?

I reached for another box of less chocolatey cereal. It felt full, so I took it out. Dad usually did the grocery shopping, but during Brentwood University's basketball season, he wasn't the greatest at keeping everything stocked. Coaching the team kept him plenty busy.

I left the pantry and got a couple of clean bowls and spoons from the dishwasher, then set them on the counter.

"Can you make mine with almond milk?" Mom asked.

I was pretty sure that was the only carton that was left, but I said sure anyway. "What are you working on?" I asked as I filled our bowls.

"A research project about ROTC students." The instant Mom talked about her work, she seemed to brighten. Both she and Dad loved their jobs at the local college—her as the dean of engineering and Dad as the men's basketball coach. "They're some of the brightest at the university, but for some reason, the out-of-staters struggle more than their peers who came from California."

"Why?" I asked, passing her a bowl. I leaned against the counter, taking a bite of my cereal.

The second she opened her mouth, I knew I'd hit pay dirt. Mom could talk about work for *hours*, which would be an excellent excuse to stay up even later. "I think it's a lack of connection caused by moving away from home," she said. "They get here, and they don't know a lot of people, and they can't get home easily to be around their support systems. Plenty of my advisees have told me how difficult it can be. I don't even need a research project to know it's hard on them."

"That makes sense."

She nodded. "But proving causation could have huge implications for program funding, and I have everything in place to get my study started, but one of my students just backed out!" She let out a heavy sigh and set her spoon down. "Which means I have to delay the project—yet again to look for another volunteer."

"Can't you leave one of the soldiers without a partner? Use them as a control?" I asked. Growing up with a professor for a mother, I'd learned to speak research right along with English. Now, as the dean, she still took on research projects she believed would help her students succeed.

"The review board said because if we think connection is going to help them succeed, it's not ethical to let one go without." She rubbed her temples again. "This sets us way back and totally blows my schedule. Classes don't start back until next Monday, and the odds of finding another volunteer to start tomorrow are iffy."

"Why?" I asked. "Can't you just email your advisees?"

"I could. But open rates are low, and even if they opened, no one wants to sign up for daily emails. Even though it would take less than ten minutes to send. It took us forever to find the volunteers we do have." She shook her head and took another bite of cereal. "What a mess. Unless..." Her eyes landed on me, and I instinctively backed away from the counter, taking my bowl of cereal with me.

"Oh no," I said. "No, no, no. Do you remember the time you had me volunteer as a taste tester for the Food Science Department?" I shuddered. "I smelled like garlic for weeks!"

"That was just one time!" she said.

I pursed my lips. "Uh-huh. What about the time I volunteered for the Athletic Training Department? Huh? I thought I'd never walk without a limp again!"

"You got extra money for that! And you walk just fine now," she said. "Plus, no chance of bodily injury on this one."

I raised my eyebrows.

"I'm telling the truth!" she said. "Besides, having some humanitarian-type research on your résumé would look really good to MIT."

"I already got in!"

"But what about the internships you could get once you're there? You'll be competing with the best of the best from all over the world. It won't be like Emerson Academy."

I bit my lip. She had a point. Emerson Academy was one of the top-ranking high schools in the country, but I was still a big fish in a small pond here. College would dump me right into the ocean.

"Plus, it would be a huge help to me," Mom said softly. "Please?"

If we stuck with the nautical references, it was like I was a fish and she'd just jerked the line. (Which was one of the reasons I didn't go fishing with my dad anymore. Cruel and unusual.) "Fine." I set my cereal down with a sigh. "Fine. What do I need to do?"

Her lips spread into a relieved and slightly manic smile, and she got up to hug me. "Thank you, thank you!" She stepped back and rubbed my shoulders. "All you have to do is maintain contact with one of the soldiers for thirty days. One email a day is all that's required. I just have to get a screen-shot of the timestamps when you're done!"

My cringing face relaxed slightly. "That's it? Emails? No word-count requirement or anything?"

She nodded.

"No smell testing? No taste testing? No workout routines?"

She shook her head. "Easy as pie, right?"

I gave her a relieved smile. "Yes. Now I'm taking my cereal to my room so I don't get roped into any other projects."

She laughed quietly. "I'll send you the email tonight. Would you mind emailing your soldier before you go to bed?

"Sure," I said, my foot already on the first stair. "Night, Mom."

When I got to my room, I sat in bed with my cereal and got my phone from my nightstand. There was already an email waiting from my mom with the ROTC student's email address.

From: D.harris@bretnwoodu.edu
To: mitbound321@gmail.com

A.banks@brentwoodu.edu

Be sure to send before midnight.

Love you!
Mom

I glanced at the time on my phone and realized I only had twenty minutes left. Without much time to think, I began typing.

From: mitbound321@gmail.com
To: A.banks@brentwoodu.edu

Hi there,

I just learned about this research project a few minutes ago, so I haven't had a lot of time to think about what I would tell a complete stranger about myself. Here goes nothing.

I should probably get this out of the way first. I'm captain of the Mathletes at my school. Mostly because no one else wanted to be captain, but also because I'm good at it. I got a 35 on the math portion of my ACT and a 23 on the English part. My mom made me retake it, and I got the same score all over again. Writing bad, numbers good.

Despite my terrible writing skills, I still got into MIT, so that's good. I'm excited to get out of California. (Not sure why you came here from out of state. Maybe you could answer that question?)
My mom's really smart, and everyone says I look like her, but it's hard to tell with all the pant suits she wears. My dad's a basketball coach, and my brothers are really good. I think God gave me an extra scoop of brains and forgot the brawn when She made me.

I'm sorry you have to spend the rest of the month writing a high school student, but my mom sometimes talks about students getting paid to participate in research. I hope this is one of those times.

What are you majoring in? I'm planning to study aerospace engineering. Everyone tells me that major is hard work, but they've never seen me try to make small talk.

Best wishes,
Nadira

I read the email over for typos, then added A.Banks's email address and hit send.

My cereal was somewhat soggy, but I finished it up and still couldn't get myself to go to sleep—or stop thinking about my impending last semester at Emerson Academy. The last three and a half years had been...three and a half years.

There hadn't been anything too special to mark the passing time. Sure, there was the girl who'd gotten covered in cupcakes at a homecoming game. Or the time the school bully changed his ways to be the kind of boyfriend my best friend deserved. Or watching my brothers win the state championship in basketball two years ago. But all of that had happened to *other* people. I was only a spectator.

There were only four months—give or take— left of high school, and what did I have to show for it? I was a never-been-kissed Mathlete with a skin condition and a one-way ticket to life as a perpetual nerd. This research project might be the closest I ever got to regular conversation with a male who wasn't in my family. If A.banks was a male...

Out of curiosity, I went to see if I could find whoever he or she was on social media. Mom insisted my brothers and I kept our accounts ultra-private, so all anyone would find if they searched my name was a faded blue avatar. But most people didn't have the privilege (liability?) of a parent so involved in career placement.

That was evidenced by my search for "A Banks." Several people populated the search results, but there were only five in California. One who said they attended Brentwood University. Apollo Banks. The small profile photo showed a guy in front of an American flag. Below it, his location information displayed Austin, Texas and Brent-wood, California.

I clicked through to enlarge his profile picture, and my mouth fell open.

Apollo was in a uniform, looking into the camera, with tan skin and mossy-green eyes and a breathtaking smile with straight white teeth. A small shiver of excitement raced through me, but I quickly tamped it down. My tired mind was messing with me. Guys like that did not date girls like me. Even if their profile did say they were single.

The fact that he was a million miles out of my league and I had barely started emailing him did nothing to deter me, though. In the next half hour, I learned he had a younger sister, an older brother, and looked incredible in hiking shorts. He had several photos with him and his brother atop peaks along the Pacific Crest Trail.

I drank in the information, poring over every word until I noticed the clock telling me it was nearly two in the morning. I might have hated school, but I'd already done plenty to make sure tomorrow would be miserable and require multiple iced coffees. At least I'd be able to see my friends again in the morning.

I clicked off my phone, thinking of handsome smiles and everything I couldn't wait to tell my friends about my pen pal for the month.

TWO

NADIRA

WHEN I WOKE up in the morning, I was exhausted, but thankfully Mom had a strong pot of coffee downstairs, which I poured over ice with plenty of cream and sugar while my brothers did what they could to eat an entire box of cereal between the two of them. They were bottomless pits during basketball season. Meanwhile, I could *look* at sugar and gain weight, no matter how many home workout videos I did.

I found Mom leaning against the counter, looking at her phone, and said, "Any food left?"

"Toast and cream cheese," Mom said, "but Dad's coming home from the tournament tonight, so we should be stocked up soon."

I put my hands together and pretended to pray.

"Oh hush," she said with a chuckle, dropping a couple of slices of bread into the toaster. Then she whispered, "Just in case..." She reached into her purse and got out a couple of twenties. "Can you stop by Ripe and pick up a few easy things?"

"Sure," I said, "not like I'm doing you other favors already. Hint, hint."

She teasingly batted me with her hand. "Brat."

I laughed and began spreading cream cheese over my toast.

"I forgot to tell you," she said. "I can't get out of that meeting Thursday, so I won't be able to make it to the Mathlete competition. I'm sorry, baby."

Disappointment rocked through me, but I tried to keep a brave face.

Not brave enough, though, because she said, "I know it stinks, but career women have to juggle a lot of balls. Some are rubber and some are—"

"—glass, I know," I said. I put the toast together and called to my brothers, "We need to get going."

Mom frowned. "Someday you'll understand."

"Sure. See you later." I picked up my bag and walked to the car, fighting tears. I knew I was over-reacting (probably because I'd hardly slept last night), and I knew Mom couldn't miss work, but it sucked having two parents so involved in their jobs. This was my last year as a Mathlete, my last year in the house, and they'd only made it to one meet. It was better than none, but I'd seen them go to game after game of my brothers'. Just because my sport didn't involve a ball, why wasn't it as important?

I got in my car and turned it on, waiting for my brothers to come out. Eventually, they did. Terrell sat in the passenger seat, and Carver sat in the back, spreading his legs out. Even though he was only a sophomore, he was already well over six feet tall, like our dad. Of course, I'd gotten our mom's short genes and was permanently stuck at five four. I wouldn't have minded a few extra inches to help disguise the extra pounds.

"Why do we always have to leave so early?" Terrell grumbled as he buckled in.

I ignored him and pulled out of the driveway, heading toward Emerson Academy. Ever since Terrell hit his junior year—and began leading the state in points scored during the season—he'd gotten a real attitude.

"You know why," Carver said. "It would be terrible if she missed a *second* of one of Mr. Aris's lectures. She might get dethroned as the Mathlete god."

"Goddess," I corrected, giving him a look over my shoulder. "You're just jealous because you can't add up all the points Terrell's scoring." He kicked the back of my seat, and I gave him another glare. "You're such a child."

He stuck his tongue out, proving my point, and got back to texting. Both of my brothers had a revolving door of girls interested in them. They'd even dated some girls in my class, which felt weird to me. Guys were already so immature; why would a girl want to date someone *younger* than her?

Not that I had anyone lining up to take me out. The closest I'd even been to having a guy's number was Mom giving me Apollo's email address the night before, and he hadn't even emailed me back yet.

As I drove the familiar path to school, I couldn't help but replay everything I'd sent to him. Had I come across as lame? Quirky? Boring? I knew it was a long shot he would even become interested in me, but I let myself fantasize that he might. For once, I let myself pretend that *I* was the girl guys were interested in.

We pulled up to our parking spot, and the boys got out without giving me a second thought. That was fine, because I usually waited for one of my friends to arrive so we could walk in together. Before the school bully, Ryker, fell in love with my friend Cori, I never knew what kind of torture awaited me on the hundred-yard walk into the building, much less in the hallways. Even if Ryker couldn't be our personal bodyguard throughout the day, something was better than nothing.

Emerson Academy prided itself on producing the best students, and that included the bullying category. Even with Ryker off my back, there were plenty of threats, like the two girls who thought they ran the school or my archrival on the Mathlete team, Regina.

Adriel pulled into the parking lot a few spaces down, and I noticed her boyfriend, Carter, sitting in the passenger seat of the car. Even though they weren't on a date, he got out and opened her door for her. It was adorable. And I was jealous. No guy would ever do something like that for me.

Noticing me, Adriel waved, and I waved back, opening my door myself to get out of the car.

"Hey, girl, hey," she called, walking closer to me with her hand linked with Carter's.

I glanced up from their hands to her face. "Hey," I said back, smiling because she seemed so happy. "How was break?"

"Good," Carter said. "Got our trophy in the mail from nationals."

My mouth dropped open. "That's amazing! I didn't know it would come so soon."

He and Adriel had competed together in a national dance competition, just to prove Adriel's old dance instructor wrong. That a plus-size girl *could* dance well enough to own the stage.

"Thanks," Adriel said. She tapped at her phone screen and held out the photo of the award.

I took it in, marveling at the glass like I'd marveled at all of Apollo's photos the night before. "You two definitely earned it... I actually have something to show you too."

"What's that?" she asked, hitching her backpack over her shoulder.

As we walked toward the school, I tapped on my phone screen, pulling up Apollo's profile photo. I passed the phone to her, and she and Carter stared at it.

Adriel giggled and said, "No offense, Carter, but this guy is hot."

"It's not just you. I can see it too." Carter chuckled and pulled on his collar.

Shaking her head, Adriel handed the phone back. "Who is he?"

"He who?" our friend Faith called from behind us.

I waved her over and showed her the phone.

Her mouth dropped open. "A Greek god?" she asked, pretending to wipe drool from her chin.

I shook my head. "My new pen pal."

Each of them gave me a confused look, and I explained Mom's research project and how I'd gotten voluntold into participating at the last second.

"Sorry," Carter said, "I have to go. Besides, I'm not the best at girl talk." Carter kissed Adriel on the cheek and waved goodbye to us.

"See you," she said, then turned to me and clapped her hands together excitedly. "Your mom is the best wing woman ever."

Faith nodded. "Maybe this is your chance to make our New Year's resolution come true."

I closed my eyes, thinking of the silly promise I'd made—that I'd have my first kiss by the end of the year. It seemed bleaker and bleaker every day, and it was only January 3. "I don't think so. I'm just going to enjoy looking at his picture and move on."

The warning bell rang, and I told them goodbye so I could grab my books from my locker.

Standing next to my locker, though, was Tatiana

and one of her many boyfriends, connected at the lips.

Ugh.

Quickly following my disgust, there was the jealousy. Why did relationships seem so easy for people like her? She wasn't nice—not in the slightest—but she still had guys all over her. The only thing I could gather was that being nice didn't matter; looking good did.

I kept my eyes off them as I hurriedly got my books and left. They didn't even notice I was there.

THREE

NADIRA

STEPPING into the math room was like a breath of fresh air. It felt like the closest thing to home I had at Emerson Academy. Seats were assigned, so I always knew where to sit, and Mr. Aris had decorated the room simply, with a few posters of famous mathematicians spread about.

Two things are infinite: the universe and human stupidity; and I'm not sure about the universe. – Albert Einstein

---

Beans have a soul. – Pythagoras

Mathematics reveals its secrets only to those who approach it with pure love, for its own beauty. — Archimedes

If I had more time, I would write a shorter letter. – Blaise Pascal

"Where were you last night?" I muttered to Blaise's portrait hanging over my desk, thinking of the rambling email I'd sent Apollo.

"Are you talking to yourself again?" Regina asked from the seat next to me.

I glared at her. "Are you talking to *me* again?"

Mr. Aris came into the room then, cutting off Regina's retort as she smiled at him, her nose turning browner by the second.

"Good morning, Mr. Aris," she said.

"Good morning," he said and began passing out stapled packets of paper. Louder, he asked, "How was everyone's break? Did you spend it doing math or more boring things like beach vacations?"

I chuckled while the rest of the class stayed silent. Most people didn't like Mr. Aris—aside from brown-noser Regina—but that was probably because he taught some of the hardest subjects at Emerson Academy. I, on the other hand, adored him as a teacher. He was tough, but fair, explained things well, and gave clear guidelines. Not like English, where the teacher could ask for your *opinion* and still tell you you're wrong.

"This is a short assessment," he explained. "We'll be digging deeper into the material this semester, and I want you to be able to see how far you've come at the end of the year."

"Great idea!" Regina said, as though Mr. Aris had invented the concept of a pre-test himself.

"Thank you," he said, not even looking up from his stack. "Now, I'll give you the entire period to work through it. If you finish ahead of time, you can get out a book and read silently. If you don't have a book, you may have ten minutes to visit the library and pick one." He passed out the last of the papers and then came to my desk. "Hey, Nadira, can you come to the hall with me?"

"Oh, sure." I immediately worried that I'd done something wrong, even though it was only the first day back from break. My heart beat quickly as I followed him out, feeling like everyone's eyes were on my back.

We stepped into the empty hallway, and the door echoed as he closed it.

"Am I in trouble?" I blurted nervously.

He chuckled. "Not at all. In fact, the school board just approved funding for my travel to a research conference at MIT."

My eyes lit up. "You have to go on a tour to see the campus! You know they have a nuclear reactor there, right?" I'd only been to MIT once on a tour, but it had felt like a magical place. I couldn't wait to go there in the fall.

He chuckled. "Don't start quoting the brochure to me. I'm still a Harvard fan, through and through."

"Only because you haven't toured MIT," I retorted.

Shaking his head, he said, "Don't make me change my mind about what I'm going to say next."

"What's that?"

"I also got budget approved to take two of my brightest students with me to the campus. You're one, and Regina is the other." He looked at me, waiting for me to be excited, and I was, but Regina?

"That's... great," I said, forcing joy into my voice. "When are we going?"

"During spring break. I'll send an email to your parents to let them know, but I wanted to tell you the good news!" He reached for the door. "I better let Regina know."

I walked through the door, feeling everyone's eyes on me as I went back to my seat and he called Regina out to the hall. That was fine because I had the perfect distraction in front of me. I got a pencil out of my backpack and dove head first into the math problems. It was the best way to forget the worst class of the day coming up next.

FOUR

NADIRA

YEARBOOK WAS my least favorite class. I'd joined because it counted as an art class, but everyone else signed up so they could put pictures of themselves across the pages. Plus, instead of holding a vote amongst the student body, the yearbook class assigned the "best" and "most likely to" pages every year. And that torturous day was today.

Mrs. Johnston teetered to the front of the classroom in too-tall designer heels and began writing the list on the board. Best Smile. Best Hair. Most Likely to Become President. (We'd actually had a few U.S. presidents graduate from Emerson Academy, and even some foreign exchange students who went on to become prime ministers.)

I sat behind my computer, looking up at the

board and wishing I was literally anywhere else. If I had a choice between sitting in front of a room full of middle schoolers who'd pick on me for my vitiligo and being in this room, I'd say, hello middle schoolers.

Not only did seeing the "bests" every year remind you of who the beautiful people were, but *not* seeing your name in the yearbook reminded you that you weren't. Because, let's face it—most funny never went to the actual funniest person. It always went to the hottest guy who could make you laugh sometimes.

Mrs. Johnston clapped her manicured hands together and said, "Who wants to nominate someone for Best Smile?"

Isabella raised her hand high and then said, "Obviously, Tatiana needs to get that title."

Tatiana batted her hand and pretended to be surprised. "Are you sure, Bella?"

Now would have been a good time to bring up the fact that barf bags should be available at every desk.

Isabella wrapped her skinny arms around her friend. "I couldn't imagine anyone more beautiful, inside or out."

Mrs. Johnston put her hands over her surgically

altered chest. "How sweet to see girls lifting each other up. Any objections?"

The room stayed silent, not that anyone would willingly encounter the wrath of the IT girls. (That was what my friends and I called Isabella and Tatiana since they practically ruled the school.)

Mrs. Johnston led the class through the rest of the categories in which beautiful people were celebrated and regular people, people like me, were reminded of just how worthless we were.

At the end of the list, Mrs. Johnston said, "We usually create a wild card category each year. Last year we had 'High School Sweethearts Most Likely to Live Happily Ever After' for Beckett Langley and Rory Hutton. Any suggestions for this year?"

Tatiana raised her hand, and when Mrs. Johnston pointed at her, she turned in her seat and looked at me. "I think we should have a 'Most Unique' category, and I nominate Nadira. There's *no one* like her."

Suddenly, all eyes were on me. This was even worse than being ignored for all the other categories. Instead of being skipped over, I was being focused on for nothing other than my skin condition. I knew it wasn't about my personality because most of the people in the room didn't know anything about me, other than the fact I was a Mathlete, and they bullied me mercilessly for it.

I hated the white patches on my black skin almost as much as I hated the stretchmarks that spread over my hips and stomach. Almost as much as I hated the girls in front of me.

Almost as much as I hated that I wished I could be like them.

While everyone proceeded to give me the pity vote of "Most Unique," Isabella and Tatiana got the beauty vote. They never had to worry about going to a school dance without a date. They never had to stand with their friends and worry about being the DUFF. Never had to deal with children staring at them at the mall and loudly whispering questions to their parents.

The bell rang, and Mrs. Johnston said, "Let me take a picture of the board before we open the door! Remember, this list is *top secret*! No one outside of this room finds out."

As though the winners of any of the categories would come as a surprise.

She snapped a picture with her phone and quickly erased the board while the rest of us packed up our bags. I kept my head down as I walked past my classmates and out the door. When you looked like me, the only way to be safe was to disappear, to make sure no one noticed you at all.

In the hallway, I kept my eyes peeled as I usually did. For allies, for enemies. I brushed past Tatiana greeting her momentary boyfriend (again) with a very public display of affection, then found my friend Des.

We were complete opposites, had been since we met in sixth grade, so it was somewhat of a miracle we'd come to be such good friends at all.

"How was yearbook?" she asked.

I rolled my eyes toward the ceiling. "It was pick-the-best day."

She shuddered. "Let me guess. Tatiana won Best Smile?"

I pretended to be shocked. "How did you find out? Mrs. Johnston said it's *classified information*."

Giggling, Des said, "Some things never change. Can you believe this is our last semester here?"

"Graduation can't come soon enough," I muttered. I only had one semester—two quarters, eighteen weeks—until graduation and early admittance to MIT. (Not that I was counting.) People on the East Coast were different, colorful, unlike our whitewashed private school. Heck, even my black skin was fading away at Emerson Academy.

"I don't know," she said. "I feel like we should savor our last semester, right?"

"That's what people who had fun in high school want you to do," I said. "The rest of us know it's best to just keep your head down and make it out alive."

We reached the English classroom and took our seats near the front. From her desk, Mrs. Peters looked at us and said, "How was your break, girls?"

A lot of people thought Mrs. Peters was strange, but I liked her. She wasn't as obsessed with beauty as everyone else seemed to be—any time I caught a peek of her legs, they were unshaved, and she never seemed bothered that her glasses were out of style. Like if she just waited patiently enough, they'd come back in vogue—not that she'd care.

"Rang in the new year with milkshakes," I said.

She chuckled. "Not bad."

As more students came into the room, she greeted them, and I got lost in thought about Apollo. Part of me wished I'd never seen his social media profile. Now just the thought of writing to him made me all jittery. I didn't talk to guys who looked like him. Even when Dad brought his players over to the house to watch film, I just stayed in my room.

Guys said the meanest things about girls they didn't find attractive. Like somehow not being pleasing to the eye made us deserve verbal vitriol.

Rustling sounded around me, and I looked to see everyone was packing up their bags.

"What are we doing?" I asked Des quietly.

"Computer lab," she said, hitching her backpack over her shoulder.

"For what?" I began packing my bag too and followed her out of the classroom and into the hallway where Mrs. Peters reminded us to be quiet as to not disturb the other classes.

On the way, Des whispered to me we were supposed to write a self-portrait. *Great.*

She and I sat at two corner computers, and I couldn't help but check my email when Mrs. Peters wasn't looking.

My mouth fell open. Apollo had written back.

I glanced up to make sure I had time, and when I found Mrs. Peters helping another student, I clicked it open.

From: A.banks@brentwoodu.edu
To: mitbound321@gmail.com

Dear Nadira,

It's nice to "meet" you. I've only been at Brentwood U for a semester, and I haven't had much of a chance to meet anyone outside of my roommate or ROTC. I stayed on campus over break and I have more time than ever now, but everyone else is at home until next week when classes start up again. It's nice to have someone to email with, and I don't mind that you're in high school. :) I was there just a few months ago.

You asked what brought me to California, and I have to give a boring answer and say that I'm a legacy student at Brentwood U. My dad went here, and my grandpa did too. I'll be the first person in my family in the military though. Air Force, specifically. I'm majoring in chemical engineering, and I'll be an officer when I graduate. (If you don't know much about rankings, it means I'll have a little more authority than if I just enlisted. And some extra pay too.)

Why did you choose aerospace engineering?

V/r,
Apollo Banks

PS - I thought I should include a picture of me so you know who you're writing to. Can you send one back so I know you're not a random 35-year-old man who Dean Harris accidentally let in on the study?

Next to me, Des sucked in a gasp. "Holy hotness, who is *that*? And why are you smiling so big?"

Fighting the heat in my cheeks, I looked around to make sure Mrs. Peters wasn't looking. Thankfully, she was still helping someone else across the room.

"It's my new pen pal," I explained, giving her a shorter version of the story I'd told my other friends this morning.

She squealed quietly and shook my arm. "Dir, what if this is how you two fall in love? Can you imagine telling your kids someday?"

"Whoa, whoa, whoa," I said. "Hold up. First of all, I'm not having children. And if I do, it's child, singular. Second of all, I don't even know if he's looking for a relationship. And third of all, if he *is* open to a relationship, there's no way he'd even look twice at a girl like me." I frowned, thinking of my "Most Unique" moniker and the girl who'd given it to me. "He'd go for someone like Tatiana or Isabella without a second glance my way."

My heart ached as I said the words, because I knew how true they were. No one had ever asked me on a date. No one had flirted with me. I was just a Mathlete. The girl you talked to for answers on the math homework, not for a date to the dance.

Des gave me a look. "You need to be nicer to yourself. Can't you see that you're beautiful?"

I rolled my eyes. Des had been on a self-love diatribe ever since discovering Lizzo and Meghan Trainor, but it wasn't like I could flip a switch and stop seeing my patchy skin colors or the way my school uniform pulled tightly around my stomach.

She pursed her lips together. "When this guy sees you, he's going to think you're stunning. Mark my words." She turned back to her assignment, not even entertaining any more arguments from me.

Des might have mastered self-esteem, but I sure hadn't. There was no way I could ever let Apollo see me. If he kept talking to me, it would only be because of a research project. And knowing he was only speaking to me because he was forced to was even worse than being rejected.

While everyone else worked on their self-portraits, googled what v/r meant. Apparently, it was a common sign off in the military meaning "very respectfully" or "virtual regards." I liked that he'd used it with me.

With a smile, I began typing an email back.

From: mitbound321@gmail.com
To: A.banks@brentwoodu.edu

Dear Apollo,

Thanks for emailing me back. I hope you're having a nice break. I'm supposed to be working on an English assignment, but this is writing too, right? Besides, emailing is a much more practical skill than writing an essay about myself. Although... I guess I am kind of writing about myself.

I'm majoring in aerospace engineering because I've been interested in space for as long as I can remember. One of my grandparents got me an astronaut costume for Halloween, and that was it. I've watched about a million documentaries, and recordings of every historical rocket launch—the moon landing, Apollo 13—I cried for weeks after watching The Challenger explode.

I want to be a part of something bigger someday, something that draws states and countries and millions of people together. I'm hoping aerospace engineering can do that for me. I guess I've always wondered if there's something more for me out there. I don't know. Maybe I just feel a little out-of-place here on Earth.

Since I know why you came to California, now I want to know why you joined the military. Did you know anyone outside of your family who joined, or did the school recruiters convince you with that *awesome* swag? It sure is hard to say no to free pens and notepads. ;)

Nadira

PS-I'm not a 35-year-old man.

With the email still in my drafts, I used the trick every student knew to get past the school's blocks on social media and logged into my page. But when I saw my profile picture, I frowned. It was a photo from homecoming, but the thought of sending it to Apollo made me queasy. I could easily see the indent of my belly button where the silk dress strained against my stomach. My double chin was on full display. The dimpled fat under my arms was as prominent as ever. I couldn't send that picture to him. My fingers wouldn't even move to let me download it.

Why did he have to ask for a picture of me anyway? This email program was for a *research project*. Not a dating profile. Why did it even matter what I looked like? I could send him a picture of any person on the internet and be fine. Be more than fine, because I wouldn't have to deal with the change in tone that would surely come after he found out what I looked like—if he even kept emailing me at all.

And that would affect Mom's research... She would be so upset if I was the reason her research project was ruined. Sending him a picture of someone else would just be helping her, right?

I was grasping at straws now, but I knew one thing for sure: I didn't want him to see me as Nadira. I wanted him to see me as one of the beautiful girls. Someone he would actually be interested in instead of repulsed by.

Someone like Tatiana.

I went to her profile and downloaded her profile picture. No matter how much I wanted to deny it, she looked beautiful, with her relaxed hair falling around her face in pretty layers and her perky chest highlighted by the low neckline on the dress she'd worn to the winter dance. Her smile was bright, and her eyes even had a spark of light that looked like it could have been edited in.

This was what I wanted Apollo to see when he thought of me—someone beautiful. Someone worthy of a guy like him.

I attached it to the email and hit send.

FIVE

NADIRA

AFTER SCHOOL, we had our first Mathletes practice of the semester. Since only five people had joined Mathletes this year, Mr. Aris always treated us to our favorite coffee order.

I picked up my iced coffee filled with cream and sugar and sat as far away from Regina as I could. Still, it didn't stop her from serving up an underhanded compliment.

"I get so tired of drinking black tea," Regina said loudly to me. "I'm so in awe of how you just eat and drink whatever you want."

The three guys on the team were completely oblivious, and Mr. Aris had just gone to get extra batteries for the buzzer system, so I was on my own. I rolled my eyes and sat down at the table, checking my phone for another email. Ignoring her seemed like the best option at this point.

Arguing with Regina would only give her more fuel and more chances to be mean. I had bigger things to worry about. Like had Apollo seen the message I sent him? Would he reply today? Or would he stick to the one email a day requirement and call it good?

I felt a little guilty for using Tatiana's picture, but not guilty enough to send a real photo of me. In one month's time, the research project would be over. In four months' time, I would be on the East Coast, thousands of miles away from him and a distant memory in his email inbox.

Mr. Aris breezed into the room, holding a packet of batteries. "Sorry, took a while digging through the supply closet to find the right size." He began plugging them into the equipment, while a freshman on the team, Donovan, pressed the end of a D battery to his tongue.

Another guy chuckled and said, "Ha, you had a D in your mouth."

"Come on fellas," Mr. Aris scolded, humor in his eyes.

They guffawed even more.

I shook my head. Teenage boys were some of

the grossest beings in existence. I should know—I had two brothers who left towels stiff enough to break in half.

Mr. Aris plugged in the buzzer system and handed each of us a button to press. "We have three meets left this season—four if we can qualify for the state competition, which... drumroll please."

Donovan banged loudly on his desk.

"Will be held at Emerson Academy for the first time in forty years!" Mr. Aris announced. "If we don't qualify, we'll be charged with volunteering. Otherwise, we can pass it off to your classmates and focus on winning."

Regina clapped excitedly, but I only nodded. We had plenty of work to do if we wanted to make it to state. We'd been sloppy at the last meet, struggling especially with logarithms and geometry proofs.

"We're practicing sudden death today," Mr. Aris said. "It's been a while since we've ended a match in a tie, but you never know. Since Nadira's the captain, she'll be going head-to-head against the other team's captain. To practice, you'll each compete against Nadira, and whoever comes out on top wins a prize." He bent to retrieve something from behind his desk, and when he picked it up, I couldn't help but laugh.

"A pie?" Donovan said.

"No," Mr. Aris replied. "A *pi*." He lifted the lid to show the pi symbol cut out of the crust.

"What flavor?" I asked.

"Only the best: peach."

It was *on*.

For the next hour, we faced off against each other, seeing who could get the most points on the whiteboard. Soon, it came down to Regina and me.

Mr. Aris held his fist to his mouth, pretending to have a microphone. "In the final two, we have Nadira Harris, Mathlete captain and soon-to-be aerospace engineer. On the other side, we have Regina Granger, Emerson Academy senior soon to dominate the world of finance. Who will win? Let's find out!"

The boys drummed their hands on the table, but I focused in on the question Mr. Aris was writing on the board, furiously copying it down to my own page.

My mind buzzed, pulling equations and patterns from the problem and from previous classes. I took turns tapping furiously on my graphing calculator and writing on the page, so close to cracking the equation.

A buzzer sounded and I looked up, seeing Regina's pompous smile. But instead of waiting for her answer, I kept solving. Any good Mathlete knew that you never stopped until you knew the answer.

She read off her response, and Mr. Aris pushed his own red buzzer, showing the answer was wrong.

"Nadira, you have fifteen seconds," he said.

I kept writing and typing and with three seconds to spare, I buzzed in and read my answer from my page.

With a grin, Mr. Aris extended the pi(e) my way. "Winner, winner, peach pie dinner."

I sat at the kitchen counter, my iPad propped up with Cori on the screen while I ate my pie and helped her with math homework.

Except, we'd finished her homework half an hour ago, and now we were just snacking and chatting. My brothers were in the other room, tearing into the pizzas I'd gotten at the store, completely oblivious to us.

"You have to send him the right photo of you," she said.

I shook my head and took another bite of peachy goodness. "Not a chance."

"Dir, come on."

"What?" I asked, getting frustrated. "Why does it matter that he knows what I look like anyway? Huh? No part of the research assignment mentioned photos."

"It's not *required*, but what if he likes who you are and wants to take you on a date?" Cori asked. "What then?"

"What interest would he have in dating me anyway? I'm moving thousands of miles away this summer."

"Long distance relationships can work," she said.

I shook my head. "What is it with you guys and being so obsessed with relationships anyway?" It seemed like all day my friends had questioned me about Apollo, making the situation into more than it needed to be. He was just a cute guy whose picture was fun to look at. "I'm happy you and Adriel found the loves of your lives—I am—but a relationship's not that high on my radar. My parents lived 'happily ever after,' and where are they now? They're both working overtime, not even spending time with each other!"

Cori frowned. "It's not that."

"What is it then?" I asked, genuinely curious. I

didn't need more pressure to date than my perpetual singleness had already given me.

"We know how much we like our boyfriends. We just want you to be happy."

"And I can't be happy on my own? I need a man?" I had a weird, twisty feeling in my gut even as I said it.

She gave me a suspicious look. "Are you happy?"

I looked down at my pie for a moment, then back at her. "Why don't you let me worry about that?"

"Okay," she said gently. "Can I just say one more thing before we drop it completely and forever?"

I dropped my chin and gazed at her. "Am I going to regret saying yes?"

She gave a halfhearted smile. "I just want you to know that I think you are absolutely beautiful, and I think you deserve to feel comfortable in your own skin. Any guy, if you choose to have one, would be lucky to have you."

My eyes stung because she'd landed on everything I'd been struggling with. Growing up with vitiligo wasn't easy. Not when my pubescent years were filled with people calling me a Dalmatian or

Michael Jackson or a Rorschach test. Top it off with being fat and getting completely ignored by members of the opposite sex, and you had the cherry on top of an I-feel-ugly-all-the-time sundae.

She brushed a strand of wavy red hair behind her ear. "I better get going, though. I told Ryker I'd call him."

I waved at her and said goodbye before ending the video chat. Why did I feel so bad? Why couldn't I just see for myself what my friends said they saw in me?

Not finding any answers, I packed up my school stuff and went upstairs to get ready for bed. After a quick shower, I changed into my pajamas and lay down, checking my email for the thousandth time to see if Apollo had replied.

He had.

SIX

NADIRA

From: A.banks@brentwoodu.edu
To: mitbound321@gmail.com

Dear Nadira,

That costume must have been really good to inspire an
entire career. Once you're a famous astronaut or start a
new colony on Mars, I'll brag and say I knew you
before you got famous. But, you know, not in the Challenger, Christa McAuliffe way.

As for me, my story of how I decided to join the Air
Force isn't quite as interesting. I played football in high
school, and I was an offensive tackle. Basically, my

entire job was to block guys who tried to get our
running back and take hits for him if I could.

I wasn't amazing or anything, not good enough for a
college scholarship, but I loved playing football. Mostly
because I loved being part of a team. When we were
out on the field, it was all about the game. There wasn't
any drama about who was dating who or who had the
best car in the parking lot. We all worked toward the
same goal, putting the good of the team above
ourselves.

Then an Air Force recruiter came to the school and
talked to our class, and without even knowing me, he
spoke to everything I loved about football, but in a military context. I'd been planning to study engineering in
college, and when they told me about ROTC and helped
connect me with the ROTC program at Brentwood U,
everything just fell into place. I don't believe in coincidences. I was meant to be here, doing what I'm doing.

Added bonus, I have a guaranteed job after graduation
and no student loans. Grandpa promised to pay for my
college if I went to Brentwood U, so that made him
happy that the bill was already taken care of. My mom

wasn't as thrilled though. I think she heard military and immediately thought war and saw me dying in battle. She got so mad she hasn't talked to me since I started at BU... I'm hoping she comes around someday.

How do your parents feel about you being an aerospace engineer? Not worried about rocket ship explosions?

V/r,
Apollo

PS - Wow, you are absolutely beautiful. Are you sure you want to slum it emailing with a guy like me?

I read over his words, drinking them in like a thirsty woman in the desert. Compliments? Nice conversation? I'd take it. And then when it came to the last line, I couldn't help but smile. So this was what it felt like, having a guy think you're beautiful?

No one but my parents or friends had ever called me that. And for him to think I was "slumming it" with him? It gave me a strange, heady rush. Sure, he thought I looked like Tatiana, but this relationship was virtual. For fun. He could picture her while getting to know *me*. The real me, not the me he expected after seeing my looks.

I tapped reply on the email and started typing.

From: mitbound321@gmail.com
To: A.banks@brentwoodu.edu

Dear Apollo,

I don't play sports, but when you explain football like that, you make it sound way more endearing than a bunch of guys in tight pants crashing into each other. Who knew you were a poet? I'm on the Mathlete team, and even though we play as a team, it's really an individual game. And the drama never stops. There's this girl who wanted to be captain instead of me, so she's always trying to score more points than me to prove she's better than I am. Funnily enough, it just helps everyone win.

My mom's the academic type, so she's really happy I'm going the engineering route. My dad always says what makes me happy makes him happy. As long as I'm trying my hardest and excelling in what I'm interested in, he's okay with that.

I'm really sorry about your mom. If she's afraid to lose you, cutting you off like that seems counterproductive. Like she's wasting the limited time she thinks she has left. I know it's not that simple, though. Are you close to your dad or grandpa? Siblings maybe? I bet it's lonely being in a new town without anyone to talk to. It's going to be weird for me going to school out of state next year. I'm worried about what it will feel like to be alone.

Sincerely,
Nadira

PS – Thank you, but I'm definitely not "slumming it" with you. :)

Soon after I sent the message, a soft knock sounded on my door. I looked up to see my dad peeking his head into my room.

"Hey!" I said, sitting up. "I feel like haven't seen you in weeks!"

"These tournaments are tough stuff." He came in and gave me a hug, then sat on my bed.

"How'd the games go?" I asked.

He shrugged, rubbing his hands over his face. He looked tired but excited at the same time. "We placed third in the tournament. Not bad. I'm hoping we can improve by the time the conference tournament comes up."

"I'm sure you will." I drew my knees to my chest, wrapping my arms around them and the blanket.

"We got a call from Mr. Aris about the trip to MIT." He rubbed my forearm. "That's amazing, Dir!"

My lips spread into an easy smile. "I'm definitely not turning down another visit to Cambridge."

"This is what it's all about. You be the best and surround yourself with the best, and you'll be amazed at how far you go."

His words made my heart beat faster, and I imagined he had the same motivational effect on his players. "Thanks, Dad."

"Any time." He stood from the bed. "I need to go say hi to the boys. Make sure they get off the video games." He began walking away, then paused in the doorway. "Oh, and thanks for helping Mom with her research project."

I smiled and shrugged. "It's not that big of a deal." Especially considering who I got to message for a month.

"It is," he replied. "You're an amazing young woman."

I didn't quite feel amazing, but I settled back into my bed as he left, and I fell asleep dreaming of the handsome guy in front of the American flag, entering into a fantasy world where he could someday be mine.

SEVEN

NADIRA

EMERSON ACADEMY HAD a uniform for Mathletes. Or rather, a jacket. A navy-blue corduroy one
(which always showed any speck of lint). The
Emerson Academy seal was emblazoned on the
front pocket and the words Emerson Academy
Mathletes stood out in bright gold letters on the
back.

I plucked it from the hanger in my closet and
felt the fabric ripple under my fingertips. Most of us
didn't wear them to school and chose to only put
them on once we were in the safety of the school's
white van, surrounded by other Mathletes.

Not Regina, though. She wore hers all day, not
caring about the comments people slung her way.
Although we normally didn't get along, I had to

admit I admired her confidence. And maybe I was baffled by it too. I wondered why she insisted on wearing it when skipping it would result in much less notoriety.

Shaking my head, I folded the jacket and stuffed it in my backpack, along with a small lint roller. As I walked down the stairs, I caught the hints of bacon frying and moaned. I loved it when Dad was home. So much better than toast with cream cheese.

He stood in front of the stove, teasing the bacon in the pan. The crisp crackles of sizzling grease hit my ears, a comforting sound all its own.

He looked up from the skillet and said, "Morning, baby girl."

"Morning." I glanced around to see if Mom was around, but she was nowhere to be seen.

"Mom left for work already," he said.

"Oh." I slid into a bar stool at the island. "How was morning weights?" I asked him. His team had to work out from five to six in the morning every day to get strength training in before classes started. That on top of their afternoon practices had to be brutal.

"Good," Dad said. "You have a Mathlete meet today, right?"

"Yeah, I do." I perked up, flattered that he even remembered.

"I'm going to see if I can get Tom to take over practice so I can make it."

My lips spread into a smile. His assistant coach was more than capable of handling one practice. I just hoped he followed through on his word. "That would be great. The meet's at Clearwater. And you know they always have people come in through the west entrance of the school."

He nodded, bringing the bacon from the pan to a plate full of paper towels. Grease immediately spread across the dotted white surface. "What time?"

"Three," I reminded him. Although, one glance at the magnetic whiteboard calendar on the refrigerator showed me I'd already written it there.

Feet pounded on the stairs behind me, and I turned to see my brothers thundering down, shoving each other and arguing over whose cologne was whose.

Carver flamboyantly picked at his hair and said, "You're just jealous the ladies like my scent better."

"Please." Terrell shoved him, making him stumble down the last step. "I got that for Christmas from Nadira. Ask her."

I blanched, not wanting to be in the middle of the argument but knowing my memory could settle it in a second.

Carver leaned over the counter next to me. "Who did you buy that blue bottle of cologne for? Huh?"

I closed my eyes, knowing exactly who I'd given the blue bottle to. "I gave you the blue bottle—"

"Hey!" Terrell yelled.

"—and I got you a green bottle," I finished, pointing at him. "I saw it in the drawer with my brushes the other day."

With a roll of his eyes, Terrell pushed off the table and bounded up the stairs. Dad winked at me and handed me a few pieces of bacon wrapped in a makeshift holder of paper towels.

Carver tried to grab the rest of them, but Dad batted his hand away and gave him a few pieces, then launched an apple at him, testing Carver's reflexes.

Carver snatched it out of the air and said, "Ha!" sticking out his tongue.

"Nice," Dad said, saluting him. "Ready to crush the Bears Friday?"

"Of course." Carver bit into his apple. "Think we can make the point guard cry again this year?"

Dad snorted with laughter. "It's not his fault the tallest guy on his team was only five foot eight."

I shook my head. "Y'all need to pick on someone your own size." It wasn't really fair for that school to even be in the same league as Emerson Academy. They were a small country school farther inland and didn't have the privilege of money like we did.

From behind me, Terrell snorted, and a fresh wave of cologne filled my nose as he sat beside me. "Kind of hard to do when you're six-six."

I rolled my eyes. "Maybe that means don't pick on people."

He tugged a piece of my hair. "Or just you."

I batted his hand away just as Dad lobbed another apple.

Terrell picked it out of the air and bit into it. "Try harder next time, old man."

Dad just chuckled.

I finished the rest of my bacon and said, "We better get going."

"Yeah," Terrell said. "Wouldn't want to keep Mr. Aris waiting."

Dad launched another apple. This one found its mark on Terrell's forehead.

I sniggered as I picked up my backpack and made my way out to the car.

"Have a good day!" Dad called after me. "You're going to do great today!"

"Thanks!" I said and walked outside. As I waited for my brothers in the car, I took off my blazer and put on my Mathletes jacket. Maybe if my dad could believe in me, I could believe in myself.

As I got out of my car wearing the jacket, I felt more self-conscious than ever. The corduroy material itched at my arms and strained around my shoulders as I walked toward Adriel and Carter. As soon as Adriel saw me, she whistled and said, "Work it, girl!"

Blushing, I shook my head and pulled my backpack on so at least it would cover the giant MATHLETE on my back. It was practically a kick-me sign.

"I don't think I've seen this jacket before," she said.

I shrugged off the comment and walked toward the school. Even though it was cold outside, Isabella and Tatiana leaned against Grant's truck, a sad imitation of Ryker's. Why anyone in our school needed a vehicle that got less than ten miles to the gallon was beyond me.

Catching my gaze, Tatiana lifted her hand and waved, cooing, "Hi, Mathlete!"

My cheeks went pink as the rest of them laughed at the word. At me. I kept my eyes on the pavement, trying to block out their laughter.

Next to me, Adriel muttered, "Don't listen to them."

But then Grant called, "Do you ever use your calculator to get off?", making the guys around him guffaw with raucous laughter. "You can spell 'boob' on it."

Carter growled, "Cut it out."

"That's cute," Tatiana said. "How nice of you to share your boyfriend, Adriel. Since we all know Nadira can't get one of her own."

Adriel kept her gaze forward. "Don't react. You'll just give them what they want."

But my fists were clenching at my sides and my eyes were stinging, and I just wanted the ground to swallow me whole.

Carter bit back, "It's called common human decency, Tatiana. Why don't you try it sometime?"

I closed my eyes, knowing what Adriel had said was true. His retort only made them laugh harder at him. At us. At *me*.

As we drew closer to the school, the giant *Ad Meliora* engraved in stone over the entrance mocked me. The phrase meant "toward better things" in Latin and was supposed to remind every student at the Academy that we were always to strive for better.

Except the "better" part didn't apply to every aspect of our lives. We didn't strive to be better people or to treat one another in a better way. No, we strove to be better than others, whatever the cost.

Before we walked inside, I took off my jacket and put it back into my backpack, trading it out for the blazer. I never should have worn it anyway.

EIGHT

NADIRA

WE GOT into the school van that would take us to the Mathlete competition, and I sat in the front passenger seat, the space reserved for the captain. It was the best seat in the car, with enough leg room to fit my entire backpack by my feet. But instead of getting out the English homework I should have been working on, I took out my phone.

One new email from Apollo.

I happily tapped to read the message, my English homework a long-forgotten memory.

From: A.banks@brentwoodu.edu
To: mitbound321@gmail.com

Dear Nadira,

I'm flattered you think I'm poetic. If you could hear it in my Texas twang, you might not find it so lyrical.

I was always a mama's boy, which my siblings love to pick on me for. I have a younger sister and an older brother. My dad's a banker at the biggest chain in Texas, and my mom's a stay-at-home mom. We basically live in Mayberry. There aren't a lot of hiking trails at home like there are here, and we weren't close to a beach either. So I feel like I'm always out trying to soak in what I missed out on growing up.

Last weekend, I went to Seaton Pier because I heard there was good fishing off the dock. Even though the people at BU act like Seaton is the cheap part of town, I loved it. The waters were clear dark blue, like the Air Force colors. I even rolled up my pants and put my feet in the water. It felt wrong not to, you know?

My mom and dad met at Brentwood U, and I can't help thinking that every spot I go might be special to them somehow. Dad's told me a bit, but I wish I could ask Mom about it. I guess it's better not to think about it too much.

What about you? Are you close to your brothers? Your parents?

V/r,
Apollo

I smiled at my phone, hardly glancing up as Mr. Aris started the van and drove us away from Emerson Academy.

From: mitbound321@gmail.com
To: A.banks@brentwoodu.edu

Dear Apollo,

My parents met in college too, although, they went to a small private college in Illinois. I've never visited it before, but I think someday I might like to. Their jobs brought our family here. I was in sixth grade when we moved to the area, and I met best friends who are more like siblings to me than my own brothers.

My two best friends are Cori and Desirae, but we call

her Des. I'm pretty sure Des is going to be a famous singer someday. Cori's going to rule the world, whatever she does. And we met two other girls this year, Faith and Adriel, who are the sweetest people ever. Whenever I get made fun of at school, they're always on my side.

As for my brothers... I love them to death, but it feels like we live in different worlds a lot of the time. They're obsessed with basketball, and even though I understand the game well enough, it feels like always being on the outside of an inside joke, watching them and my dad talk about it.

I've gone to a few parties at Seaton Pier, but the last one was busted up by the police. I don't drink, but I was still lucky I got out without being caught. If my parents ever knew I was at a party like that, I'd never see the beach—or the outside of my room—again. We went to the pier a couple weeks ago to get corn dogs and walk around, and I still felt panicked, just from the memory. Pretty sure I'll be lying low until graduation.

My mom is very smart. Analytical. Cunning. And she has a good heart. Even though we should get along the best in our family, sometimes it feels like she just doesn't get it. Like she skipped being a teenager and was born in a pant suit, ready to take on the world without any insecurities or doubts. I've never felt that level of confidence.

Maybe someday.

Sincerely,
Nadira

I sighed as I hit send. I needed to remember who I was. I wasn't the picture of Tatiana I'd sent him. The girl blessed with beauty and charisma. No, I was Nadira, the girl gifted with mathematical skills and literally nothing else. Maybe someday a guy who was more interested in brains than beauty would take notice, but until then it was best to just lie low and not get my hopes up. It was the only way I knew to keep from being disappointed.

I moved to set my phone in my bag, but it vibrated in my hand. This time, though, it didn't signal an email. No, an instant message awaited me, from none other than Apollo Banks.

Apollo: Hey, I noticed you were online.

I stared at the phone as though it were from another planet. Somehow, seeing the letters pop up in front of me, appear on my phone screen, seemed so intimate. So *real*.

Suddenly, he wasn't just words in an email inbox or a requirement for a research study or a photo on a social media page. No, there was a person on the other end of my phone. One who cared enough to message me. Who was waiting for a reply.

Apollo: Are you there?

Nadira: Hey, sorry.

I frantically racked my brain, looking for something, anything, to say that wouldn't let on to the screaming inside my mind.

Nadira: What's up?

Apollo: Just finished walking the path between my classes so I'm ready for Monday. You?

Nadira: On the way to a Mathlete meet. Which classes?

Apollo: Philosophy and human geography.

Nadira: Those don't sound like engineering classes...

Apollo: Getting my gen eds out of the way first. It was my advisor's idea. She wanted me to ease into the harder classes.

Nadira: That's dumb.

Apollo: What do you mean?

Nadira: I mean, you went to college to study engineering. You should at least get to taste it before it's too late to change your major... Who's your advisor?

Maybe I could hint about it to Mom without letting on who'd told me.

Apollo: Dr. Harris. Do you know her?

My lips parted. My mom was Apollo's advisor? I knew she kept on a few advisees so she could interact with students, but this was too real. My fingers hung over my phone screen as I contemplated a response.

Nadira: Yeah, we've met.

Apollo: But next semester, I'll hit the ground running with my engineering classes.

Nadira: Same here. :)

Apollo: Are you excited for college?

Nadira: That's an understatement.

Apollo: Why?

Nadira: I mean, why not? High school is awful. Everyone here has a superiority complex. There aren't that many people of color in my school. I've taken every advanced math class I can get into, and I'm still bored half the time. Not to mention I get asked if I make love to my calculator on a daily basis.

Apollo: ...what?

Nadira: It's a long story.

Apollo: I have half an hour until I need to get to a meeting.

Nadira: Well, in that case... I wore my Mathlete jacket to school today and got made fun of before I even hit the building.

Apollo: Ugh. People are awful. If you went to school in Texas, as beautiful as you are, you would have been homecoming queen.

A nasty pang went through my stomach. He was right. Tatiana had been the homecoming queen, and her friend Isabella was sure to be prom queen. I wished I looked like Tatiana, with her rich russet skin and eyes as wide and charming as a fawn's. Not to mention her narrow hips and thin arms. She could have used my jacket as a parachute —if she'd ever stoop that low on the fashion scale. I bet she checked that all her life-saving devices were designer before ever stepping foot on a plane.

Apollo: I got made fun of a lot my freshman year...

Nadira: Yeah?

Apollo: I was 98 pounds and tried out for the football team.

My eyes boggled at the message. How had that Greek god ever been ninety-eight pounds?

Nadira: WHAT?

Apollo: Uh-huh. I was a...late bloomer. I grew six inches and fifty pounds the summer after freshman year. Got another couple inches and forty pounds the year after that.

Nadira: Wow. Didn't it hurt to grow that much? When my brother shot up from 5'9" to 6'6" I felt like he was always taking Tylenol and hot baths because of the growing pains.

Apollo: I still have stretch marks on my calves and shoulders from it. I hurt all over for like a year and a half...Yeah it sucked.

Apollo: You know, until people stopped treating me like crap.

Nadira: Ugh. Why can't people treat you well because you're a person and not because of how you look?

Apollo: If someone doesn't feel good about themselves as they are, they need to find reasons they're worthy. One way is making themselves look "better" than someone else.

Nadira: What if they are actually better?

Apollo: Everyone has their strengths and weaknesses.

Nadira: Well, math is it for me. I'm screwed.

Apollo: Depends on who you're asking. The people

who build your house. The people who run the stock market. The people who rule the world. I bet they don't think math is such a worthless skill.

Nadira: Yet all the awards that count in high school are based on social standing.

Apollo: Yep. They *really* prepare you for the real world.

Nadira: Do you like college?

Apollo: Yes.

Apollo: And no.

Nadira: What do you mean?

Apollo: It's fun to be on my own. But there's no consistency. One day you have lit class, then next is philosophy. Some days you're up until midnight studying for three tests and the next week you don't even have homework. You meet so many people you can't remember all their names, yet it's hard to make any real connections. It's lonely and chaotic. If I didn't have ROTC, college would be a lot harder than it is.

Nadira: I never really considered that.

Apollo: Yeah?

Nadira: I guess I never thought having freedom could be a bad thing.

Apollo: Me neither. There are definitely upsides too. There aren't really cliques in college. And I don't have to get permission to go on a midnight ice cream run.

Apollo: Sorry, I need to get going. But I'll talk to you soon?

Nadira: Definitely. Have a good day. :)

I rested my phone in my lap, staring out the windshield at the highway passing before us and the houses passing on either side.

Part of me wondered if Apollo would have messaged me if he knew what I really looked like. If he would have talked to me if he had met me as a high schooler.

Then I thought I shouldn't ask questions I didn't want to know the answers to.

NINE

NADIRA

SOON, the van pulled into Clearwater High School's parking lot, and I looked around, quickly recognizing vehicles from surrounding schools. Some we had competed against before, and some I'd only heard of. A small jolt of energy coursed through me as I donned my corduroy jacket and got out of the van.

Mathlete meets were one of the few places I felt at home. Everyone else here understood me in a way not many people did. They saw the fun side of math, the competitive side. I wondered if I would feel the same sense of acceptance at MIT. I hoped so.

We walked through the west entrance, the door

banging open in the wind. I cringed, and Donovan covered his ears.

"Sorry," a woman at a table said. "We're getting that fixed on Friday."

Mr. Aris said, "We do like to make an entrance."

Regina cackled.

The woman gave a polite chuckle and looked over our jackets. "Emerson?" Mr. Aris nodded, and she gave us a welcome packet similar to the ones we got at all the other meets. "Cafeteria is that way." She pointed down the hall.

Not that she needed to tell us. I'd been in so many different schools thanks to the Mathletes, and I'd memorized them all by heart. Sometimes I wished I could try attending a different, bigger school, just so there would be more variety in the people surrounding me. But then I wondered if there would be just another version of Isabella and Tatiana waiting for me. Or if I would have as good of friends.

The problem with my imaginary scenarios was that it was always *me* moving schools. As if I was the problem and not the people around me who liked to make others feel small.

We reached the cafeteria, buzzing with students

from all over the state, and Regina hunted down an open table like a hawk. She dropped her bag down and immediately asked Mr. Aris about the schedule.

He read off the schools we'd be competing against. A few of them were easy, but I blanched when he listed Brentwood Academy.

"They're here?" I asked, looking around for them. I hadn't seen their bus, but it only took two seconds to find the smug group. They were always surrounded by a doting group of parents, and they came with an exorbitant array of snacks, massive coolers, slow cookers, and trays upon trays of food that they never shared with anyone else. "Ugh," I said, turning back toward my own team.

Not only did they show off in the cafeteria, they showed off in the matches with flamboyant pushes of the button and bogus challenges against obviously correct answers. (And if that sounds ridiculous to you, you've obviously never been a Mathlete. They were the *worst*.)

We'd beaten them a handful of times over the last couple years, and they'd handed it to us just as often. Our rivalry in sports like football and basketball was alive and well in the academic realm too.

Mr. Aris quirked one side of his lips and said,

"If you want to be the best, you have to beat the best."

I shook my head. "Did you read that on a poster?"

"Ha ha," he said. "Our first match is against Credence, so let's head down to classroom..." He peered at the schedule. "Twenty-seven."

We left a few things at the table so we could mark it as our own and then left the cafeteria, heading toward our first match of the day. The classroom had been rearranged to have a table up front for each team and a few chairs set up for spectators.

There were a few parents there, but none were my father. My heart sank as I realized how much I'd been hoping to see my dad in one of those chairs. I shook the thought, taking a seat and hoping he could be on his way, just late. There were still a few matches left. Besides, I couldn't focus on Dad right now. I had to keep my attention on doing the best I could.

For the next forty-five minutes, we went head-to-head with the opposing school. They actually weren't bad, but between the five of us and our different strengths, my team came out on top, sealing our first win of the day.

With that match behind us, we went to the next room, and again, I found the seats vacant of my father. Match after match, it went that way, winning but feeling like a loser inside. Dad hadn't made a single one of my meets. Did I need to make it to the state competition for him to see how important it was? Or would that even matter?

I sighed as I took my seat for the final match of the day against Brentwood. We had to go to a larger room than scheduled because so many of their families had come to watch. One person even had a sign with glittery letters that said KICK THEIR MATH.

The sign was lame, but their enthusiasm made my heart ache that much more.

I replaced that painful feeling in my chest with focus, staring down the people at the opposite table and swearing to crush them with everything I had. If they lost, they had their families to lean on. Who did I have but an empty seat?

For the next hour, we faced off in one of the most intense matches of my Mathlete career. For every answer I had, they had one too. For every time we guessed wrong, they were buzzing right on in with the correct answer, and we did the same to them.

Finally, it came down to the last question. The one that would decide the winner and the loser. My pencil scribbled furiously over the provided scratch paper, and when I buzzed in, I spoke my answer clearly, confidently.

But the judge looked at me and said, "That is incorrect."

My heart sank, and I heard Regina sigh beside me. Instantly, the opposing captain's buzzer rang. I closed my eyes, listening to him say the answer I'd gotten wrong. And I knew he was right before the judge confirmed his accuracy.

The judge cleared his throat. "Brentwood Academy wins an incredible match. One hundred twenty to one hundred ten. Great job to both teams."

Tears stung my eyes as I realized maybe I hadn't deserved to have my dad there after all.

We drove home in relative silence. Two of the underclassmen shared a Nintendo Switch, battling against each other in the back seat. Regina helped Donovan with his history homework. And I sat with my forehead against the cool window, wondering how on earth I'd gotten the answer wrong.

Sensing my mood, Mr. Aris said quietly, "It happens to everyone."

I couldn't bring myself to look at him. "I'm the captain. I'm supposed to be better than that."

"Exactly," he said. "You're the *captain*. Not a calculator. You can't always be right. Winning is a team effort, no matter how much you contribute."

Tears stung my eyes yet again, and I closed them to dam the flow. "You should make Regina captain."

From the back seat, Regina instantly said, "I'm up for it, Mr. Aris."

He cleared his throat, readjusting his seat. "No such thing will happen." He spoke to me now, but louder, as if he wanted Regina to hear this too. "I made you captain because you understand what math is all about, Nadira. It's logical. Straightforward. But also a challenge. If you respect math, it will respect you."

I nodded to show I understood, but sometimes Mr. Aris spoke about the subject like it was the love of his life instead of his wife. And if I continued being so pathetic, it might end up being mine as well.

Okay, I was crossing the line into wallowing, and I knew it. I needed to get out of this funk.

I got out my headphones and listened to music the rest of the way, getting lost in the beat until I made my way home. Mom's car was gone, which I expected, but Dad's car was there in the driveway. When I walked in, he was sitting on the couch with the boys, playing video games, having the time of his life.

When he heard me walk in, he turned, his smile falling. "Sorry I couldn't make it, baby girl. One of our players had an emergency come up I needed to help with."

I nodded. Of course, his team, his job came first.

"How did it go?"

"We got second," I said flatly.

"Pretty close to first," he said. "Sounds like you did a good job."

Terrell yelled, "Dad! They're about to get you!"

Dad turned back to the game, playing with my brothers.

I, on the other hand, went to my room and cried myself to sleep.

TEN

NADIRA

ON THE WAY into school the next day, Terrell leaned over to me. "I need your help."

I glanced toward the back seat, wondering why he was being vulnerable in front of Carver, but saw Carver had his ears covered with headphones. If I strained my ears, I could hear fast paced music coming out of the bulky device.

"What's up?" I asked, confused. The last time Terrell had wanted my help was on a math assignment, and he didn't have his folder out in front of him at the moment.

"I'm seeing this girl..." he began.

He wanted girl advice? "Do you know who you're talking to? Carver would probably be more help."

"He's not a girl," Terrell pointed out.

I pressed my lips together. "True. I'll do my best."

"Okay, so I'm seeing this girl, and I want to ask her to be my girlfriend—"

"Who?" I asked. "Is it someone I know?"

Terrell sat lower in his seat. "Never mind. Forget I asked anything."

"Wait, wait, wait," I said. "Who is it?"

He gave me a look before letting out a sigh and saying, "You're not going to be happy about it."

"Is it one of my friends?" I asked, getting worried. The only single two left were Des and Faith, and I wasn't sure how I'd feel about either of them dating my baby brother.

"Not exactly."

"Then who?"

"Tatiana."

It was like all the wind had been sucked out of the car in a single word. How could my brother want to date the girl who'd made it her life mission to make me (and girls like me) completely miserable? Despite the betrayal, my sisterly instinct kicked in, and strong. I didn't want Terrell to be just another one of her conquests—making out in front of the lockers one day and a castoff the next.

"You like Tatiana?" was all I managed to say.

He shook his head again, reaching for his own headphones. "Forget it. I thought you might be able to help me with what would impress a girl, but obviously it's too much to ask for any advice."

"Wait," I said, keeping my eyes trained on the road. I didn't want to see how much this mattered to him, even though I could hear it in his voice.

"What?" he asked skeptically.

"She loves dance. Maybe something related to that? Adriel's always looking for good scrunchies to keep her buns in place."

"Okay, I can do that." He nodded. "Thanks." He put on his headphones, and I blinked quickly, fighting tears as we arrived at school.

The boys got out of the car, and I leaned forward, resting my forehead on the steering wheel while I rubbed my temples. How could my own brother want to date Tatiana? She was sneaky about her meanness, making sure there were never teachers around when she bullied me, but Terrell had to know.

Maybe it just didn't matter to him.

A horn honked as Des's red convertible passed by, jerking me out of my self-pitying stupor. I unbuckled and got out, walking toward her and trying to act like I wasn't completely crushed. My own brother preferred Tatiana, knowing how cruel she could be.

Des was out of her car, putting her sunglasses into the case, when I reached her. She looked me over. "What's wrong?"

I shook my head. "My brother has a crush on Tatiana."

She made a gagging sound.

"I know." I readjusted my backpack. "He asked me for advice."

"Ew."

I shook my head, trying to breathe deeply. "Can you blame him for liking her?"

"Um, definitely." She smacked her knuckles into her hand. "If my baby brother even *looked* her way, I'd take him out."

"I'm not that strong, I guess."

She put her arm around my shoulders. "It'll be okay. She has the attention span of a gnat when it comes to guys."

"But what about Terrell?" I asked. "What if he gets hurt?"

Her lips twisted to the side. "Everyone has a first love. And a first heartbreak. He'll be okay, especially with a sister like you."

Mrs. Johnston stood in front of the board, writing as I walked into the classroom. Tatiana and Isabella were already in their seats, and I looked at them with fresh eyes, wondering what my brother saw in Tatiana beyond her appearance. Or was it really just her looks that caught his attention?

Tatiana jerked her chin toward me, whispering, "Take a picture. It'll last longer." She flipped her hair. "This is my good side."

I rolled my eyes, muttering, "Original," and went to my seat behind her.

The bell rang, and Mrs. Johnston turned toward us, pressing the cap onto the marker. Her long nails crackled against the tray as she set it back in place.

"We've completed our fall pages, but now it's time for our editors to assign spring pages. Tatiana and Isabella, can you come up here and begin divvying them out?"

Isabella crooned, "Of course, Mrs. Johnston." She and Tatiana walked to the board, passing Mrs. Johnston, who teetered on spiky heels to her desk at the back of the room.

They went down the list, giving the best pages to their friends and leaving the leftovers to everyone else. At last, they reached the 'Best of' page, and the two of them stared down the room, their eyes calculating. Then they turned toward each other, whispering something the rest of us couldn't hear.

Finally, they faced the room again. With an evil grin, Tatiana said, "We're giving the 'Best of' page to Nadira. We're hoping for something extra *unique*."

I glared at them. Not only were they insulting me with my title, they were making sure I would have to see it and focus on it until the page was complete.

Mrs. Johnston clapped her hands together. "Fabulous idea, girls. Now let's get to work, class!"

I shook my head, frustrated. I had gotten the measly quarter-page dedicated to the Mathletes and the "Best of" page, which didn't leave me a ton to work on for the *rest of the semester*. I hated this class. With a passion.

And since I didn't know how the Mathlete season would end yet, I only had the "Best of" page to occupy my time.

I pulled up the spread in the design software we used and began adjusting the type to fit the names of each student until I finally reached the wild card category.

Most Unique.

I willed my fingers to type the letters, but they shook over the keyboard. Typing in my name would only mean Isabella and Tatiana had won. I wanted no part of their victory.

The bell rang, and I let out a relieved sigh. But my relief was short-lived, knowing by the end of the year, I would be on that page and in everyone's yearbooks, memorialized by their disdain for me.

ELEVEN

NADIRA

ALL MY FRIENDS and I sat around a table in the AV room for our Curvy Girl Club 2.0 lunch. For whatever reason, someone sponsored fat girls to get together and eat once a week.

Yes, I know it sounds ridiculous.

No, I'm not making it up.

It was our crazy guidance counselor's idea, if that means anything.

Besides, I wasn't going to look a gift horse in the mouth. Once a week, I got food catered from some of the best restaurants in Emerson *and* avoided the cafeteria. That was a win-win for me.

Today we were eating Italian from La Belle, and I swirled one of my noodles around my fork, lost in thought.

"What's up, Dir?" Desirae asked me. "You seem off."

I glanced up at my friend, realizing how much I must have missed as my thoughts wandered. "Sorry, I'm just having a hard day." I set my fork down.

Faith frowned. "That stinks. What's wrong?"

I shook my head. "It sounds dumb out loud... but my parents haven't come to any of my Mathlete meets, and Apollo thinks I'm Tatiana, who my brother has a crush on, and I guess I'm just feeling sort of pathetic."

Cori reached across the table and rubbed my arm. "You are *not* pathetic. You're one of the smartest people I know."

"That's the problem," I said. "Smart doesn't mean interesting. Smart doesn't mean beautiful. If anything, it means *unique*." I groaned.

Adriel practically growled. "Don't let Isabella and Tatiana get to you. I danced with them for years. They treat everyone that way."

"Not their boyfriends," I said. "Not skinny people."

"So what?" Des asked. "You want to be skinny? Do you really think that would make anything better?"

"Maybe if you cured my vitiligo too," I muttered. "Then we're in business."

Des groaned. "Can you make me a deal?"

"What?" I asked.

Her eyes twinkled. "You have to agree to it first."

I closed my eyes. "Why do I feel like I'm making a deal with the devil?"

"Want to win that fiddle made of gold or not?" she asked.

I snorted. "Sure. Sign me up. It's not like I have anything better to do anyway."

Her teeth gleamed as she smiled. "This weekend, you and me. We're going to a party. A college party. You're going to talk to boys, and one of them is going to get your number."

My eyebrows drew together. "That's the best you got? Some drunk dude's going to ask for my number?"

Her lips pursed. "I bet within the first half hour, a *sober* guy is going to be interested in you. And he's going to see the real you, not some picture of Tatiana you grabbed off the internet."

"Fine." I rolled my eyes. "But if no one asks for my number, you'll drop this self-love nonsense and let me be a realist?"

"A cynic?" she corrected. "And sure."

Cori's eyes pinballed between the two of us. "Okay, you have to text us and let us know what happens."

Faith nodded in agreement. "But I know that doesn't fix what happened with your parents. Sorry, Dir."

Her thoughtfulness made my heart hurt. I managed a "thanks" and got back to eating the food in front of me. People always said that exercise gave you endorphins. Well, you know what else gave you endorphins? *Carbs*. And I was going to eat plenty of them before enduring whatever nonsense Des had planned for tomorrow night.

I came home to an empty house. My parents were working, and my brothers were at practice. Which meant I had the television—and the newly stocked pantry—to myself. I popped a bag of popcorn and played something on the TV while I worked through my homework.

I had it done in under an hour and sat back on the couch with my popcorn and soda, thinking about the romcom on TV and the tragedy of my life. Des had been so confident someone would ask for my number at this party she was dragging me to, but how would it feel when I got there and everyone acted as though I were invisible?

Past experiences had taught me that was an eventuality. No one at my own school or any of the Mathlete competitions I'd been to had ever acted remotely interested in me. Why would that change now?

I shoved down the disheartened feeling spreading in my chest and looked at my phone for a distraction.

Apollo was online.

I bit my bottom lip and sent a message before I could chicken out.

Nadira: Hey, how are you doing?

Apollo: I was actually just writing my email to you. This is easier. :)

I smiled at the screen. At the realization he had been thinking of me at the same moment I'd been thinking of him.

Nadira: Instant gratification for the win.

Apollo: Haha. How was your day?

Nadira: It was okay. You know, besides comments from the mean girls and my brother's new crush on said mean girls.

Apollo: Ugh, I'm sorry.

Nadira: It's not your fault.

Apollo: You know what I mean.

Nadira: I know. How was your day?

Apollo: It was okay. I just finished at ROTC. We had a back to school meeting, and it felt like drinking through a fire hose.

Nadira: I bet.

Apollo: And my professor completely called out this couple in front of the entire class. I was embarrassed FOR them.

Nadira: What happened?

Apollo: We were sitting in a lecture hall, so there's like a hundred people in the class. Maybe more? And there's this couple in the middle of the room. He has his arm around her, and she's resting her head on his shoulder. It was cute, but also, I was kind of jealous, and then the officer just snapped at them. "This is a lecture hall, not a movie theater! If you want to be romantic, take it out of my classroom." blah blah blah. It was a little harsh.

Nadira: It sounds harsh, but... what about *ROTC* got them in the mood for that?

Apollo: I don't know. I feel like when you love someone, you always want them to know they're loved, whether you're in a class or a restaurant or just watching TV.

Nadira: You're a romantic.

Apollo: Well, my mom thinks I'm sweet.

Apollo: ... thought I was sweet.

Nadira: Ouch. Still no contact?

Apollo: That would be a negative.

Nadira: Doesn't Brentwood U have Parents' Day in the spring? Maybe your dad can talk her into coming?

Apollo: I wouldn't count on it. My sister said they're sleeping in separate bedrooms now. Have been for months... I guess she was upset that Dad supported my decision.

Nadira: Apollo... I'm so sorry.

Apollo: Don't be. It's good practice, right? Sacrificing for my country?

Nadira: Soldiers don't get paid enough.

Apollo: We don't do it for the money. Or, most of us don't anyway.

Nadira: Well, thank you in advance. When you're a big-time sergeant, I'll be able to say I knew you before you got famous. ;)

Apollo: Name dropper.

Nadira: Definitely.

Apollo: What are you doing now?

Nadira: Sitting on the couch, watching a movie, eating too much popcorn. What about you?

Apollo: Hanging out in my dorm room. My roommate's watching *Sex and the City* without headphones while playing video games.

Nadira: Are you rooming with a girl? I didn't know that was allowed.

Apollo: Oh, no, it's a guy. He says he's doing "recon" on the female psyche.

Nadira: I just laughed out loud.

Apollo: He's convinced it will help him meet girls.

Nadira: How's that working out for him?

Apollo: It's not, but he's only on season two. I'll let you know if anything changes by season six. And he said he's going to start going to parties.

Nadira: I'll be standing by for that.

Apollo: I hope so.

TWELVE

NADIRA

FRIDAY MORNING, I packed my bag to stay at Desirae's and carried it downstairs with me. Dad had French toast going on the griddle, and Mom sat at the counter, sipping coffee and reading on her tablet. She liked to get the news that way instead of by newspapers.

They both looked up and greeted me as I joined them.

"Good morning," I returned. I felt like I'd hardly seen either of them this week. Although that may have been slightly on purpose.

Mom pressed the side of her tablet, making the screen go dark. "I heard you did great at the Mathlete competition."

I bristled, not really wanting to talk about it

with them. It was becoming clear that they didn't care.

"I can't make the next one," Mom continued. "But I'm hoping I can get to the last one before state."

"Sure." I sat down at the counter and grabbed a plate from the stack. I topped it with a couple pieces of French toast and doused them in syrup.

I could feel my parents looking at each other as I cut into a slice, but I kept my eyes down and focused, not even looking at them until I'd taken a bite. Which turned out to be delicious.

Dad was a good cook. And outside of basketball season, he would make these elaborate meals for us. He always said any job around the house was a job for someone who lived in the house. Nothing was too big or small for him, whether it was dishes or cooking or dusting off family photos.

We basically grew up seeing him and Mom juggle our home in a way that I'd never seen my friends' parents do. I didn't even realize it wasn't normal until we moved here and I saw Cori's mom operate as a stay-at-home mom. She did so much around the home while her dad handled all of the business dealings.

I wondered if I would ever find a partner who would help share the load like my parents did.

"So," Mom tried again, "you're going to Des's tonight?"

"Yeah. I'm gonna stay over there, and I should be back sometime tomorrow afternoon."

"Remember that Dad has a game Saturday night," she said.

"Right." How could I forget? It had been on the calendar just like my Mathlete competition.

Dad said, "Remember to wear your badge and they'll let you in." As though I hadn't been to hundreds of his games before.

"Okay," I replied. Part of me wondered if I would see Apollo at the game. Of course, he wouldn't recognize me because he'd never seen a photo of the real me. But then a new problem crossed my mind. If I sat by Mom, he'd know I was her daughter. Maybe he'd say hi. Maybe she'd introduce me....

"Mom, are you going to the game?" I asked.

"I'm going to live-stream it from my office. See if I can't get my work done fast enough to catch the last quarter or so."

Okay, at least that gave me a little bit of time.

And if she came and Apollo walked over, I could always run to the concession stand or something.

Dad began talking to Mom about something around the house that needed to be fixed while I ate my breakfast, thinking about my conversation with Apollo the day before. He'd talked about how being around the Brentwood campus reminded him of how his parents met, but now I couldn't think of BU without thinking of him.

When I went to the game Saturday, I would surely see the places he ate or studied or the pond he walked past on the way to class. Maybe I had already seen him without knowing it. A small shiver went down my spine, but I quickly suppressed my excitement. I was *not* allowed to think these thoughts. Not when I'd been so dishonest from the outset, and definitely not when I knew it would go nowhere once he saw my face.

Instead of dwelling on it, I focused on school. On my day. On putting one foot in front of the other until it was time for my volunteer period. Each Friday, I spent the afternoon in the teachers' lounge grading freshman math assignments for Mr. Aris. Although teaching wasn't my ideal occupation, it was nice to be able to help him out.

Especially since I basically had the whole room

—and coffee pot—to myself, aside from the teachers who meandered through for drink refills or to grab a snack in between classes. Mr. Aris even said I could use my phone to play music while I graded.

I was nodding along to a song by Jude Santiago when the music stalled for a moment. One new notification.

Since all my friends were also volunteering and my parents didn't typically text me during school hours, there was only one person I thought it could be...

I picked it up, knowing I shouldn't be slacking, but decided to check the messages anyway. The school was getting free work out of me on top of the tuition my parents paid. They could spare a few of my minutes.

The second I saw Apollo's instant message, my face split into a grin.

Apollo: Working hard?

Nadira: More like hardly working.

Apollo: Haha. How are you?

Nadira: I'm supposed to be grading freshman math papers. Feels good up here on my high horse.

Apollo: Crushing dreams, are you?

Nadira: Wouldn't have it any other way.

Apollo: You're cruel.

Nadira: Some might say I'm helping them.

Apollo: By breaking their hearts?

Nadira: Setting realistic expectations for their grades?

Apollo: Haha. I can feel the ice all the way from here.

Nadira: And where is here? What are you up to?

Apollo: Just got back from a run, and now I'm procrastinating my human geography homework. I'm supposed to be doing a three-minute video on an aspect of California for the class to watch. I can't believe I have homework before classes even officially start.

Nadira: And you don't want to be on camera?

Apollo: I'd rather run another six miles.

My eyes boggled at the phone. A six-mile run? That was almost as shocking as the fact that he wouldn't want his beautiful face on screen.

Nadira: I'd rather pluck my toenails out than go on a run of any length.

Apollo: Oh, come on, it's not that bad.

Nadira: I could say the same thing about talking to a camera.

Apollo: Touché.

Nadira: Do you ever pronounce that word likes it's spelled? Try it.

Apollo: LOL I just said toosh in front of my roommate.

Nadira: hahahaha

Apollo: Don't laugh.

Nadira: I didn't tell you to say it out loud!

Apollo: It's a little late now.

Nadira: What did he say?

Apollo: Well, now he's grilling me about the girl I'm talking to.

Nadira: What are you telling him?

I bit my lip, waiting for his reply, when the bell rang. My first hour of grading was over, which meant teachers would soon be in the lounge. I shoved my phone underneath me on the couch, wishing I could just watch the screen and the three little dots until he answered.

But I needed to get back to grading. I'd spent too long messaging, and Mr. Aris would know if I wasn't doing what I was supposed to.

I kept my head down while teachers came in and out. My phone vibrated under my hip, and I itched to get it. To read what he'd said. But I couldn't without getting caught.

The door opened again, and our guidance counselor, Birdie Bardot, swept into the room, her pleated skirt flowing around her legs. It was bright pink and clashed horribly with her bright orange top.

"Hi, Nadira," she said to me, chipper as usual.

"Hey." I turned back to my stack of paper and continued grading papers.

She went to the coffee pot, carrying her mug that looked like a cow, udders and all. The teacher that had been in there left the room, leaving just the two of us, and Mrs. Bardot said, "How are you doing? And the real answer, not the typical, 'good, how are you, good' nonsense."

My eyebrows lifted, torn between giving her a real answer and giving her a quick answer so I could attend to the phone under my hip. "I..." I let out a sigh. "I have amazing friends."

"But?"

"But, I'm stressed about a guy. Why is it always a guy who throws a wrench in things?" I said, frustrated with myself more than Apollo. He'd never been anything other than himself. "Can you tell me that I should be more focused on my studies or my future career? Please?"

Replacing the coffee pot, she leaned against the counter and held her mug with two hands.

"Growing up stinks. I know everyone here wants to be an adult and move on, and I'm supposed to be helping you realize your full potential. Well, no one ever tells you that when you grow up, you're going to have bills and nieces' events that you can't attend because you have to work, and that you might even get your heart broken a time or two."

"What would you know about heartbreak?" I muttered. "I've seen all the happy pictures in your office of you and your man."

She shook her head. "In fact, I have not always been this 'happy.' Do you remember the protest? It's been about six years ago now."

"Vaguely?" I said. When I was in sixth grade, there had been a massive protest that had gotten the elementary and middle schools shut down. At the time, I was so preoccupied with adjusting to a new town that I hadn't realized what the protest was for.

Birdie frowned. "I fell in love with a students father, which at the time was strictly prohibited. I was already on rocky footing before I started dating my Cohen. No one prepares you for getting dumped by your *fiancé*."

I raised my eyebrows. "Mr. Bardot dumped you?"

"I was engaged before him." She laughed manically. "Of course, no one would have known that back then because instead of an engagement ring, the guy gave me a new bird cage for Ralphie. To keep him here since I couldn't bring him home. I should have known he was the wrong guy for me then."

My head was spinning in so many ways.

"Luckily I have my Cohen now... But it wasn't always like that. You'll get through this, dear. I know you will." She shook her head and walked toward the exit, musing to herself. "Why do they make condoms when the real thing that needs protecting is your heart?" She shut the door behind her, and I burst out laughing. She had a good point.

I picked up my phone to text my friends about what Birdie had said, only to see Apollo's message staring back at me.

THIRTEEN

NADIRA

I GOT out of volunteer period and hurried to Des's house, needing her feedback on the message. When I got there, she was standing in front of her closet, looking at rows of dresses with a contemplative expression.

"Des, step away from the clothes," I said, holding out my phone. "I need you."

Looking confused, she came to me and took my phone, reading the message from Apollo out loud.

Apollo: I told him I'm talking to a beautiful girl. And that I'm liking her more every day.

Her lips spread into a grin. "He said that about you!"

I nodded quickly. "But I'm freaking out!"

"You haven't responded." She looked from my phone to me. "Why haven't you responded?"

"I don't know how to flirt!" I cried, pacing her room. "Anything I say would sound stupid!"

"Oh nonsense." She put her hands on my shoulders and sat me on her bed. "Here's what you do." She pushed my phone into my hands. "You text him back and say 'back at you.' Throw in a wink, and he'll go gaga."

"That's it? Three words? I've been stressing about this for *hours*."

She sat beside me on her bed. "Boys are easy. It's overthinking that makes things complicated."

I tilted my chin down, looking up at her. "Do you know who you're talking to? Overthinking is my middle name. They wanted to make it my first name, but the doctor said no."

She chuckled, shaking her head. "You'll see, tonight. College boys aren't like high school guys who just want to play games. If they like a girl, they'll go for it. Like Apollo just went for it with you." She gave me a pointed look. "Or Tatiana."

I stood from her bed, feeling a guilty swirl in my stomach. "But he said he's liking me more every day. If it was just about my looks, he would have liked me the most from the beginning, right?"

"Which is exactly why you should cut the act and tell him you were too chicken for the truth on day one."

I gave her a look. "Can you just help me get ready for this party so I can prove to you no one's going to ask for my number?"

"Uh-huh." She shook her head. "Hope you like the taste of crow."

She sat me at the mirror in front of her dresser and began painting this ridiculous makeup on my face.

"This wasn't the deal," I said before she could apply too much. "I thought you were going to give me an outfit, maybe a pair of shoes. But if you can't even recognize me, it doesn't count. The guy's supposed to be interested in me just as I am."

"Fine, you're right." She set the eyeliner down and left it so that the only makeup she managed to do was thick black lines over my eyelids. I had to admit I liked the way it drew out my dark brown eyes, but the look didn't feel like me.

The door cracked open, and Mama De poked her head in. "*Hola, chicas.*" She grinned at me and held out a platter of chips and different dips. "Thought you two might want some snacks."

Des grinned at her mom, and I nodded.

"*Muchas gracias*," I said, putting the two years of Spanish I'd taken in high school to use. Unfortunately, that was about all I could do other than ask where the bathroom was.

"*Claro*. Of course," she said. "*Eres bonita.*"

The words brought a smile to my lips. "*Eres amable.*"

Mama De set the platter down on Des's dresser and then left the room.

"Your mom is the best," I said.

Des nodded. "She's one of my best friends." She winked. "Aside from the CGC of course."

I took a chip and dipped it in the guac. "She'd be my best friend too if I ate like this every day," I joked. But really, I wondered what it would feel like to have a mom I could really confide in. The last time my mom and I had talked about anything other than school or work was... never. We just didn't relate like Des and her mom did.

I went to the mirror again and finished my look by sweeping mascara over my lashes. "So who are we meeting anyway? Please tell me it's a different guy than the one from New Year's."

"It is. His name's Devon," she said. "I've been talking to him for a couple weeks."

"That was fast," I said. "How do you find so many guys?"

"There are billions of them on the planet." She chuckled. "I don't know. I feel like all of our friends think that dating in high school is supposed to lead to happily ever after, but I just want to have fun. Besides, any relationship is doomed to fail once I get a record deal. We won't be on the same level."

I sat back in the chair in front of her vanity, slightly jealous of the way Des viewed the whole relationship thing. For whatever reason, she had this magnetic field around her with guys of all types, even really attractive ones who I never could have gotten to notice me. And it wasn't that she wasn't beautiful... but she had full hips and cellulite and a double chin just like me.

I was curious to see what Devon looked like, but also a little nervous. "Please don't leave me at the party just to hang out with that guy."

She pursed her lips. "What kind of wing woman do you think I am?"

"One with a very high predatory instinct."

She rolled her eyes at me. "He has some cute friends too. You wouldn't be alone."

"Hey!" I said. "That's not part of the deal. If

you put someone up to asking for my number, it doesn't count."

"I know," she replied, "but you're gonna have options is what I'm saying."

I shook my head. "Getting one guy to ask for my number was a bit of a stretch, Des. We're not living in a fairy tale here."

She let out a heavy sigh and then walked to me, putting her hands on my shoulders. "Dir, this has got to stop. I know you don't feel beautiful and middle school was really hard on you. I get it—I do —but you are absolutely beautiful in your own way."

I gave her a look, but she fired right back.

"Hear me out. If you ever have a daughter—or a niece—she's going to look like you. Do you really want her to think the same things that you're thinking to yourself?"

Just the thought of a sweet, innocent girl, feeling a fraction of the insecurities I did made my heart hurt. I closed my stinging eyes and shook my head. But how could I turn off the way I'd felt about myself for years? It seemed impossible.

Des dropped her hands from my shoulders and turned back to her mirror, taking a napkin and blotting her lips on it while I gathered myself. "Are you ready to go?"

"Sure," I said, reaching for my purse. It didn't have much in it—just my phone, some money, and some hand sanitizer. (If this party was at some guy's frat house, I didn't want to get whatever bodily fluids were sure to be everywhere on my hands.)

"Let's go," she said. She hooked her arm through mine, and we left the house, waving to her parents on the way out.

Des's parents had always been less strict than mine, letting her go to parties and stay out late. They trusted her in a way my parents never would because my parents had never even been tempted to place trust in me. I didn't do much of anything except spend time with my friends. My brothers, on the other hand, were a different story.

When we got into her car, she said, "Do you want the top down?"

It was finally starting to warm up like it always did this time of year, but it was still a bit cold for me. Besides, I always felt like I was in a fishbowl when we drove around in her car with the top down.

"Not right now," I said.

She nodded and turned on the music just a little

bit too loud, singing along as we drove toward Brentwood. She took us to the streets lined with housing that students typically rented for the affordability and proximity to the college. There were at least a few parties going with people walking in and out of houses and crowding the sidewalks, but she pulled in front of one of the biggest crowds.

Just looking through the open windows showed me there had to be at least a hundred people there, and the house didn't look like it had more than four or five bedrooms. She parked along the street and got out, walking over the uneven sidewalk in her spiky heels with confidence. It made me wish that I had worn more than my Vans. But then again, if someone was going to hit on me, I wanted it to be on me, not some made-up version.

Not that it was going to happen, I reminded myself. I couldn't get my hopes up that today was going to be different than literally every other day of my life, no matter how confident Des seemed to be.

We walked into the house, and the music was even louder than it had been in the car. It practically vibrated my bones, and I immediately wanted to leave. To lie on the couch and watch movies and message Apollo instead of being here, in this place where I so clearly didn't belong.

The girls here seemed happy, free in their revealing clothes as they giggled and fell all over each other. And the guys looked to be having just as much fun. There was a ping-pong table out with cups lined into pyramids and another table where people were flipping quarters around, and another group of people sat on the couch, laughing and talking. There were even people dancing in the middle of the open-concept living area.

Was this what it would be like at MIT, or would I still feel like an outsider? Would I ever feel like I fit in outside of a math classroom or the Curvy Girl Club 2.0?

A guy approached us, taking Des into a hug. She hadn't been lying—he was very attractive. Tall and lean with a shadow of a beard that accented his strong jaw line. He kissed her cheek and turned to me. "Is this your friend?"

She nodded. "Isn't she cute?"

My cheeks immediately heated as he gave me an assessing look. I cared more about his response than I wanted to.

He nodded, then said, "I'll go get us some drinks. What do you want?"

Des asked for a beer, and I told him I just wanted a soda. I never quite understood the allure of making your brain work under its full potential. If anything, I wanted mine to work faster so I could understand more.

As he walked away, Des shimmied her shoulders to the music. "Didn't I tell you he was cute?"

"Yeah," I said, "he's cute, but how old is he?"

"Twenty-one. Not that much older than us."

She made a good point, but I bet most people would have judged her for dating an older guy. It was so weird to me that as a high schooler, you couldn't date a twenty-one-year-old, but the first day of college, it somehow became okay.

"Age is just a number," she said. "It's what's in your heart that matters."

Apollo was only a year older than me, I thought. Then I shook my head. I shouldn't have been thinking about him or his age, but now that I was, I had a hard time stopping. What was he doing tonight? Was there a chance he was here, at this very party?

I was looking around, wondering if I would recognize him from his profile picture. His strong jawline and full lips would be hard to miss.

In my scan of the room, I didn't see anyone

who looked remotely familiar, aside from Des. Maybe that was a good thing.

Her guy brought back a can of soda for me and a red cup for Des. "Wanna dance?" he asked her.

She looked at me first. "Is that okay?"

"Sure," I said, nodding. I could always go and hold up a wall for a couple of hours until it was time to leave.

They weaved through the crowd and began dancing with the group of people off the living room. I went and leaned against a wall near the entrance door so people wouldn't notice me as they walked in. As I watched all these people around me, having fun and living their lives, an over-whelming feeling of sadness and loneliness washed over me.

Why did I feel so out of place here?

I got out my phone, if only to distract myself, and saw a new email from Apollo waiting.

From: A.banks@brentwoodu.edu
To: mitbound321@gmail.com

Dear Nadira,

I started reading, but next to me, someone said, "Not a party person either?"

I looked up from my phone into the face of a guy I could only describe as artsy. He had shaggy, wavy hair and wore dark jeans with a paint-splattered white T-shirt that hung a little too loosely on his shoulders.

"Not really," I said.

"Me either. But I'm really bad at meeting people in class, so I thought I'd try this."

I chuckled. "I'm the same way. My friend dragged me along as a third wheel."

"Nice. My roommate wouldn't come along. Said he had assigned reading to do before Monday."

I nodded. "And is there any reason you're not studying?"

"I'm an art history major." He chuckled. "All my work's going to be crammed into the last two weeks of the semester." Though his words were lighthearted, he seemed guarded as he said it, as if worried about my reaction, and I guessed that made sense.

Multiple people had probably already told him that it wasn't a very viable major. But if my mom had taught me anything, it was that keeping all fields of education alive mattered and that there would always be positions open for people with knowledge.

"That's cool," I said, meaning it. "What made you choose that?"

Seeming surprised by my reaction, he relaxed a little and said, "I went to a class during a campus visit and fell in love. I'm hoping to work in a museum someday or a gallery."

"That sounds fun. Would you do it in California?"

He shrugged. "Anywhere that would take me."

I laughed. "I love a man with standards."

"What about you? What's your major?"

"Aerospace engineering. Or at least it will be in the fall."

He lifted his eyebrows. "A high schooler *and* a masochist? Way to slip that info in early."

I laughed again. "Some of us actually like math," I retorted. I couldn't believe I was actually having a decent conversation with a guy. Maybe Des had been on to something; maybe college would be my time to shine.

"I don't believe that," he said. "Who's paying you to say that?"

He acted as if he was looking all over my body, and I said, "What are you doing?"

Giving up the search, he said, "Checking for wires."

I snorted.

"You have a cute laugh," he said.

I blushed.

"Do you think you might want to go get coffee sometime?" he asked.

Butterflies swirled in my stomach. Had I just been asked on a date? A real date? That was even better than a phone number. I bit my lip, trying to stifle the massive smile that threatened to split my lips apart. "Maybe. Are you sure you want to go with a high schooler?"

"I was a high schooler last year." He got out his phone and had me type in my number. Once I entered my name and handed it back, he tapped on the screen. "There. I sent you a text."

The vibration in my pocket confirmed.

He put his phone away. "This music's giving me a headache. I'm gonna head out. Unless, you want to join me?"

I shook my head, nodding toward Des. "She's my ride."

"Okay." He smiled. "I'll text you sometime. Nice to meet you, Nadira."

I pressed my lips together, nodding, and watched as he left through the front door.

My lips parted in shock as I took in everything that had just happened.

Within seconds, Des walked up to me, squealing. "Was that what I thought it was?"

I glared at her, not wanting to admit that she'd been right, but I couldn't hold the expression for long without smiling.

"He got your number," she sang, grinning like the winning fool she knew she was.

"Yes, yes, okay?"

I hadn't thought it possible, but her smile grew even wider. "Okay, time to start Project Love Yourself. But until then..." She glanced over her shoulder at Devon, who was still waiting on her. "I've got someone to dance with. Do you want to come with me?"

I bit my lip and nodded, thinking for the first time that maybe, *maybe* I belonged.

FOURTEEN

NADIRA

I AWOKE the next morning in Des's bed, hearing her soft snores and the sound of the ocean rolling outside. I'd slept amazingly and felt well-rested, even though we'd been out until midnight and had stayed up talking for a few hours after that.

A glance at my phone told me it was only eight in the morning. Outside of Des's room, I could hear the sounds of cooking—or maybe cleaning—as pans softly clanged against each other.

The sun coming through her gauzy curtains was bright, and I decided a walk on the beach in the sunshine sounded amazing. After using the bathroom and showering, I walked out of her room while Des slept away, finding food and a note on the countertop.

Have a great breakfast, chicas. – *Mama De*

I smiled at the note and took one of the burritos from the plate. It was still warm.

As I went outside, the breeze was cooler than the bright sun let on, so I wrapped my jacket more tightly around myself and let my feet sink into the sun-soaked sand. I walked and ate my breakfast, thinking about the night before.

A guy had asked for my number, unprompted. I didn't even care if he changed his mind the next day and never texted me again. He had known literally nothing about me and had still approached me. That had to mean he liked the way I *looked*.

A nasty thought in the back of my mind said he probably thought I'd be easy, but I shook it off. If he'd thought I was easy, he would have pressed harder about leaving the party with him. No, he'd said he would text me instead.

I smiled at the thought and got out my phone to see if he had texted me yet. No messages, but since I had my phone out, I took a picture of the beach, of the waves and the sand and the sun glancing off the water.

In the back of my mind, I heard a voice curiously close to Des's telling me to turn the camera around. Which made sense. I was supposed to be loving myself, not hiding behind a screen. The wind blew through my hair and I smiled at the screen, parting my lips so my gap teeth were visible.

The second I saw the picture, I cringed, but I immediately wiped the expression. If I was going to love myself, I had to set boundaries. Be disciplined, just like I was in school. I sat down in the sand and forced myself to look at the picture. To notice all the white spots on my black skin. To see the dark gap between my two front teeth. To notice the way my full cheekbones pressed into my eyes, making them look squinted with my smile. This was me. And I desperately wanted to like what I saw.

Having had enough, I got out of my photo reel and checked my email instead. My eyes widened as I remembered I'd gotten a message from Apollo the night before. In the excitement of the party, I'd completely forgotten to read it!

I went back to the email and began reading.

From: A.banks@brentwoodu.edu
To: mitbound321@gmail.com

Dear Nadira,

Did you know that you can actually buy stars? It seems a little silly to me since I'm from Texas and we think any land we buy you should be able to put cows on. But for someone who's interested in that kind of thing... you could own a giant ball of gas in the sky and name it whatever you want. Here's the website in case you wanted to check it out.

V/r,
Apollo

My lips parted as I tapped through to the website. Sure enough, there were a selection of stars available to choose from, and you could actually name the one you bought whatever you wanted, as long as the name wasn't already taken.

I lowered my phone and put my hand over my heart. The very fact that Apollo had seen this and sent it to me meant he'd been thinking of me. That something in his world had reminded him of me.

With my heart melting and a smile on my face, I began typing back an email.

From: mitbound321@gmail.com
To: A.banks@brentwoodu.edu

Dear Apollo,

I need to save my money so I can buy one for myself.
And eventually all the cows here will release enough
methane to make the earth a big gas ball anyway.

What are you up to this weekend? You know, other
than casual intergalactic window shopping.

Sincerely,
Nadira

I sat in the sand for a moment, looking over the
email I sent and smiling to myself. Things were
starting to look up. If one person had been interested in me, there were surely more, right? It
couldn't have just been a fluke incident. At least, I
hoped not.

A notification for a new email slid down my
phone screen, and I tapped it, eagerly reading Apollo's words.

From: A.banks@gmail.com
To: mitbound321@gmail.com

Dear Nadira,

I'm trying to catch up on studying this weekend. I swear my professors got together and decided to torture us all with tests on the same week. I'm a little bummed too because my roommate invited me to a party, but I couldn't go. I'm sure there will be other parties, though.

What about you?

V/r,
Apollo

I smiled at the email and went to the messaging window. I almost sent him a picture of me on the beach. But the night before was too good. I couldn't ruin the high I was on yet. So I sent him a picture of just the beach instead.

Apollo: Where's that? It's beautiful.

Nadira: By one of my friend's houses. They live right on the water.

Apollo: Jealous.

Nadira: Same here. At least I can come crash any time I want. Being outside is nice.

Apollo: I know. I'm sitting out in the courtyard with my books for a change of pace.

He sent me a picture of his books spread out on a table on campus. I recognized it as one on the patio area outside the library. I'd been there a few times during finals weeks when I needed somewhere to study.

Nadira: Don't your classes start Monday? Why do you have homework already?

Apollo: A lot of my professors assigned reading to complete for the first day. I don't want to get caught unprepared for a pop quiz.

Nadira: That stinks. Well, it looks like you have a reading paradise set up there.

Apollo: You're the one looking at paradise. :) If I could, I'd put the books away and be at the beach with you in a second.

My heart stalled. Had he just said what I thought he did? That he would rather be with me?

I shook my head. It was about the beach, not me.

"What are you doing out here?" Des called.

I looked up from my phone to see her several feet away. "Went on a walk... and then I got an email from Apollo."

Her face lit up as she sat in the sand next to me. "Show me, show me, show me."

I passed my phone over to her, waiting until she saw the last message there. Her mouth fell open. "He wants to be with you!"

I shook my head. "He wants to be with *Tatiana*."

"But he knows *you*."

"That's a problem, then, isn't it?" I said with a sigh. I sent Apollo a message saying I'd talk to him later and put my phone away in my pocket.

Des leaned back, resting her hands in the sand behind her. "When are you going to send him an actual photo of you?"

"I almost did today," I admitted. "I just couldn't do it. Couldn't ruin it."

She stared over the water. "Why does it matter so much what he thinks of you? If he doesn't think you're pretty, so what? We'll both know he's wrong. And isn't it better to know now, before your heart gets involved?"

"My hearts already involved." I let out a shaky breath, following her gaze. I didn't want to like him, but he was nice, thoughtful. My eyes stung, and my throat felt tight. "I don't think I can take another rejection."

Instead of speaking, Des put her arm around me and rested her head on my shoulder. "I'm going to love you enough for both of us until you learn to love yourself."

FIFTEEN

NADIRA

I PUT on my Brentwood U jersey and swiped a mascara wand through my eyelashes. The jersey hung low enough that I wore leggings underneath without worrying anyone would see the ever-present dimples on my bottom.

Dad had already been at the college for a few hours now, along with Mom, so Carver, Terrell, and I loaded into my car. As soon as the doors closed, I was overwhelmed by their cologne. My throat constricted, and I coughed against the strength of the smell. "Do you guys think you used enough cologne?"

"No," Carver retorted.

Terrell snorted. "He wants the girls to smell him coming."

"It's better than the way they'll smell you coming," Carver said. "I don't know why Tatiana agreed to go to the game with you."

My eyebrows rose, and I looked at Terrell out of the corner of my eyes. He was meeting Tatiana at the game? He never took girls to the game, instead trying to chat up the pretty college girls.

He didn't meet my eyes, so I shook my head and turned up the music. They took the hint and got out their phones. Part of me wished I wasn't driving so I could do the same. I wanted to distract myself and message Apollo to ask if he was going to the basketball game. If I would see him there.

Instead, I kept my hands on the wheel and my focus on the road until I reached the crowded parking lot at the university. Dad had put a parking sticker in my car, so at least I could park up close.

We got out of the car, and the boys ambled ahead, ready to check out the concession stand and the college girls. People streamed around me as I walked toward will call and told them my name.

They handed me a ticket, and I continued into the building. Families of the players and coaches got to sit pretty close behind the home team's bench. I made my way to the familiar place, waving at the people I knew as I went.

Sitting in my usual seat, I watched as the players warmed up. I glanced around the gym, looking for my brothers, and found them already sitting with a group of girls. Of course. Except I recognized one of the girls this time. Tatiana sat in Terrell's lap, running her fingers along his short curly hair, down his cheek.

"Is anyone sitting here?" a guy said, drawing my eyes away from the nightmare.

I looked up to see a super cute guy waiting on me patiently, and I almost couldn't speak. "Um, no, it's free."

"Awesome." He smiled. "Would you mind scooting down so we have some room?"

It was then I noticed the cute girl behind him. "Oh, sure."

If they hadn't been right next to me, I would have facepalmed so hard. Instead, I had to act like I wasn't completely pathetic as the warm-up clock counted down and the game began.

My phone vibrated, and I got it out, wondering if I'd forgotten something at Des's house.

Unknown number: Hey, it's Josh from the party Friday. Are you at the basketball game? I think I see you.

My cheeks instantly heated as I straightened to

a more attractive posture. Where was he? I looked around but couldn't see him.

Nadira: Yeah, where are you sitting?

Josh: Look to your right.

I turned my head and saw him standing in the aisle. My face instantly lit into a smile, and I waved him over, feeling a lot less lame than I had earlier. As he walked toward me, I noticed his outfit—dark jeans and a blue Brentwood U T-shirt a size too big.

"Hey," I said as he sat down. "I didn't take you for a basketball fan."

"I'm not. My roommate talked me into coming."

"Your roommate sounds pushy." I looked around for a friend but didn't see anyone. "Where is he?"

Josh pointed toward the student section. "Second row, three down."

As Josh sat next to me, my eyes landed on his roommate. I could have picked him out anywhere. My heart stalled, and my breath shallowed. Josh's roommate was *Apollo*.

I couldn't help but take him in, every bit of him, from the jeans that fit too well to the Brentwood U T-shirt that clung to his muscled chest.

Josh said, "Do you see him? He's in a white shirt? Short hair?"

"Oh, yeah," I said, slamming my jaw shut. My mind was racing, and I didn't know how to act. How to behave. What if Apollo saw me? What if Josh told Apollo my name? There weren't that many Nadiras in the world. Would he know I was a fraud? Would he hate me?

Then I looked a few rows behind Apollo to see Terrell and Tatiana were still absorbed in each other. And I panicked. Apollo might not have known what I looked like, but he had seen a picture Tatiana. She was only ten feet away from him.

"Holy crap," I muttered.

"What?" Josh asked.

"Oh, I, um." How did I get out of this? How did I keep Apollo from looking just a little behind him and to the right? "I need to use the bathroom. I'll be right back."

"Sure," Josh said.

I scrambled up and edged along the bleachers, rushing to get to my brother. I had to find a way to get Terrell and Tatiana *out* of there.

The second I was out of sight of Josh, I pulled my phone out and dialed Terrell's number. "Pick up," I muttered as it rang. "Pick up." I hurried along the track on the back side of the bleachers, preparing myself to go up and get him if I needed to.

Just when I thought it was going to voicemail, Terrell answered with an annoyed voice. "What?"

I raised my eyes toward the ceiling, biting back a retort. "Hey, I was wondering if you and Tatiana might want the car keys? You could make out in the parking lot." That was safe, right? It wasn't like they could get naked on a college campus.

"What's the catch?" he asked.

"No catch. Except for the one where I don't have to see you two suck each other's faces off the whole game." There was a bite to my voice, but considering my brother was dating my bully, I felt pretty proud I wasn't screaming and dragging him away by his ear right now. "Are you in?" I asked impatiently.

A loud cheer swept through the crowd, echoing in my ears and then a second later in the phone.

"Sure," he said.

"I'm behind the bleachers."

The call ended, and I looked down at my phone, bouncing from foot to foot and praying that Apollo wouldn't see them on their way out. A few minutes later, they stumbled out from the bleachers,

Terrell's arm hooked around Tatiana's shoulders, her giggling up at him. I wanted to punch something, throw up, and breathe a sigh of relief at the same time.

But since all of those things would have been awkward to do in front of them, I extended the keys, and Terrell took them, not giving me a second glance. Shaking my head, I turned away and walked back to the bleachers where Josh had been sitting.

With a million excuse-mes, I sidled toward him and sat down again.

"Hey," he said with a warm smile.

"Hey," I said, looking over the court and not wanting to be here at all. I was exhausted, the lights were bright, Apollo could see me, and there was no way I was going to be able to keep my eyes off him. Not to mention, adrenaline still raced through me at the fear of Apollo seeing Tatiana making out with my brother. "Do you want to go to the coffee shop?" I asked. "I was up a little late last night."

"Sure. Basketball's not really my scene either. Want to go to the one in the library?" Josh asked.

I nodded. "Unless you know of another one nearby?"

"That's the closest one," Josh said. "Let me text Apollo."

My heart stumbled as his name fell over my ears. Josh didn't seem to notice as he tapped at his phone. I watched as Apollo got his phone out of his pocket, checked the screen, and then waved our way.

I blanched as his eyes traveled across his friend to me for a second time, that same slightly crooked smile turning up his lips. Apollo had smiled at me. *Me.*

Completely oblivious, Josh turned and walked away down the bleachers. I sucked in my stomach as I crossed the full bleachers again and finally reached the freedom of the stairs.

I followed Josh out of the stadium, my heart hammering and my stomach turning and my body *changed*.

I'd seen Apollo. And he'd seen me.

SIXTEEN

APOLLO

I NEEDED to watch *Sex and the City*.

That's what I thought as I watched Josh walk away with his girl. He hadn't even told me her name, but her face was caught in my mind. He'd spotted her across the gym and pointed her out. She had big curly hair framing the most unique face I'd ever seen. She was beautiful, one of a kind—I could tell from twenty feet away. But she had left the game with my roommate. And here I was. Alone.

The game didn't seem so interesting anymore.

I decided to get up and grab some food, maybe get some air.

The line at the concession stand was long, so I skipped it, heading toward the exit. There was a couple ahead of me. A guy who looked tall enough to be on the basketball team and a slender girl. He had his arm around her waist, and she looked up at him.

She almost looked like the photo I had of Nadira, but I shook it off. I'd been talking to her so much lately, every girl with dark skin and black hair looked like her at first glance. Maybe because I wanted it to be her so badly.

Eight months without dating was a long time after a two-year relationship, and I was ready to move on. I wanted to move on with Nadira.

Which was crazy considering I'd only known her for a week, but I just had a feeling. My gut was hardly ever wrong.

I pushed through the exit and turned left. The couple ahead of me was too close. I was too jealous.

I walked along the sidewalk by the stadium, taking deep breaths. I reached for my phone and went to my messages. I was tired of texting Nadira. I wanted to hear her voice instead. Know what her laugh sounded like.

But I was worried too. Would how much I wanted to talk to her scare her away?

I let out a sigh and dialed a different number. My brother's.

He answered after a few rings, and I heard bird-song in the background.

"What's up?" he said.

"Just left a basketball game. You?"

"Bette and I went camping," he said. "I can't believe I have enough service for a call to come through."

I felt lucky he had service, but now I realized how pathetic I sounded. I was just jealous of Josh meeting a pretty girl. The way she had smiled across the gym at me had made my stomach turn upside down. Would it feel the same way when Nadira looked at me? Would she ever look at me?

"So," Colby said. Which was code for *why are you really calling*.

I let out a sigh. "I've been talking to a girl."

He whooped loudly, and I imagined the birds from earlier taking flight. "What's her name? When can I meet her?"

"It's not like that."

"Then how is it?" he asked.

I let out a sigh. "You know how I signed up for that research study?"

"Yeah?"

"She's my pen pal."

He laughed. "You been writing love letters?"

"Okay, I'm hanging up."

"No no," he said. "What's the deal? Are you dating her? Did you ask her out?"

"I haven't even met her in real life," I said. "But I want to. We've been talking for a week, and I don't know how to ask without being weird, you know?"

"Yeah..." Colby was quiet for a moment. "Can't you just ask her out on a date?"

"She's in high school."

"Cradle robber."

I scuffed my shoe over a weed growing through the sidewalk. "I hate you."

"How old is she?"

"Eighteen. She's a senior."

"She pretty?"

"Colby."

He chuckled. "What? It's an honest question."

"She is," I said, but it kind of annoyed me. I didn't want to date a *pretty* girl—someone obsessed with makeup and appearances. I wanted to date someone real. Someone unique. Someone like the girl Josh had left with earlier. But Nadira's personality more than made up for it. "And she's funny and smart. We can actually talk about math without her getting bored."

"Sounds like a winner," Colby said. His voice crackled.

"Colby," I said.

But his voice broke up even more before the line went silent.

I sighed and sat on a bench along the sidewalk. From here, I could see the building where I took most of my classes. It was brick. Plain. But I didn't see it—not really. I was thinking of what it would be like to meet Nadira in person. What it would be like to have her smile at the sight of me.

I took out my phone and opened a new email, deciding to practice what I would send her.

Dear Nadira,
I've enjoyed talking with you. What do you say we continue this conversation in person? Maybe at a restaurant?

I groaned, quickly deleting the text. How lame could I sound?

Dear Nadira,
I want to hear your voice.

Okay, that was creepy. Delete.

Dear Nadira,

I've been thinking about you a lot lately. Have you been thinking about me?

Too needy.

I let out a sigh and shoved my phone in my pocket. I really did need to watch *Sex and the City*, see what the scripted, perfect guys on TV said to get a girl interested, because I was *definitely* rusty. If I'd ever been good at all.

I stood from the bench and walked back to the game, but instead of paying attention to basketball, my mind was filled with thoughts of one person.

SEVENTEEN

NADIRA

"WHAT KIND of coffee do you like?" Josh asked, stuffing his hands in his pockets as we crossed the quad toward the coffee shop.

I tucked my hands into my own pockets, not used to talking to boys who weren't my family members or teachers. "Usually iced coffee with extra cream and sugar."

"Same," he said. "But I like mine black."

"How very artsy of you," I teased.

"No, no, artists are supposed to drink herbal teas steeped with tufts of lavender."

I laughed. "That's a good point." I could even picture it in my mind.

We were quiet for a moment, and I asked, "How long have you been rooming with Apollo?"

"Just this year," Josh said. "I was a little bummed when I got paired with a soldier, because I'm just about as opposite from a military guy as it gets, but he's been really nice. Not what I expected."

"Yeah?" I asked, thankful for every drop of insight he gave me to Apollo's life outside of emails with me.

"He's actually gotten me out of my shell a bit."

I thought of what Apollo told me about Josh watching *Sex and the City*, and my cheeks heated slightly. It must have worked, because Josh was easy to talk to, even if I wasn't attracted to him in the same way I was to Apollo.

"Are you going to live in a dorm next year?" he asked.

"That's the plan, although I haven't been assigned a roommate yet."

"Nice. I'm hoping I can talk some friends into getting an apartment or something next year. The dorms are getting a little old."

"Why is that?"

He shrugged, fumbling with his zipper. "It would just be nice to have my own place."

I nodded, and we continued up the library steps in awkward silence. It struck me that this was kind of like a date. He had asked me to coffee at the party, and now we were going. The thought made me slightly nervous. What were people supposed to do on a date? Kiss?

I wanted my first kiss. But with Josh? I didn't feel that kind of chemistry there. If that was something people really felt.

And besides, I probably shouldn't kiss someone when all I could think about was his roommate. As we checked out at the coffee shop, I wondered what Apollo had thought of me when he saw me across the gym. Had he been interested? Thought his friend could do better? My fingers itched to get out my phone and email Apollo to see if he'd tell me about it.

"Nadira?" Josh asked. It was clear this wasn't the first time he'd said my name.

"Sorry," I said. "What's up?"

"It's okay. I was just asking if you wanted to sit in here or outside?"

"We can sit in here," I answered. That seemed to be the safer answer in case Apollo decided to go back to the dorms early. If he caught up with us and we started talking, it would only be a matter of time before he discovered my true identity.

Josh went to a small table in the corner near a window that overlooked the quad. "How is this?"

"Good." I sat in one of the seats and wrapped my hands around the cold cup.

For the next hour or so, Josh and I just talked. We had some things in common, and he told me about different art principles he was learning in class. I wondered again if this was what dating was supposed to feel like? Like hanging out with a friend?

All the ice in my cup had melted by the time Josh looked up and said, "Hey, man, how was the game?"

I looked behind me and gazed straight into the eyes of Apollo. No photo of him had done his eyes justice. They weren't just green. They were moss with flecks of gold star bursting around the irises. And his lips seemed to be in a perpetual soft smile.

Apollo shrugged. "We won by ten."

That statement, spoken in his voice, snapped me out of my shock. "I'm sorry, Josh, I have to go." I scrambled to stand, grabbing my purse, and left the coffee shop.

Behind me, Josh called, "Wait, I'll walk you."

"It's okay," I said, backing out the door. "I'll see

you later." I hurried to the gym, hoping I could make it back before Dad noticed I'd been gone. Luckily, people were still leaving the stadium as I walked in, and I hurried to the court to find Dad standing with my brothers. Thankfully, Tatiana was nowhere to be found. But there was what looked like a small bruise on Terrell's neck...

Dad raised his eyebrows at me. "Where have you been?"

I bit my lip, not sure how to answer.

Carver blurted, "I saw her leave with a boy!"

Dad's face went ashen. "What?"

I raised my eyebrows. "Is it really that big of a shock that a boy would want to talk to me?"

Dad stuttered. "Who—what—why—where did you go?"

"I went and got coffee with a boy. It was very PG, I promise," I said. "And what about Terrell, huh? He went off with Maleficent and she gave him the mark of the beast."

Terrell glared at me.

Dad shifted, grumbling slightly, as if not sure what to make of it or who to chastise first.

"Congrats on the win," I said, hoping for a change in subject.

"Thank you," he said, "But we'll talk about this tonight."

I let out a sigh and waved at my brothers to follow me. "Let's go home."

EIGHTEEN

NADIRA

I COULD HEAR Mom and Dad start talking through the crack in my door the second she got home.

"Do you know what your children were doing today?" Dad asked her.

Mom chuckled a little, and I heard her thick purse fall on the counter. "It must have been something bad if they're *my* children and not our children."

"Terrell spent the game making out with some girl. And Nadira was with a boy, not even in the building," Dad said, as if he were telling her I'd been doing drugs or rooting for the other team. Both would have been equally as bad in his mind.

"I know about Nadira," Mom replied lightly.

"What?" he asked, just as stunned as I was.

"One of my TA's went to the coffee shop and told me that she saw Nadira there with a boy. Said they were sitting across from each other and talking. Not even close enough to touch. It sounded kind of sweet."

Dad was silent for a moment. "She was with a college boy."

"She's going to be in college in just a few months. Honestly, I'm glad she's dating now while she's at home so we can talk to her about it."

"But she was sneaking around," Dad said. "She wasn't even going to tell me about it until the boys ratted her out."

I sighed, looking toward the ceiling. Terrell had a love bite on his neck! Why was *I* the topic of conversation?

With a smile in her voice, Mom said, "You're worried about your baby girl."

There was silence for a moment, and Dad said, "She's growing up, hon. I can't believe she's going to be gone so soon."

I smiled lightly and sat back on my bed, getting out my phone. They cared. And even if it had been out of panic, I'd been on a date today. I'd spent time with a boy.

I'd seen Apollo.

How had it been only this morning I'd been messaging with him? It felt like a lifetime had passed, and I just wanted to email him again.

I forced myself to wait until the next morning to message him. After we had brunch—with plenty of hints from my parents about me dating—I went up to my room and checked my computer. Luckily, Apollo was logged on.

Nadira: Happy Sunday.

Apollo: Do you mean happy almost-Monday?

Nadira: You're a pessimist, aren't you?

Apollo: Maybe... Who's asking?

Nadira: No need to put your guard up. You're talking with one of your own kind.

Apollo: Is that so?

Nadira: Mhmm.

Apollo: How did you discover you're a member of the dark side?

Nadira: Some people think I was born with it.

Apollo: Some people think it's Maybelline?

Nadira: Exactly.

Apollo: How was your day yesterday?

Nadira: It was okay, you?

Apollo: Not bad. Went to the basketball game and hung out with my roommate the rest of the day.

My stomach bottomed out. He'd brought up the subject of the game. How could I ask the right questions to get him to tell me what he thought of me?

Nadira: What did you think of the game?

Apollo: It was pretty good until my roommate bailed on me to hang out with a girl.

Pay dirt.

Nadira: Oh?

Apollo: He's been talking about her nonstop since Friday night and apparently, she was at the game.

Nadira: What do you think of her?

Apollo: She's stunning. Totally his type.

My mouth fell open. Stunning? He thought I was *stunning?* But then my happiness fell at the second sentence. If I was Josh's type, did that mean I wasn't Apollo's?

Nadira: What does that mean? Stunning and his type?

Apollo: She seems a little shy. Really unique.

I pushed back from my computer and got up, pacing the room. Unique? I let out a shaky breath. Why couldn't I get away from that freaking word? Why did the one guy I liked have to use it on me?

My computer chimed with a new message, and I went back to look at the screen.

Apollo: I'm bad at describing people.

Nadira: Okay.

I couldn't quite bring myself to sit down yet. To fully engage with the person who called me the least desirable word on the planet.

Apollo: Okay... did I say something wrong?

Nadira: I don't know.

Apollo: You're being cryptic.

I bit my lip, slowly sitting in the chair. It wasn't Apollo's fault. He probably thought I was ugly and didn't want to say that outright. He was a nice guy, after all. He wouldn't insult his roommate's girl like that. And I couldn't blame him for saying what everyone already knew. I wasn't easy on the eyes. I wasn't the kind of girl guys liked for her looks. I was the kind they got to know, slowly discovered they liked my personality, and then decided they could live with my looks. It wasn't Apollo's fault.

Nadira: Not on purpose. Was she nice at least?

Apollo: I don't really know. I feel like I scared her away. I seem to have that effect on women.

Nadira: What do you mean?

Apollo: I haven't dated anyone since I've been at BU.

Nadira: Really? Why not?

Apollo: Just hasn't felt right yet. I don't want to date a girl just for fun and get our hearts involved. I want it to be something real.

Nadira: Isn't that the point of dating? To see if it could be something real?

Apollo: I don't think so. That's what friendship is for. When I ask a girl out, it's because I like her. A lot.

Nadira: That's an interesting way to look at it.

Apollo: So I take that to mean you're a heart-breaker, dating around and whatnot?

Nadira: "Whatnot?"

Apollo: You're dodging the question.

Nadira: No, I've only been on one date before.

Yesterday, in fact. With your roommate.

Apollo: And? Was it awful?

Nadira: No. Not really. It was just... not what I expected.

Apollo: In what way?

Nadira: I don't want to sound lame.

Apollo: Lamer than a college freshman who hasn't been on a single date in eight months?

Nadira: Fair. That is pretty lame.

Apollo: Hey!

Nadira: Just kidding.

Apollo: ... I'm waiting.

Nadira: I don't know how to describe it. I always thought when I went on a date, I would get butterflies and be giddy and want him to kiss me.

Apollo: But you didn't feel those things?

Nadira: No. And I can't tell if I'm hoping for too much or if that's what dating is. Just like hanging out with a friend.

Apollo: That's not what it is... when you do it right.

Nadira: And you've done it right?

Apollo: Once. Kind of.

Nadira: Kind of?

Apollo: She was my high school sweetheart. We started dating the beginning of my junior year and dated all the way through senior year.

Nadira: What happened?

Apollo: She went to college in Houston. I went to college in California. I told her I would do long distance, but she said no, she didn't want to go to college with a boyfriend. Even if that boyfriend was me.

Nadira: That sounds awful. I'm so sorry.

Apollo: It was. In the beginning. But eventually, I realized all the ways we were wrong for each other. Moving here turned out to be a blessing.

Nadira: How?

Apollo: Well, first of all, I'm going into the military. Any girl I date is going to have to be okay with long distance from time to time. And whenever I started talking about the military, my ex would just kind of... zone out. Or change the subject. She didn't seem to be interested in it at all. And she didn't ever spend time with my mom when I wasn't around. Whoever dates me has to like my mom.

Nadira: You didn't notice any of that when you were dating? Two years is a long time.

Apollo: I did. But I just wrote it off. Now I know better. I know what I want.

Nadira: And what is that?

Apollo: A beautiful girl who's smart, with goals and dreams and a stubborn attitude who'll survive distance and deployments and whatever else life throws our way.

Apollo: What about you?

Nadira: What do you mean?

Apollo: What kind of guy are you looking for?

Nadira: I'll let you know when I find out.

The problem was, I thought I already knew.

NINETEEN

NADIRA

APOLLO and I hadn't been talking long, but I already felt like I knew him better than half the people I went to school with. I looked forward to messaging him every day. I was eager to hear his opinions on things I didn't let most people have opinions on. I'd never been so excited to check my messages in the morning or smiling so often as I went to bed.

I was pathetic.

By the time this was over, I'd be a distant memory to him while he'd be at the front of my mind, the comparison to every guy I met.

Even Josh. He was kind, but there wasn't any chemistry there. But how could Josh stand a chance next to Apollo? It wasn't fair comparison, for either of us.

Part of me wished I'd never talked to Apollo so I could be satisfied with the attention Josh was giving me. But that wasn't real life. No, real life was thinking about Apollo all day and then running to my computer the second he messaged me that evening.

Apollo: Happy Monday.

Nadira: HAPPY Monday? I thought you were a pessimist.

Apollo: You're right. Sad Monday.

Nadira: Terrible Monday.

Apollo: Awful Monday.

Nadira: We should just cancel Monday.

Apollo: Yeah. Where can I sign?

Nadira: I'm starting a petition now...

I sent him a link to a petition to cancel Mondays from here on out.

Apollo: Omg you actually did. I'm going to be the first one to sign it.

Nadira: Not if I sign it first.

Nadira: HA!

Apollo: How did you do that so fast?

Nadira: Skills.

Nadira: And good Wi-Fi.

Nadira: But mostly the skills.

Apollo: Okay, so we have two signatures. 999,998 until we can submit it to Congress.

Nadira: That should be easy. Everyone hates Mondays.

Apollo: What should we name not-Monday once we get it cancelled?

Nadira: Sunderday?

Apollo: Satunday?

Nadira: Extra Sunday?

Apollo: Early Tuesday?

Nadira: We'll find something good.

Apollo: I hope so. Because Mondays stink. I'm pretty sure I failed my philosophy quiz today.

Nadira: Isn't philosophy literally the study of thinking? How could you fail if you have a brain?

Apollo: So you see my problem.

Nadira: Haha. I bet you got a decent grade.

Apollo: How was school for you?

Nadira: I hate Yearbook.

Apollo: What happened?

Nadira: So there are two girls in the class who are basically queen bees at school. And today we're deciding on the layout for the senior pages, and they basically want whoever wins royalty at homecoming and prom to get an entire page out of the layout.

Apollo: Which means they'll be on both pages?

Nadira: Bingo. And of course they're the editors, so the teacher lets them make the decisions. It just stinks because so many of my classmates are incredible. Like one of my friends won at a national dance competition. The judges literally created a new category for her and her partner because they were so amazing. Why isn't that going to be front and center? Or another friend got signed to play college sports. Is that not important? I'm pretty sure the Mathletes will go to state this year. Can't that be a big deal?

Apollo: That's just the way high school is. I know it might sound crazy, but next year, when you're at MIT covered in guys and learning about something that will change the world—nay, universe, Miss Aerospace Engineer—you won't even be looking at your high school yearbook.

Nadira: Maybe, but I can't see me getting much studying or universe-changing done while "covered in guys."

Apollo: Multi-tasking is an important skill in any career.

Nadira: I'm rolling my eyes.

Apollo: I'm laughing.

Nadira: I'm signing off.

Apollo: I'm looking forward to talking to you tomorrow.

Nadira: Goodnight. :)

Apollo: Goodnight, beautiful.

I read that last line again. And then I screamed.

Feet thundered up the stairs, and my cheeks heated as I closed my laptop and turned toward the door.

Carver stood there, chest rising and falling, and he said, "You okay?"

"Yeah—yep, never been better." I couldn't even hide my grin.

He eyed me skeptically, stepping into the room. "You're blushing."

"No I'm not," I said, looking away. "I'm just, uh... exercising."

"In your desk chair?" he asked.

"Totally." I pretended to do an exercise I'd seen Dad do in a chair before, and then toppled over, crashing to the floor. "Well, I'm still mastering it."

Carver burst out laughing. "You're a terrible liar, Dira."

I glared at him, pushing myself off the floor.

"Does this have anything to do with that skinny kid you were with at the game?" he asked.

"Rat," I muttered.

"It does!" He clapped his hands together, then covered his mouth. "We were starting to wonder if you had something going on with Des, and then—"

I glared at him. "So what if I was gay? Would that be a bad thing?"

His eyes widened. "No, totally, it's fine if you are. I mean. Wow. Are you... gay?"

I rolled my eyes. "Pull your foot out of your mouth. I'm straight."

"So this boy..." he began.

"Goodbye, Carver," I said, walking him to the door.

"Is he a good kisser?"

"Goodbye," I repeated and shut the door behind him, hearing him laugh all the way down the stairs.

"He said WHAT?" Des asked at lunch.

I'd waited until all my friends were together, including Cori and Adriel's boyfriends so I could get the male perspective too.

"He said, 'Goodnight, beautiful'!" I cried, so ridiculously happy.

Carter frowned. "But he doesn't have a real

picture of you."

Des nodded. "Because she's too chicken."

I glared at her.

Faith said, "You have to send him a real photo. I'm sure you can say you grabbed the wrong one from your computer or something."

"Yeah, that'll work great," I said. "It'll be kind of like ordering a swimsuit off the internet to find out it's only big enough to cover one boob instead of two."

Ryker's eyes widened. "That happens?"

"Don't be so excited," Cori said. "And that's beside the point. You guys are emailing. It's not like he's been seeing the wrong person every single day."

I frowned down at my untouched tray of food. "That's not the biggest problem. You know the guy who asked for my number Friday?"

They nodded.

"That's Apollo's roommate."

"What!" Des cried, then covered her mouth, realizing how many people were now staring our direction. "You didn't tell me that!" she hissed.

"I found out Saturday, and I'm so mortified I didn't even know how to process it."

Adriel shook her head slowly. "Oh, what a tangled web we weave..."

Des finished, "When first we lie to our super-hot internet pen pals."

Ryker snorted, but I shook my head, asking, "What does it mean? That he said goodnight beautiful?"

Cori and Ryker smiled at each other, then Cori turned to me and said, "That he likes you."

Ryker smirked. "You mean, Tatiana."

Cori hit him.

Leaning forward, Carter put his elbows on the table and said, "You have to tell him, Dir. You're what? A week? Two weeks into this thing? You're not in too deep to tell him you got nervous. If he's a good guy, he'll understand."

"And if he's not?" I asked. "What if he stops emailing me and ruins my mom's research project?"

Faith gave me a look. "Your mom's smart. I'm sure she assumed some people would drop out."

I sighed. "I don't know."

The bell rang, and Des said, "You do know. It's just hard to admit we're right."

With that, we stood from the table and I walked my untouched plate of food to the trash. What a mess.

TWENTY

NADIRA

APOLLO: Happy Tuesday.

Nadira: You mean Sad post-sunderday.

Apollo: We haven't decided on a name yet.

Nadira: You mean you haven't decided.

Apollo: Uh-huh. What are you up to?

Nadira: Just finished homework. Hanging out on the couch and watching TV until my brothers get home from basketball practice.

Apollo: How late do they usually stay out?

Nadira: Well, practice ends at 5:30, but they usually stay longer to work on free throws. They have a friend drop them off here around 6 or 6:30.

Apollo: Do your parents work late?

Nadira: Depends on the day. Mom loves her job, so usually. Dad stays pretty busy during basketball season. What about you? Were your parents home most of the time?

Apollo: My mom was. She made it to every one of my games, videotaped them even. Now that I'm in college, I appreciate her more than ever. She always made the best breakfasts for us, and dorm food just doesn't compare. Dad worked late a lot, but he was usually home before I went to bed.

Nadira: Is she talking to you yet?

Apollo: Nope.

Nadira: I hate that.

Apollo: Me too. So we should talk about something happier.

Nadira: And you call yourself a pessimist.

Apollo: Just not a masochist. :) How was school today?

Nadira: Oh, you know... One of my friend's YouTube videos went viral, overheard the mean girls talking crap about me in the bathroom, got an A on my calc test. The usual.

Apollo: I don't even know where to start with that.

Nadira: You're saying you're surprised by the A? Oh ye of little faith.

Apollo: No... I just... what did the girls say? I'm so sorry.

Nadira: It's nothing I haven't heard before. Called

me fat. Said no guy would ever be interested in me. That scientists should put me in a lab... blah blah blah.

Apollo: Nadira, that's awful. I don't understand why anyone would say that about you. You're beautiful. And definitely not fat.

I read the words again, then put my phone down, tears stinging my eyes. This was my chance. I could send him a picture of me and let him know who I really was. That I wasn't some skinny girl with flawless skin. I was a freak. And people were right when they insulted me that way.

I began typing out the message to tell him. To put this farce to an end before it went too far. But then he sent me another message.

Apollo: Call me. 555-0213. I'll take your mind off it. :)

I stared at his number, then stood up and put my phone on the couch, staring at it like it was a viper.

Maybe it was.

What would happen if I took this relationship with Apollo out of text? Would hearing his voice make it real? Could he hear my fatness in my voice? Was that even a thing?

But my heart longed to talk to him. To let him comfort me from the things Tatiana and Isabella had said. Apollo was quickly becoming my favorite distraction.

I took a deep breath, tapped on his phone number, and called my pen pal.

It only rang a couple of times before he picked up and said, "Hello?"

I didn't know what I'd been expecting, but it wasn't the twist in my stomach at his voice, which sounded as warm as melting chocolate and as strong as steel.

"Hello?" he said again, and I realized I'd been clutching the phone so tightly to my ear I'd forgotten to speak.

"Hey," I said, suddenly self-conscious of how the words sounded coming out of my mouth. Would Apollo be as entranced by my voice as I was by his?

He chuckled low, and if I thought I liked the sound of his voice, his laugh was even better.

"You sound just as beautiful as your picture."

The words lifted me up before pummeling me to the ground. He thought Tatiana was beautiful, but my voice was too. For a moment, I wondered if there was a chance he could find the real me beautiful as well.

"Thank you," I said quietly.

There was a pause, and he chuckled, which made me chuckle in return.

"I guess I'm not as good on the phone as I am online," he said.

I smiled, thinking he was completely wrong. "You did promise a distraction."

"True," he said. "What are you watching on TV?"

"An old episode of *Survivor*."

"*Survivor*?"

I paced on the living room carpet. "You seem perplexed."

"You just don't seem like a *Survivor* person."

I rolled my eyes. "I'm not. Sometimes I like to watch reality TV to make myself feel better about my life. They're sleeping on sand out there. My bed looks *way* better in comparison."

"That's brilliant. You should give life advice," he said with another laugh that warmed me from the inside out.

"I have plenty of it, just none for myself, apparently."

"You and me both," he said. "So I have an idea for the next time you hear those girls being mean."

I trailed my toe in a circle on the carpet. "I'm all ears."

"Punch them in the face."

I laughed out loud; the answer was so unexpected.

"Bet they won't run their mouths anymore," he teased.

"Yeah, and I won't be valedictorian either," I retorted. "I *never* get in trouble."

"So you're a good girl?" The flirty undertones in his voice made butterflies take off in my stomach.

"You could say that," I replied softly.

This. This is what had been missing from my date with Josh. There was something about Apollo. The way he spoke, the words he said, that took me completely off balance in the best possible way.

The front door opened, and Carver and Terrell ambled inside, crashing into each other. Terrell saw me first, a grin spreading on his lips. "Is that lover boy?"

Carver began making kissing sounds.

"Apollo, I've got to go," I said. But before hanging up, I added, "Call me tomorrow?"

"You can count on it."

I couldn't wait to hear his voice again.

TWENTY-ONE

APOLLO

I HELD the phone to my ear for longer than I needed, wanting to catch every sound on the other end of the phone before she ended the call.

Nadira's voice—talking to her—was incredible. I wanted to pound my fist in the air. I wanted to run ten miles. I wanted to jump on the trampoline in my parents' backyard and fall happily on my back.

"You have it bad," Josh chuckled from where he sat in front of his TV. He had his video game headset on and was tapping on the controllers, but apparently that hadn't stopped him from noticing me.

"How much of that did you hear?" I asked, my cheeks getting got.

He made his voice all breathy and crackly like a pre-pubescent teen. "'So you're a good girl?'"

"Oh shut up." My ears were hot now. My neck too.

He grinned, still not looking at me. "You have a crush. It's cute."

I got up from the chair and grabbed my jacket.

"Where are you going?" Josh asked. "A convention for lovestruck schoolboys?"

I gave him the finger and left the room, not quite able to hide my smile. As I shrugged on my jacket and walked toward the elevator, I wanted to call my mom and tell her about Nadira. How talking with her made me feel.

But I already knew she wouldn't answer, and part of me was mad enough to hold out until she called me first. So I went down to the parking lot and drove to see the woman who'd been my surrogate mother ever since I moved to California.

Just a few miles away, Brentwood Senior Community came into view. My dad's parents still lived in their home and my mom was estranged from her folks, so at first going into a nursing home had been strange. But now, the people there were like my second family.

I parked close to the front, since the visitor

spaces were always open, and walked to the front door. I tapped in the entry code and said hi to Rosie, the woman who always parked her wheelchair in the sun coming through the front windows.

"Hi, baby." She extended her arms.

I went and gave her a hug. She squeezed me tight, placing a big wet kiss on my cheek that I'd wipe off later—out of her sight, of course. I wondered how many hugs she got a day, if she even got one, and my heart tore just a little bit.

Miss Honey, one of the CNAs, passed by, pushing a cart of laundry and said, "Hi, Apollo! Aunt Tilly's in the dining room. I bet if you ask Amanda, she'll grab you a plate for supper too."

"Thanks," I said, then gave Rosie my biggest smile. "See you Saturday, Rosie."

She smiled and waved, then I went in search of my aunt. I'd almost forgotten it was supper time. My stomach tied in knots from my conversation with Nadira, but maybe it would help to sit and eat with my great-aunt.

I made my way to the dining room where Aunt Tilly usually went to play Skip Bo with some of the other people here. The nurses called them residents, but that made me uncomfortable. The term seemed too formal. This was their home. They lived here.

I found Tilly at the end of a table wearing one of the big covers they put on some of the people here before eating. Since Tilly's stroke, her left hand didn't work as well, and the shaking could cause some issues.

As I drew closer, I said, "Hi, Aunt Tilly."

She looked up at me, giving me a lopsided smile. She couldn't speak, but her eyes focused in on me. I leaned over and gave her a hug before pulling up a chair beside her. Most of the people at her table were nonverbal, which made me sad. Tilly's stroke had taken her ability to talk, but not think. She probably would have loved hearing others' conversations. At least, I would have if I were in her shoes.

Amanda, the cook at the nursing home, came out of the kitchen carrying three trays. Catching sight of me, she grinned as she set the trays down at a different table. "Tilly, you have a visitor?"

Aunt Tilly smiled at me.

"Do you want some supper, honey?" Amanda asked.

"If it wouldn't be too much trouble," I replied.

She put her hand over her heart. "Not if you keep talking with that southern charm."

The tips of my ears got hot, but I smiled and

turned back to Aunt Tilly. "I just had great news and wanted to come tell you." I swore I could see the spark of a question in her eyes, so I continued. "You know that girl I've been emailing with? I called her on the phone tonight and..."

And what? I thought, not sure how to finish. How could I even describe this feeling in my chest that was somewhere between flying and soaring.

"I like her," I finished.

Aunt Tilly put her good hand on mine. There was a bit of food on her fingers, but the gentleness of it nearly brought tears to my eyes. I missed my mom, but having Tilly step in made it a million times better.

Amanda set a tray in front of me. "Here you go, honey. Mashed potatoes, chicken fried steak, and extra corn. Just for you." She winked.

I smiled and thanked her, then ate alongside Tilly. She might not have been able to talk, but she spoke to me more than she'd ever know.

TWENTY-TWO

NADIRA

THE NEXT MORNING when I came downstairs, Dad already had a breakfast casserole made and was sitting at the table eating a slice. As I approached the table, he took a plate from the stack and lifted a serving of casserole onto it.

"Thanks," I said, settling into a chair. "Mom already gone?"

"Yeah, had an early advising appointment," he replied, taking another bite. "I have a question for you, baby girl."

I raised my eyebrows. "What's up?"

"I want to take you out tonight. Show you how a man should treat a lady on a date."

My cheeks instantly felt warm with embarrassment, and I almost checked to see if my brothers had heard him. They would never let me hear the end of it if they thought the only date I could get was with my dad.

"How does that sound?" he asked.

"Like taking a cousin to prom. But worse."

He laughed. "It's not like that, Dira! You're growing up, getting ready to move out, and I'm realizing all we haven't taught you. Indulge your old man, will you?"

I looked toward the ceiling. "Did you ask Mom if she thought I'd say yes?"

"No..." He fought a smile, and I pointed at him. "Shut up!" He used his hand to wipe the smile from his face.

I laughed. "What are we doing on this 'date'?"

"Dinner, a movie. Pretty standard."

"Glad to know you're making it special," I muttered.

He rolled his eyes. "So leave the car for the boys to take home from practice, and I'll pick you up by the school entrance after you get out."

Behind me, Terrell called, "We get the car?"

"That's right," Dad replied.

Once they got down the stairs, Carver fist-bumped Terrell. "Can we hang out at Waldo's for a while?"

Dad shrugged. "I don't see why not."

The boys crowded around the table, taking twice the amount of food I'd had. Since I knew we'd be going out after school, I excused myself to my room to get an outfit that would be more comfortable than my uniform. I always changed out of it as soon as I could.

As I went upstairs, a new message came across my phone.

Josh: Hey, how are you?

I looked at it for a moment, guilt twisting my stomach. How could I tell Josh I didn't like him? That no matter how friendly he was, I would always compare him to Apollo? Since I couldn't find the words for that, I texted him something different.

Nadira: Hey, I'm fine. Getting ready for school.

I set my phone on the bed and went to my dresser, reaching for a sweater and some leggings. I wished they would make leggings part of the dress code at Emerson. Regular pants were the worst. Skirts were only marginally better.

I stuffed the clothes in my backpack and then looked at my phone again.

Josh: Want to hang out this weekend?

I looked at the letters, my fingers hovering over the digital keyboard. Now that Apollo and I had talked on the phone, he knew what my voice sounded like. It would only be a matter of time before he found out who I was. Then Josh would hate me too.

I sighed and typed out a reply.

Nadira: Sorry, but I can't.

I bit my lip. How did you turn someone down without hurting their feelings? I'd ask Des, but I had a feeling she didn't give emotions a second thought when breaking up with a guy, especially since dating was all about fun to her.

Nadira: I'm going to be moving in a few months. I don't think now is the best time to start something.

The second I sent it, a guilty feeling worked through my chest, but I locked the screen anyway and tucked my phone in the side pocket of my backpack. I needed to get to school.

On the drive there, I couldn't help thinking about this "date" with my dad. If Apollo ever heard of it, I'd sound like the biggest nerd alive. But a part of me was thankful, too, that Dad was finally taking an interest in me.

No matter how much I hated high school, and no matter how much I looked forward to MIT, I would miss my family when I was gone. I hoped they'd miss me too.

After school, I changed into the leggings and sweater I'd tucked away earlier and then went outside to wait for Dad. Part of me was worried he wouldn't show, so I breathed a sigh of relief as his car pulled up along the building.

He got out of the car, wearing nice clothes, not the sweats he usually dressed in throughout the week.

"What are you wearing?" I asked.

He lifted a finger. "Rule number one. A good guy should dress nicely for a date. If he's going to run around in rags, you don't want it."

I shook my head, picking up my backpack from where it had been resting on the ground by my feet. "Any other obscure rules I should know of?"

"Yes." He reached for the door handle. "A lady should *never* touch a door on a date. Car door or otherwise."

"That's so antiquated," I said as I threw my backpack to the back seat.

"Chivalrous," Dad corrected, waiting for me to get in. Once I was, he said, "Fingers out of the way?"

"Yeah." I reached for my seatbelt as he shut the door and buckled in while he walked back around the car. Once he was inside, I said, "If you ask me, this was all a waste of time. We could have been on the road by now."

"Dating isn't about efficiency," Dad said. "It's about two people enjoying time spent with one another. If it's with the right person, you'll never want to cut it short."

I looked out the windshield, thinking of Apollo and how, no matter how long I talked to him, it was never enough.

"Now," Dad continued, "your date should ask you what kind of music you like to listen to or turn it off completely so you can talk. I happen to know you like 97.9, so I turned it there. If he plays it too loud and isn't singing with you, you don't want it."

I rolled my eyes. "Noted."

"Now, if a guy is always making you make plans for a date, you can just nope on out of there. In a good relationship, you take turns choosing so all the maintenance work doesn't fall on one person."

"Maintenance work?" I said. "You make relationships sound hard."

"Trust me, when you've been together as long as Mom and I have, maintenance work is necessary. Even the best car will quit being good if you don't change the oil every now and then."

I pretended to be disinterested, but honestly, all the thought that had gone into this was flattering. Dad was really trying.

As we drove across town to LaBelle for supper, Dad told me about the appropriate ways to interact in a car. When he began talking about the... activities that were strictly off limits, my cheeks burned.

"Dad!" I cried.

"What?" he said. "I coach a college basketball team! I know more about teen boys than you do."

I couldn't disagree. "But that doesn't mean I want to talk to my *dad* about it."

"I'd rather you learn it from me than a magazine," he retorted, pulling alongside the restaurant.

As he parked along the curb near the valet stand, I asked, "What sort of restaurant-arriving etiquette do I need to know?"

"Plenty," Dad said. He handed the valet the

keys, then walked alongside me toward the door. He put his hand on my shoulder blades. "Their hand goes any lower than this, and they're just looking for one thing. You don't let them get close."

"Dad! Why are we talking about..." I lowered my voice. "That?"

Shaking his head, he said, "The good guys might not be thinking about it, but the wrong ones will be thinking *only* about it."

The thought made me all squirmy. Were there really guys out there who only thought about sex? And what if I wanted the right guy to think about it? And if they *did* think about it, how did they bring it up? How did a person go from pen pals to phone callers to lovers?(Asking for a friend.)

Either way, I wasn't about to ask my dad. "So, hand in an appropriate position," I said. "Moving along."

"Right," Dad said, "so when we walk in, the waiter's going to take us to the table. Your guy needs to pull the chair out for you."

Thankfully, Josh hadn't done that on our impromptu date. The thought of having a guy pull a chair out for me, and then try to push it in with my weight on it was... ugh. "Pass. Next." We reached the door, and Dad held it open. "Gen-tlemen must be obsessed with doors," I muttered.

Before Dad could reply, a host took us to a table. We sat, and Dad began looking over the menu.

"Now's the part where it can get really bad," Dad warned.

I raised my eyebrows. "You're right. He could be a vegetarian." My eyes widened. "Or lactose intolerant. No chance to share cheesecake!"

He snorted. "That *would* be awful."

"Or if he talks with his mouth full."

"Gross," Dad said.

"Or if he's *boring*."

Dad chuckled. "Okay, so you've got this part down. But you know what definitely has to happen while you're on a date?"

"What's that?"

"He needs to ask about you. You're too inter-esting to let that opportunity pass."

I smiled, but that insecure feeling rose inside my chest, threatening to overpower the good time I was actually having. But if I really was that interesting, why did my parents always put me last? Why had I gone alone to every single school dance?

"Dira, you okay?" Dad asked.

I blinked quickly, trying to stem the new onslaught of tears.

He scooted his chair closer and rubbed my back. "What's going on, baby girl?"

I shook my head, the words coming out of me as unbidden as my tears. "Dad, look at me."

Dad's mouth fell open, then closed.

"I don't know if you've noticed, but I haven't had that many dates. Guys aren't interested in this." I gestured at myself. "That guy I went to have coffee with? He's the first person who's even looked my way without throwing up in his mouth."

Dad tilted his head, his forehead creasing. "Honey, that's not true—"

"It is," I argued, wiping at my eyes with the cloth napkin. "Guys don't want to date a girl who could sit on them and literally suffocate them, Dad."

"Dira..."

"And my skin?" I said, the lump in my throat aching. "Dad, guys think it's *contagious*. People have called me herpes girl. Dalmatian. Leper. They've asked if my mom *had sex with a panda*." I choked over my sob, each of the words marking my heart like vitiligo did my skin.

"Nadira," he said, his voice hard. "You look at me, and you look at me right now."

His harsh tone snapped me out of the sobs, and I sniffed, looking at him. His black eyes were hard, and the muscles around his jaw were tight.

"Just because someone can't see your worth doesn't mean it's not there."

"But, Dad—"

He shook his head and repeated, "Just because someone can't see your worth doesn't mean it's not there. *Even you*. Do you understand?"

His words blindsided me, took the ground out from underneath me, but he kept speaking.

"Your body is not anything you have to apologize for. It is a tool that you can use however *you* choose. My players use their bodies for entertainment. Mom uses her body to carry around that massive brain." He smiled softly. "Your body is *your* tool. *No one* else's. They don't get to use it or judge it or mislabel it as something it's not. Okay?"

I nodded slowly, taking it all in. I'd never thought of my body in that way. Only as something to be fought against. Something to cover up or hide. But a nagging voice argued with him still. "What if I never get to find a guy who wants to go out with me?"

He spread his arms wide, inviting me in for a hug, and I hugged him back. Breathing into my hair, he said, "You'd never want someone to come at a bolt with a hammer, Dir. It would do more damage than good. That doesn't make your tool bad. Sometimes it takes a while to find the right fit."

The waiter arrived and looked at us awkwardly. "Do you need a few minutes?"

I nodded into my dad's chest, thankful to have him on my side.

TWENTY-THREE

NADIRA

WE GOT BACK to the house and walked inside, joking about the waiter who'd bet Dad he could speak in a British accent for the rest of our meal at La Belle. (The waiter had won, and Dad was out twenty bucks.) Once my emotions had calmed, I'd actually had a really good time.

"In here!" Mom called from their room on the main level.

We walked over that way to find her folding clothes on their king-sized bed. (Dad needed that big of a bed so his feet didn't hang over the edge.) She smiled up at us and asked, "How was dinner?"

"Ask Dad how he lost twenty bucks."

He put his arms around my shoulders and rubbed his hand in my hair.

"Hey!" I cried, beating at his arm. "That's not very chivalrous!"

He let me loose. "Date's over—you got all the learning you're going to get!"

Mom chuckled. "Sometimes I think I have four children instead of three." She shook her head. "Did you have a good day, Dir?"

I nodded. "I'm actually expecting a call, so..."

Her eyes lit up. "Go ahead."

I went up the stairs as fast as I dared. Apollo was supposed to be calling in less than ten minutes, and I didn't want to sound out of breath when I answered. Unfortunately, I hadn't accounted for him being as punctual as I was.

The phone rang five minutes before our eight o'clock time, and I took a deep breath before letting out a breathy, "Hello?"

"Hey," he said. I could hear the smile in his voice.

"What's up?" I asked, still out of breath. I decided to lie down on my bed. Surely a prone position would help in slowing my heart rate. (Although, hearing Apollo's voice only sped it up again.)

"Just failed another assignment, no big deal," he said with a slight laugh.

"What class was it this time?" I teased. "History of Rock and Roll?"

"I'll have you know I took History of Rock and Roll last semester, and it was actually pretty interesting. I now know way more about AC/DC than I ever thought I would. My dad is very proud."

I laughed. "I hope so."

"It was human geography. Everyone presented their videos, and I'm pretty sure I'm the most awkward human alive. Now we're learning about human migration patterns through U.S. history."

"Like we're geese or something," I said.

"Exactly like that."

I couldn't help but smile. "If this is how your 'easy' classes are going, how will your engineering classes go next semester?"

He groaned. "Maybe I'll be like Einstein. You know, fail my basic classes so they think I'm stupid, then just blow everyone else out of the water in calculus."

"Did you just say what I thought you said?" I asked.

"What?"

"Well, I thought I just heard you compare yourself to one of the brightest minds in history."

"Hey," he said with a chuckle, "if the failing test grade fits."

I rolled my eyes. "I'll be sure to tell my parents that next time I bring home a failing grade."

"Be honest," he said. "You've never brought home a failing test grade."

"I have!" I argued.

"When? In seventh grade?"

My cheeks got hot. "Sixth," I mumbled.

"What was that?"

"Sixth, okay? And it was so mortifying I never did it again. Besides—I still maintain that English teacher was grading unfairly."

His laugh tickled my insides with butterfly wings. "Stubborn."

The word struck my heart. That was what he said he wanted, right? A stubborn girl? I shoved the thought down, lest I get lost in fantasies and forget reality.

"You know what I want to know?" I said. "I want to know what you do besides school and ROTC."

"If I told you, I'd have to kill you," he deadpanned.

"Classified information, soldier?"

"Mostly embarrassing."

"Now I'm intrigued." I played with the edge of my comforter, weaving the seam between my fingers. Downstairs, I could hear my brothers arguing over video games and the quiet hum of my parents' voices in their room.

"I play bingo," he mumbled.

I let out a laugh. That was the last thing I'd expected him to say. "You do what?"

"I have a great aunt who lives in a retirement home here. All of her family's moved away and any Banks who attends Brentwood U goes to see her. That's the deal."

"That's the deal?" I echoed.

"Yes. My brother did before he graduated. A few cousins have done it, and well, now it's my turn. At this point, it's a family tradition."

The thought of Apollo, this ex-football player and future soldier passing his free time playing bingo with his great aunt brought a smile to my lips.

"What?" he asked. "Does that ruin my street cred?"

I bit my lip. "I actually think it's pretty sweet."

There was a small moment of silence before he said, "What about the famous future aerospace engineer? Do you just pass your time doing math calculations and blowing everyone away with your brilliance?"

I snorted. "The luxurious life of a Mathlete."

"Really," he said. "I want to know."

I rolled over on my bed, propping myself up on my elbows. "Not much. I watch my brothers' games. I go to school. I hang out with my friends."

"What do you and your friends usually do when you're together?" he asked.

"Lots of different things... eat Mexican food, lie on the beach, watch basketball games, go to dance competitions, plot payback on bullies and then fall in love with them."

"Wait, I have to hear about this." I heard the creak of springs and wondered if that was the sound his mattress made as he lay back on it. It made the conversation feel more intimate somehow.

"Well, it all started last semester..." I launched into the story, telling him about Ryker and what a jerk he'd been before Cori put him in his place.

"Remind me never to cross you or your friends," he said with a laugh. In the background, I heard a door close. Apollo said, "Hang on a sec."

I waited as the phone line went silent. I wondered if Josh had walked into his room. I felt a little guilty for turning him down, but it was for the best to break it off before we got too involved in a relationship that would never work.

He came back on the line and said, "I may need you to help me plot revenge on some girl."

I sat up straighter. "What do you mean?"

"Josh said that girl turned him down. He's pretty disappointed."

"Oh," I breathed.

"She said she was breaking it off because she's leaving for college. That's not until August. Why turn someone down before you even know how it's going to go?" Apollo said. "Why not at least give it a shot?"

My voice was small. "Maybe she thought it was for his own good."

"He can decide that too."

I wasn't sure how to respond, so I made up an excuse to get off the phone and said goodnight. Apollo made a good point.

Which got my thinking... Was it his choice to decide whether or not he thought the real me was ugly?

I didn't know, but I also wasn't ready to find out. The odds of anything working out were looking bleaker and bleaker day by day.

TWENTY-FOUR

APOLLO

ON THE DAYS I had to wear my uniform on campus, people looked at me differently. I couldn't really blame them since my ironed pants and shiny black shoes stood out pretty starkly against their sandals and frayed shorts.

One of the first complaints my mom had attempted to bring up was how much work ROTC would be on top of my regular classes, but so far it hadn't been bad. I could use my classes toward elective hours, and the extra time spent in leadership lab, where I learned drills or training, didn't take too much out of my schedule.

But today, I really didn't want to go.

Nadira and I had established a time for our next phone call before I remembered it fell right in the middle of my leadership lab today. And I couldn't call her early because I had an advising appointment with Dr. Harris.

On my way to the engineering building, I sent her a text saying I wouldn't be free until nine, and if she couldn't talk, I'd understand.

Then I put my phone in my pocket and walked up the stairs until I reached Dr. Harris's office. It was one of those nestled inside a larger office, and she had an assistant who made sure no one got to her space without an appointment.

The woman looked up at me from her keyboard and said, "Appointment?"

"For advising," I said.

She moved her mouse around, leaning closer to her computer screen. "Apollo Banks?"

"That's me," I said.

"You can head back."

I walked around the reception desk and went to the cracked door, knocking softly.

"Come in," Dr. Harris said warmly.

I pushed open the door and stepped inside. She smiled at me and gestured at one of the chairs across from her desk. "Take a seat, Mr. Banks."

I did as she asked, noting the stacks of paperwork on her desk. "Busy?"

"Just the way I like it. I actually need to leave after this for a meeting with the university president."

I nodded, trying to pay attention to her words as I noticed the picture hanging behind her desk. She and her husband stood with their three children—two really tall boys and a girl. The boys were in basketball uniforms, holding a plaque, and the girl had her face painted navy blue and was covered head to toe in navy blue clothes. But now I noticed something on the boys' jerseys I hadn't seen before. Emerson Academy.

I wondered if Dr. Harris's daughter knew Nadira. If they were friends since Dr. Harris's daughter must know quite a bit about engineering.

Following my eyes, Dr. Harris turned toward the photo and smiled. "The boys won the state championship that year. They assisted each other on the final point. We were so proud."

"I bet," I said with a smile.

She nodded and turned to her computer, tapping on the keyboard. "Since ROTC students enroll in fall classes before other students, you can pretty much take your pick. I have a few suggestions for intro engineering courses, but I'd love to hear what you'd like to take as well."

I thought of Nadira and how she'd be studying aerospace engineering in the fall. "Maybe an aerospace class?"

She nodded. "Sure. You can take one of those as your engineering elective once you finish the intro class." She began listing out classes I could choose from—which ones counted toward my major, which ones were required by the college, and then added the hours I had to take for my ROTC program. When it was all said and done, I had fifteen hours of classes and Fridays free.

"That's lucky," Dr. Harris said. "That'll be great time to catch up on homework or take a long weekend with family if needed."

My stomach sank. I couldn't go home to see family—not if my mom wouldn't even speak to me or look at me when I walked through the door.

"Is everything okay?" she asked.

I nodded, not trusting myself to speak.

"How has the research project been? Are you making a new friend?"

Thinking of Nadira made me feel instantly lighter. "Yeah, it's been great. Really."

She seemed pleased. "That's amazing."

An alarm on her smart watch went off, and she glanced at it. "I'm sorry. I need to go or I'll be late."

I stood, picking my backpack up off the floor. "Thanks, Dr. Harris." I extended my hand, and she shook it.

"Don't be a stranger," she said. "My calendar always has room for you."

I nodded and left, walking down the hallway and to the elevator. I had physical training to get to anyway.

I began the long trek across campus toward the rec center. ROTC students trained in one of the gyms there every Thursday evening. Luckily, we had our own locker area, so once I got there, I changed into my assigned shorts and T-shirt. As I tugged the shirt over my head, another guy came in.

"Hey, Connor," I said, nodding to him.

He lifted his chin. "Ready to get smoked in the relay race?"

I swore. "Why is Sarge so obsessed with relays?"

"Because it's fun to watch you lose."

I flipped him off right as a few other guys came into the locker room. After a little explanation, they too joined in on the banter. It reminded me of high school before a football practice. No matter how different we were or where we came from, there was always fun to be had.

For the next couple hours, Sarge led us through relays designed to prepare us for the PT test—push-ups, running, sit-ups. And when we finished, we played Capture the Flag to get us running back and forth across the court.

By the time we finished, I was sweaty and relaxed. Something about moving my muscles and wearing myself out calmed my brain in a way little else did.

I showered off in one of the stalls and then put my clothes back on to walk to the dorms. Connor asked if I wanted to go get a drink at his brother's apartment, but I turned him down. I wasn't about to miss out on a chance to talk to Nadira.

As I walked back to my dorm, I couldn't help but think about her. How had her day been? Were those girls still being mean to her? I didn't under-stand why anyone would pick on her or call her fat. High school was a hard place, but not usually for girls who wore a size two. She did have the Math-lete thing working against her though.

I hoped she had at least stood up to Regina today. It sounded like Regina always gave her trouble at Math-lete competitions. I made a mental note to ask her about it tonight if she called—tomorrow if she didn't.

I passed girls on campus, and I could see that they were pretty. That they looked at me like I was something special, but they didn't hold any interest to me. Anyone would fall short compared to Nadira, and I hoped that wouldn't come back to haunt me.

I reached the dorms and took the elevator up to the eighth floor. In a surprising turn of events, Josh was sitting at his desk, when I got to our room, sketching with what looked like a black piece of chalk.

"What?" I asked, stumbling backwards and clutching my chest. "You're not playing video games?" I looked around the room. "Where's the ice?"

Josh glared at me. "Ice?"

"Because hell must have frozen over."

He snorted and chucked a piece of the black stuff at me, which I easily dodged. With the "threat" on the floor, I shucked my hat and shirt and hung them up in my closet, then took off my pants, hanging them carefully as well.

"Take it off, baby," Josh cooed.

I pulled my underpants down, showing him my ass.

"Okay, going to have trouble getting that mental picture out of my head."

"You're welcome," I retorted, pulling on a pair of shorts.

"Why are you putting on clothes? Shouldn't you be sending nudes like that to your pen pal?"

"Nudes are gross, and she's probably in bed," I said, trying to take the sadness out of my voice. We'd only been talking for a couple weeks, but something already felt like it was missing when I couldn't talk to her.

"Even better," Josh said, waggling his eyebrows.

I threw a shoe at him.

He caught it and tossed it back. And then my phone started to ring.

TWENTY-FIVE

NADIRA

"YOU'RE UP LATE," Apollo said.

I smiled, hanging my Mathlete jacket back on the hanger. "We had a Mathlete meet today at a school two hours away. It ran late, and then we got supper on the way home." I yawned silently. "It's been a long day."

"How did you do?" he asked, not seeming worn out at all. Actually, he seemed interested.

"We won," I said with a tired smile. "And I finally had that conversation with Regina."

"What did you say?" he asked.

I slipped my hanger onto the bar in my closet and slid the door shut. "I told her I was sorry that she's upset about me being captain, but that she's an excellent Mathlete and we should focus our energy on getting to state and not on a feud that won't matter five months from now."

"Wow." The awe was clear in his voice. "And what did she say back?"

I rolled my eyes and held my phone between my cheek and my shoulder so I could start unbuttoning my uniform top. "Basically that the reason she didn't like me wasn't because I was captain of the Mathletes but because I'm an—and I quote—'insufferable know-it-all who somehow bewitches the teachers into liking me.'"

He sucked in a breath. "Ouch."

"Not really. Because she's wrong. I'm not a know-it-all. If I was, I would know that I was, right?"

Chuckling, he said, "You're making my brain hurt with that kind of mental acrobatics."

"And besides, the teachers just like me because I actually do my work and don't complain."

"Are you sure that's why?" he asked. "Not because you're nice or funny or smart? That's why I like you."

My cheeks warmed slightly as I shimmied out of my shirt and then began working on my skirt. "Maybe I am good at trickery if it worked on you."

"Ha ha," he said. "I'm training for the military, remember? I can't be swayed so easily."

"No one ever said that you'd be good at it," I teased, stepping out of my skirt. I turned my phone on speaker and set it on my bed as I reached for my pajamas.

"You really know how to build up a guy's ego," he said.

"I did follow your advice to stand up to Regina. That's a pretty big compliment."

"Hey, you're right. You did."

"And that's just now registering?" I teased. I pulled my shirt over my head and slipped on some shorts before sliding under my covers.

"I'm still surprised," he retorted.

"Ha ha," I said. "We've known each other for a solid two weeks. It's about time I try at least some of your advice, right?"

"It feels like I've known you so much longer," he said quietly.

My heart beat faster as I rolled to my side, my back to the door. "I feel the same way."

"Josh keeps teasing me, calling you my girl-friend. I can hardly convince him you actually exist."

I laughed softly. "Why would he say something like that?"

"Maybe because when I'm not talking to you, I'm thinking about you."

The low hum of his words sent a jolt of electricity to my stomach, and breathing suddenly became difficult. Apollo was thinking about me like I was him? I ran his words over in my mind, hardly believing them to be true.

"It's okay if you don't feel the same way," he added quickly.

"I do," I blurted. Then I steadied my voice. "I do feel the same way."

I held my phone tightly to my ear, waiting for his response, hoping to hear the smile in his voice.

"Oh," he said softly, his voice full of that exact smile I'd been hoping for. I could picture it so clearly it was almost like he was there. "Is there any chance..." He let out a breath. "Is there any chance you'd like to meet me sometime? Get to know each other in person?"

The hope in his voice nearly tore me in two, and all of the good feelings I'd had only moments earlier came crashing down.

He didn't have feelings for me. He had feelings for the girl who looked like Tatiana. Telling him the truth would also mean confirming that I'd lied. Our relationship would end before it even began. But was it a real relationship if I couldn't even be honest with him?

It was time to let him know this relationship wouldn't last and blame it on the distance. I'd rather have him forever think of me as his beautiful pen pal instead of an ugly liar.

"I..."

"Don't say no," he said. "Not yet."

"But Apollo, I —"

"Just wait, okay?" he asked, something new in his voice. Desperation. "Don't say no yet. Give me the rest of the month to change your mind."

I bit my lip, wishing desperately there was a way come clean without losing him completely. I wanted to give myself more time. Come up with a way show him the real me that wouldn't lead to sheer and utter devastation of the first guy I'd really had a crush on. Between my friends and me, there had to be a solution.

"I'll wait," I said.

"Then I will too."

TWENTY-SIX

NADIRA

FRIDAY NIGHTS WERE ALWAYS BUSY. Cori played on the girls' varsity basketball team, and then my brothers played on the boys' varsity team. I'd spent way more hours sitting in the gym than any Mathlete should. By now, I was a pro spectator.

Rule number one of surviving hours on end of high school basketball? The concession stand. Rule two? Friends.

I loaded up on nachos, hot chocolate, and Nerds Rope, and then went to the gym to find my friends Adriel and Faith in the stands. I saw them and started climbing the steps, scanning the crowd. My parents were there too—a few rows over from my friends—ready to watch the games for the night.

My chest ached, wondering if they would ever

make it to a Mathlete event before the end of the season. We had two left—if we made it to state. The odds were not in my favor. Still, I forced a smile as I reached my friends and sat beside them.

"Where's Carter?" I asked Adriel. Her boyfriend had become a fixture of our friend group lately, and it was weird not to see him around.

She swallowed her bite of popcorn and said, "He's been training for this bodybuilding meet coming up. Actually, I was going to ask you guys if you wanted to come?"

I raised my eyebrows. "Guys with muscles lining up on a stage? Sign me up."

"Same." Faith giggled. "When is it?"

"After spring break," she said. Her eyes lit up, and she nudged my arm. "Maybe you can invite Apollo."

I shook my head, looking down at my food that suddenly didn't look so appetizing. "He's going to hate me by then."

"You never know," Adriel said.

Faith nodded. "Give him some credit. He likes *you*, not just some picture."

I was about to respond when the announcer told us to rise for the national anthem. Des walked to the middle of the court, holding a microphone.

I placed my hand over my chest as she sang the words in the most beautiful rendition I'd ever heard. She sang at almost every game, but each time sounded different. I could hardly believe how talented she was.

I found myself getting jealous. She was beautiful with a talent for singing. Adriel was an amazing dancer, Cori had a scholarship to play college ball, and Faith was about to save the world in the Peace Corps. What was special about me? Anyone could memorize an equation or two.

I let out a sigh, which was covered by raucous applause for Des. She deserved the recognition.

The game began, and I split my time between hoping my phone would vibrate in my pocket, cheering for Cori (who was an absolute beast on the court), and explaining basketball as best I could to Faith and Adriel. Des had younger brothers who played sports, so when she joined us, she understood what was going on in the game.

Sitting with my friends was a nice distraction from the fact that my parents were here for my brothers but hadn't been there for me. I especially needed the distraction when the boys' game started and I could hear them cheering above all the noise in the gym. I watched my parents, their eyes intent on Terrell and Carver. Each fall made their eyes crease with worry. Each successful basket made them smile with pride.

My chest ached so badly by halftime I needed a few seconds to get away from it all. To center myself. To stifle the jealousy rising in my chest.

I leaned over to my friends and said, "I'm going to get some air."

Des asked, "Want me to come with?"

I shook my head. "I'll be back in a bit."

My feet couldn't move fast enough as I left the gym, fighting the stinging tears in my eyes. I pushed past the double doors into the cool night air and walked down the stairs, stepping around the corner so I could have a private space.

Tears dripped down my cheeks as images of my parents supporting my brothers flashed through my mind.

My brothers were the perfect children in every way. They had skills validated by the entire student body. They did decent in school. They had friends, girlfriends. They were fit and attractive.

And then there was me with my mottled skin everyone stared at and my gap teeth that my parents refused to have corrected with braces. Not to mention my large stomach and thick thighs that ruined jeans (the ones that fit).

I sniffed, the cool air burning my nose and making my eyes water even more. Hot tears rolled down my cheeks, and I squatted down, just wanting to disappear. To be someone, anyone else.

My phone rang, and I pulled it from my pocket to cancel the call, but the name had me stopping short.

Apollo.

It was time for our nightly call, and if I was being honest, I just wanted to talk to someone who thought I was special. Who felt the way he said he did about me.

I pressed the button to answer and held my phone to my ear. "Hello?"

I'd tried to make my voice sound normal, but the instant Apollo heard me, he said, "Nadira, are you okay?"

"No," I choked out, half-laughing only so I wouldn't burst into more tears.

His voice was gentle as he asked, "What's going on?"

"I feel so pathetic," I said, shaking my head. "I shouldn't have answered. I just…I don't know…I just wanted to talk to you." A small sob peppered from my lips.

"Hey, hey, hey, I'm here. What's going on?"

The tenderness in his tone took me aback like a hug that only made you cry that much harder. "My parents never come to my Mathlete competitions, but they're here for my brothers' games. They're here, and I don't know what I did to be less important to them. If I could play sports, I would. If I could be tall and skinny and charismatic, I would. But I'm not, and it sucks." I cried harder, diving in the spiral of every thought I'd been working so hard to suppress.

"Baby," he breathed. "Don't say that."

My heart hurt even worse. Here was this amazing guy calling me *baby*, talking to me like I was a treasure, and all I'd done was keep secrets from him and answer his call when I was already falling apart.

"Why do you even want to talk to me? Why?" I asked, but it sounded like an accusation. Like what was wrong with him that he wanted to spend his evenings talking to *me* instead of sending an email and being done for the day? And he wanted to meet me? If he had any sense at all, he'd be deleting my email. Forgetting my number.

Forgetting me.

The line was silent, and for a terrifying, heart-broken moment, I thought I'd convinced him. Shown him that he really was better off without me. But what he said brought more tears instead.

"Nadira, if I didn't want to be talking to you, I wouldn't be. I'd send you an email a day and move on. You're not like that. You're smart, in the scary way that says you can start a colony on Mars or destroy the universe. There's not an in-between. And you're funny, but in the sarcastic way that makes me think a second longer than most jokes do. I don't understand why, but you're easier to talk to than people I've known for years. And I'm not about to question it, because I like *you*, Nadira. Not who you wish you could be."

Tears streamed down my cheeks, but they were happy this time. All this time, when I'd been trying to hide behind Tatiana's picture, Apollo had seen the real me underneath it all.

"I like you," I admitted. "I really like you, Apollo. More than a pen pal should."

"Don't say that. Don't let 'should' get in the way. Not with us."

My lips twitched into an almost smile. "Why?"

"Can't you feel it? There's something special here."

My heart beat painfully in response. "I can," I whispered.

"Me too," he said. "So promise me? No more should when it comes to you and me?"

"I promise."

"Good." He sounded pleased, and I just wanted to hear the smile in his voice all day. But my friends were probably waiting for me. Maybe even looking for me.

"I should—I need to get back to the game," I said, not wanting to in the slightest.

"Skip it."

"I wish. Can we talk tomorrow?" I asked, hope fighting against my carefully constructed walls of what I expected my life to be like as a curvy girl with vitiligo.

"You can count on it."

I looked at his name on my screen for a moment before I ended the call and went inside.

I needed my friends to help me find a way to tell Apollo the truth once and for all, and I hoped what he said was right. That he'd fallen for the real me behind the person I thought I wanted to be.

TWENTY-SEVEN

NADIRA

I FELL asleep to a goodnight text and woke up to "good morning, beautiful."

I smiled at my phone before setting it aside to get ready for the day. My friends agreed to meet at Des's midmorning for a strategy session. As I left the house, my brothers were still asleep, and both of my parents were at work—Mom at the college and Dad at an away game, which gave me all of Saturday free.

I pulled up to Des's driveway, my stomach tying itself in knots. So much rested on what solution we came up with. I finally realized how much I wanted to meet Apollo. Enough that I was willing to risk this perfect bubble we'd made online to turn it into something real.

The logical part of my mind told me it wouldn't work. I'd lied to him—catfished him like people did on reality TV. Not only that, but I was in high school and he was in college. I would be in Boston the next semester while he continued his studies at Brentwood U. And then after that? Who knew where our careers would take us.

But for once, I didn't want to be practical. I wanted to follow my heart, and my heart was pointing at possibility.

Adriel pulled into the driveway soon after me, and I waited for her as she got out of the car. She wound her arm through mine and said, "Are you ready for this?"

Feeling queasy, I shrugged. "I think so."

"It's so exciting," she said, moving us forward. "How romantic that you found each other when you were least expecting it! You didn't even know you were going to meet him until your mom asked you to help her out. Can you imagine if that person had stuck with the research study or if your mom had never asked you?"

I blanched at the thought. "You're right." There were a million ways I could have never met Apollo. In fact, the odds were more in favor of us never crossing paths. But here we were. I didn't believe in fate, but Apollo had also told me he didn't believe in coincidences. Maybe he was right. "That has to mean something... right?"

"Definitely," she said, reaching up to knock on the door.

"You don't need to knock," I said, turning the knob. "Mama De thinks it's an insult. She wants us to feel like family."

"That's so sweet," Adriel said as we entered the house. I could hear the crashing of video games from the basement where Des's brothers were sure to be, and the TV played in the living room, her sister and Mom sitting on the couch.

They twisted toward us, and Mama De said, "*Hola, chicas!*" She pushed up from the couch. "Let me get you some food."

Adriel chuckled. "Twist my arm, Mama De."

"Where's Des?" I asked, looking around.

"Here!" Des came out of her room in a bikini, and my eyes widened.

"What are you wearing?" Usually she waited until we were at least by the water to skimp down. And I hadn't known the beach was part of our plans today.

"We're going to lay out while we talk, right?" she said. "Didn't you bring a suit?"

I shook my head.

"Borrow one of mine," she replied, like it was no big deal at all. "Top drawer of my dresser."

I looked from Des to Adriel and asked, "Did you bring one?"

Adriel lifted her hair off her neck, showing a knotted halter top.

I shook my head and headed toward Des's room. "Fine." But Des's swimsuit collection was not *fine*.

I dug through the drawer full of suits and scoffed. Was there nothing that covered a belly button in here? I pulled out a tangle of fabric, thinking I'd finally struck gold, but the one-piece had so many cutouts it was more revealing than a bikini!

I groaned, finally reaching for the suit with the most coverage. It looked like a long sports bra and spandex shorts, but it would have to do. I slipped it on and then hurriedly put on my leggings and T-shirt.

When I went back to the living area, all of my friends were there, snacking on sopapillas and honey. Mama De was already on the couch with Des's younger sister, watching a telenovela. That woman had to be magic for how quickly she could make someone feel full and loved.

Des picked up a plate with the sugary bread. "Let's go outside?"

"Sure," Cori agreed. Today she was wearing a crop top, and I admired the way she showed off her stomach despite the extra flesh there. Despite the purple stripes of stretch marks coloring her pale skin.

She smiled at me and said, "I can't believe he called you baby."

Mama De whistled from the couch, and my cheeks instantly heated. We stepped outside, and I shook my head, admitting, "I can't believe it either."

Faith said, "I'm so happy for you, but also... Forever alone."

I snorted. "Just wait until he sees what I look like."

"Ah, ah, ah," Des said, wagging her finger at me. "You promised to be nicer to yourself."

I pretended to zip my lips. Although, the sentiment stood. I dropped into one of the beach chairs near the waves rolling toward the shore. The bright sun warmed my body, even though the water was probably still freezing. It felt nice to have the saltwater breeze on my skin and be with girls who knew me—fat, vitiligo, catfishing, and all—and *still* loved me.

"So let's plan," Cori said, taking off her crop top to let the sun hit her shoulders. "Can you just call him and tell him the truth?"

Des frowned, shaking her head. She lay down, resting the bowl of chips on her bare stomach and the guac on her chest between the triangles of fabric covering her breasts.

I raised my eyebrows. "Wait, are you seriously going to use your boobs like a cupholder?"

She waggled her eyebrows. "What else are they good for?"

Adriel smirked. "I bet your man of the hour has a few ideas."

Faith nearly choked and broke into a coughing fit that had all of us laughing.

Des shook her head and dipped a chip in guac. "You can't tell him over the phone because he could get upset and ghost you. You have one week left until the month's up. Why don't you meet him in person, and then you'll be able to explain, you know? See his reaction."

Cori frowned. "She has a point."

Faith seemed disappointed. "But that's just another week of lying."

Des nodded. "But it's already been three at this point. What's one more?"

The more they spoke, the tighter my T-shirt and the swimsuit underneath it felt. I tugged at the strap. "Maybe I should just forget it."

My friends broke into outcries of dissent.

"You can't do that!" Cori said. "He likes you. The real you, remember?"

"He doesn't know the real me," I argued. "And besides. What if the real me is repulsive to him? Even if he likes my personality, we can't just have an entire relationship online!"

Adriel quirked an eyebrow. "Don't you already?"

Cori tapped her nose. "And you're not giving yourself enough credit, babe. Look at you!" She pointed at me. "We're out here on one of the warmest days since winter and you're still fully clothed! Why should *you* be ashamed of how you look? *They* should be ashamed for judging you!"

Des crunched on a boob chip. "Here, here!"

Adriel nodded. "Maybe it's like stage fright, you know? I was always terrified of getting on stage, but I kept dancing. Kept performing like I wasn't scared, and eventually it got better. I never loved the limelight, but at least going on stage didn't make me sick."

Faith said, "Kind of like fake it 'til you make it?"

"Exactly!" Adriel said. "Fake your confidence until you feel it."

"Starting now," Des said before I could back out or even think it over for that matter.

"Now?" I asked.

Cori clapped her hands together. "Take it off!"

I shook my head and gripped at the edge of my T-shirt. "What's this going to do? Huh?" I pulled it over my head. Then I shimmied out of my leggings, feeling the shorts already riding up my dimpled legs. "What is showing my fat to the world going to do?"

Des set the chips aside and sat up, leaning toward me. "This is exactly what you need to do. You need to stop covering up and show yourself, Apollo, *and* the world who you truly are."

Cori shook her head. "That's not everything."

"What do you mean?" Des asked.

Cori met my eyes, her light blue ones holding my gaze steady. "Des is right. You need to show him who you truly are. But then don't apologize. Every time you apologize or hide behind clothes, you're telling every single curvy girl that they should cover up too. That fat's something to be ashamed of. I know you love us too much to think that's true."

For once, I couldn't disagree. "So it's settled," I said, pacing in the sand and feeling exposed in more ways than one. "I'll tell Apollo that I'll meet him on Friday at Emerson Trails...maybe the north trailhead so it won't be so crowded. And when he gets there, I'll tell him that I'm Nadira. I'll explain why I showed him Tatiana's picture. And then I'll beg him to forgive me and hope he says yes."

Silence hung in the air, only broken by the soft sound of waves and wind.

Then Faith said, "You're just forgetting one thing." She grinned. "The part where he kisses you, and you live happily ever after."

TWENTY-EIGHT

APOLLO

I KEPT HOPING Nadira would agree to meet me before the month was up, but the entire weekend passed without her saying yes. Then Monday through Wednesday did too. I could tell my nerves and pacing were driving Josh nuts, but I didn't know what else to do.

When I'd asked Nadira to meet me in person and heard the hesitation in her voice, I freaked. I practically begged her not to answer me yet, because I couldn't take a no. Couldn't face a day where there wasn't a possibility for more between us.

"That's it," Josh said, getting up and dropping his controller on the couch. "Let's go."

I folded my arms across my chest, leaning against the wall. "Where? Why?"

"We're crashing an art museum. Come on."

He reached into his desk, took out his wallet, along with a baggie of plastic hooks, and shoved them in his pocket.

"We're doing *what*?" I asked.

"It'll be fun. Come on."

Shaking my head, I grabbed a jacket and my wallet and followed him out the door. We got in his car, which had fuzzy pink dice hanging from the rearview mirror, and then he took off down the road.

"We're not going to get in trouble, are we?" I asked, shifting uncomfortably in the duct-taped seat. Not only was I afraid of getting in trouble with the law, but the reprimand from my sergeant could be harsh.

"It's innocent," he said, rolling his eyes. "You worry too much."

"You don't worry enough," I muttered.

"Hey, I have straight Cs. That spells passing."

"Uh-huh." I sighed, settling back in the cracked leather seat.

"It is. When I graduate college, no one's going

to ask to see my transcripts. They'll just want the diploma. If that."

Civilian life was different; I knew that. To the officer in charge of ROTC at Brentwood U, grades mattered. It could make the difference in rankings later on, opportunities for graduate studies, and more.

But if Josh said whatever we were doing was safe, I trusted him. Even if he played video games too much, he was a good friend, and he knew how important the military was to me.

I got out my phone as he drove and sent Nadira a text.

Apollo: Good luck at the meet today!

She texted me back almost instantly, which told me she was on the way there. She usually couldn't text during school.

Nadira: Thanks! :) I hope we make it to state.

Apollo: You're going to do great.

I couldn't help but hope she made it to state and that I could go watch her. My little sister had done scholars' bowl in high school, which I think was kind of the same thing. It was always fun to listen to the trivia and see if I had guessed it right before one of the competitors rang in.

My phone came out of my hand, and I said, "Hey!"

Josh had it and dropped it in the door pocket. "No obsessing about her."

"Who?" I asked.

"You know who." He glared at me. "Your pen pal can wait a few hours."

I pressed my lips together and looked out the window, knowing Josh wasn't going to budge. A thrift store came into view, and he turned into the parking lot.

"What are we doing here?" I asked. "I don't need any clothes or anything."

He reached into his pocket and handed me five bucks. "Get yourself the most ridiculous piece of art you can find. Meet me back here."

I shook my head. Artists could be so unpredictable. Not like engineers or military members. All the aspects of my life were carefully planned, laid out—except when it came to love. Maybe that's why waiting on Nadira's answer was driving me crazy.

Regardless, the sooner I followed Josh's instructions, the sooner this would be over with. We went inside, but Josh walked the opposite way as me, going toward the bigger pieces while I checked out a shelf of trinkets.

There was some ridiculous stuff nestled in between all the out-of-date *live, laugh, love* signs.

I found a glass figurine of a pig licking out of a trough and picked it up. It reminded me of my friend Tristan from high school who was in FFA. Sometimes I'd stay the night at his house and he'd let me feed his pigs leftovers.

I flipped it over and found on the sticker it was only two dollars. I kept it in my hand, comforted by its cool weight, then found another sign. It had five stars on it and said *would poop here again.*

I laughed out loud. If this didn't come in handy for what Josh had in mind, I'd definitely save it for my bathroom later on down the road.

I went to the register and checked out, then leaned on the hood of Josh's car. I'd grabbed my jacket out of habit, but I didn't really need it. This late in January, it was already regularly in the mid-sixties. I could probably go swimming at the beach and be just fine if I wanted to. Maybe the waves would do me some good.

Josh pushed through the front door, holding up a small bag. "What did you score?"

I held up my two items, and he snorted. "Those'll do just fine."

"I'm still not sure what you're signing me up for."

"You'll see."

We got in his car, and he drove down the highway for what felt like forever, playing indie music on his radio and telling me all about bands I'd never heard of. That was one thing Josh had done this year—he'd upped my music game in a big way.

Eventually, he slowed in front of The Emerson Museum of Modern Art.

"What are we doing here?" I asked.

"Put your stuff in your pockets. And grab your student ID." Without waiting to even hear my protests, he got out and began walking toward the entrance.

"Josh," I muttered, "if we're doing what I think we're doing—"

"Shh," he said, pushing through the front door. A middle-aged woman greeted us with an overly sunny smile. It was obvious not too many people came here.

"Hi, darlings," she said. "Welcome to the Emerson Museum of Modern Art! A little background, we opened this year and we're trying to get word out." She handed us a flyer. "In case you're interested in volunteering."

I pocketed the brochure, and Josh held his out in front of his eyes, scanning it over. "We actually came to look around. Students get in free, right?"

"Absolutely." Her voice practically echoed off the walls. "I'll just need a student ID, and then you can go to the right and see the exhibit room."

I pulled mine out of my wallet, and once she had looked it over, she gave us the go-ahead. All the walls in the hallway were white and way too bright, but we entered into a big room with walls covered in various sizes of frames.

The only time I'd been to an art museum had been on a high school field trip, but this was nicer. "Is this like your mothership?" I asked Josh.

"Pretty much," he muttered, still looking at the flyer.

"You should try to get something in here," I said.

"I might."

"Or an internship."

"Maybe."

He seemed so aloof, so I let it drop. That was

until he told me we needed to find a place to hang the art we'd purchased at the thrift store.

"Seriously?" I said. "The poop art does not belong here."

"That's the point. And that's what art is all about. Shocking your senses. Giving you something unexpected to look at. If you think about it, we're doing them a favor."

I rolled my eyes. "If that lady sees us doing this, I'm pretty sure she'll lay the curse of a WASPy white woman on us."

He snorted. "We'll be forced to wear khakis and dress shirts for the rest of our lives... oh wait."

I rolled my eyes. "Because oversized ripped shirts and skinny jeans are so much better."

"Let's do this," he said, ignoring me. He glanced over his shoulder, and noticing the woman was nowhere in sight, he took a Command hook from his pocket, secured it on a wall. Then he pulled a painting from the waistband of his jeans and hung it up. Now, on the blank space next to a beautiful painting of a running stream, there was a small portrait of kittens in a bathroom with toilet paper spread everywhere.

I couldn't help but laugh. It was so ridiculous.

"Your turn," Josh said.

I looked around, my eyes getting drawn to a painting of a cupcake in front of plump pink lips. It was bright with swirling colors. I walked toward it, reading the sign underneath. *Memories by Rory Hutton.*

There was some space below her name, so I took the poop sign and hung it up with Josh's help. My heart raced, and my palms were sweaty, and I felt like I was going to puke.

I backed away from the scene of the crime, saying, "I definitely didn't get into enough trouble in high school to be doing this."

Josh snorted. "You haven't committed any crime. They can peel the Command strips off and we bought the art. It'll just make someone's trip to the museum a little more fun."

We left the museum, and I had a weird smile on my face. As we drove back to the dorm, I said, "Thanks, Josh."

He nodded. "Anytime, man. And for what it's worth, I hope it works out."

"Me too," I sighed. "Me too."

TWENTY-NINE

NADIRA

EVEN THOUGH I knew the plan and had rehearsed what I would say to Apollo a million and one times, I still couldn't bring myself to commit to a time to meet him. Something was still holding me back. Fear, insecurity, whatever it was, I needed to get over it because I only had two days until our thirty days were up.

But today I needed to focus on my Mathlete competition. This was the qualifier that would determine whether or not we made it to state.

I'd given up asking my parents to come to the meet or even reminding them of the time. If they didn't think it was important enough for them to take time off work, I wasn't going to keep begging them to come. Mathletes mattered to me, and that's what was important. (At least, I was going to keep telling myself that until I believed it.)

We pulled up to the school where we'd be competing and got out of the van. Regina waited beside the vehicle while the rest of us put on our jackets.

Mr. Aris stepped around the hood and took a deep breath. "I've got a good feeling about today, team."

I smiled, feeling jittery but excited. (Maybe that had something to do with the good luck text Apollo sent me.) "Me too," I agreed. "I feel like we have the dream team this year."

Regina snorted. "This is way better than sophomore year. Remember how horrible that was?"

I shuddered, recalling the memory of getting absolutely decimated at every meet. No seniors had joined the team that year, which left mostly sophomores and freshmen to compete. "Thank goodness it's different now."

Mr. Aris nodded and gave Donovan a look. "You'll have some big shoes to fill next year."

Regina smiled proudly, but I looked toward the parking lot under my feet.

Next year.

So much would be different.

As we walked into the building, I realized this could be the very last Mathlete competition of my life. I decided I would savor every moment, no matter the results at the end of the day.

We went into the building, and I watched the people around us as we checked in. The nervous looks on younger Mathletes' faces. The sheer confidence of older students. The bored expressions of students from this school who had been commissioned to volunteer.

And then when we went to the cafeteria to wait for the first round, I took in everyone being themselves in a way we couldn't be at school with the rest of our classmates. There was something about being surrounded by other Mathletes that felt...relaxed somehow. It was almost like being around my friends, the Curvy Girl Club 2.0. There was nothing like being in a space where you could fully be yourself, no apologies needed.

Mr. Aris approached our table with a manila envelope and pulled out the schedule. There were teams we'd faced before on the docket for the day and schools we'd only ever heard of. With the schedule—and the stakes—out in the open, he turned to me. "Any words from our fearless leader?"

Taken off guard, I mulled it over. For how much

Regina wanted to be captain, it was more or less a vanity title. I sat at the end of the table with a captain sign in front of me. If there was ever a tie, I went head-to-head with the opposite team's captain in sudden death, and if I wanted to, I could challenge an answer.

I hardly ever gave motivational speeches, but now, I looked at the other four students on a team that had meant so much to me throughout high school. Instead of speaking to them, I turned to Mr. Aris.

"Thank you," I told him. "For the last four years, Mathletes has been the one place I knew I could go where every problem had an answer, somewhere I knew I wouldn't be made fun of or ridiculed for being smart. You've made this one of the best parts of high school, and no matter how today goes, I'm grateful."

His lips quirked into a smile, and I swear I saw his eyes shining as he patted my shoulder. "It's been a privilege to serve as your coach and teacher, and after you graduate, I hope to be your friend." He smiled at Regina. "You too, Reg."

Regina grinned back at him, and for a moment, it seemed like our feud had been set aside. Today, winning was more important.

We left some of our things spread out on the table and then walked to the classroom where we'd be competing. I took my seat at the end of the table, positioned my scrap paper and pencil, and then looked up.

My parents were there.

THIRTY

NADIRA

"WE MADE IT TO STATE!" I told Apollo once I made it up to my room.

"That's amazing!" he said. "Did your parents show up?"

My lips spread into a slow smile. "They did." I savored the memory. After the competition was over, Mom and Dad offered to drive me home, and just the three of us had dinner together and talked about the meet. It was just like all those times they'd celebrated my brothers' wins, but this time the merriment was just for me.

"I'm so happy for you," Apollo replied, his voice as warm as a hug.

"Me too," I admitted. "We compete next Friday, and then I'm free as a bird the rest of the semester."

I fell back on my bed. "You know, aside from the trip to MIT over spring break and homework and prom and finals."

He chuckled. "My last semester of high school flew by. The last nine weeks, especially."

A silence fell between us, both of us lost in our own thoughts.

"It'll be a month tomorrow," Apollo said tentatively.

I bit my lip. "It will."

"Have you made a decision?" he asked. "And before you say no... don't say no."

I couldn't help the breathy laugh that escaped through my parted lips. "Yes, Apollo. I want to meet you." I heard him make a muffled celebratory noise and laughed. "Don't be too excited yet," I said, reality bringing me quickly down to earth. "I have something to tell you, and it's kind of big..."

"Whatever it is, I can't wait," he replied, his words coming out in a rush. "I can't believe I'm going to get to see you after everything. It's been the longest and shortest month of my life all at the same time."

Each of his words hit my heart differently, massaging and wounding in tandem.

"Tell me you're excited too," he said.

I chewed the inside of my cheek. I *was* excited to see him. In the moments between waking and dreaming, I imagined what it might be like to feel his arms around me. To have his lips on mine. But the trepidation of my lie outweighed even my fantasies.

"You're not excited?" he asked, his voice falling.

"It's not that. It's just..." I let out a sigh. "Promise you won't be disappointed by what you see tomorrow?"

"Babe, I could never be disappointed by you," he said.

My heart twisted painfully in my chest. "I hope so."

THIRTY-ONE

NADIRA

WE AGREED to meet at the north trailhead at Emerson Trails the next day after school.

I slept fitfully, not able to get his words or my fears out of my mind. When it was finally time to wake up, I got out of bed and slouched to the bathroom, taking my time in the shower. I worked product through my hair to help my curls stay defined and even applied a light layer of makeup to my skin.

I couldn't help but think this would be his first real impression of me. This could be how he would remember me for years to come, whether today went as well as I hoped or horribly, horribly wrong. All there was to do was hope that Apollo knew me well enough to understand.

While I'd expected the poor night's sleep, I never imagined how difficult school would be. I could hardly pay attention—even in math class. Throughout lunch, my friends tried to talk me up, but my stomach weaved itself into such tight knots I couldn't even eat. Sensing how nervous I was, they offered to meet me on the front steps after school to help pep me up for my meeting with Apollo. I gladly took them up on it.

Even though the day moved glacially slow, I still wasn't ready when the final bell rang. With my stomach in knots, I met my friends at the steps of the school while students weaved past us, toward the parking lot.

"How are you feeling?" Des asked.

My stomach quivered in response. "What if he hates me?"

Faith put her hand on my arm. "If he hates you, he doesn't know you well enough."

"Exactly," Cori agreed. "At least you're telling him the truth now, and not letting him find out on his own or just ghosting him."

I nodded slowly, and Adriel squeezed my side. "It's going to be okay. He cares about you. He'll understand."

I nodded, but then my eyes caught an unusual sight.

A guy in a military uniform was moving through the parking lot, carrying a massive bouquet of flowers.

My lips parted. I recognized him.

Des followed my gaze. "What?"

"That's Apollo," I breathed.

And it was clear where he was going. Tatiana and Isabella sat on a bench together with a couple of guys. He had seen Tatiana and was heading her way. "He thinks she's me," I choked out.

My friends' eyes widened, and Cori gave me a gentle push. "Go!"

Despite feeling like concrete, my legs sprang into action and I stutter-stepped down the stairs, going as quickly as my body would carry me.

I rushed toward him, watching in horror as he stepped ever closer to Tatiana. As he approached her and said, "Hey."

She looked up at him, and I could hear her reply a confused, "Hello?"

"It's me, Nadira." He patted his chest, right over where his name was on his uniform pocket. "Your pen pal, Apollo."

She glanced over her shoulder, her eyes

narrowing in on me. She turned back to Apollo, and I was terrified she was going to tell him the news. That she wasn't Nadira. That I was, and that I'd been lying.

But what she said was so much worse.

Her lips curled into a grin as she stood. "Apollo! It's so good to meet you."

He smiled back, handing her the flowers that had been meant for me. "You're even more beautiful than the picture you sent me."

Tatiana chuckled. "Thank you."

Isabella cleared her throat. "Who is this, Tat?"

Tatiana gestured her thin arm at Apollo. "Didn't you hear? He's my pen pal."

He extended his hand toward Isabella, saying, "Are you the dancer?"

Isabelle chuckled. "I am."

The scene unfolded in front of me like a train wreck, complete with the ear shattering sounds of crashing metal. Or maybe that was just my brain imploding. Either way, there was nothing I could do to stop it. Nothing I could do to look away.

"Sorry," Apollo said. "I know I was supposed to meet you at the trails, but I couldn't wait. I thought I would surprise you."

Hearing him speak, saying that he was excited,

snapped me out of my state. I stepped forward, saying, "Apollo, I—"

Tatiana said, "Apollo, this is my friend Tatiana!" She turned toward me and said, "This is my pen pal."

My lips parted as Apollo took me in, a cool look crossing his features.

"We've met," he said. "Kind of. She went on a date with my roommate."

Each word, the way he said it, void of the warmth he'd given Tatiana crushed my heart in two. I couldn't speak for the lump forming in my throat. Could hardly blink through the pain of growing tears.

"Want to get out of here?" Tatiana asked him.

He gave her a crooked grin that was meant for me. "Thought you'd never ask."

They walked away, his arm dropping around her narrow waist as I stared at them.

He opened the door of his car, parked in a visitor spot, and let her in the passenger side, then walked around to his side of the car, not even looking at me before getting in and driving away.

Des was at my side, breathing hard. "Nadira, what happened?"

Adriel and Faith were close behind.

"Where did he go?" Adriel asked.

Tears slipped over my cheeks. "He's gone."

Des put her arm around me, almost holding me up. "We'll figure this out. I promise."

THIRTY-TWO

APOLLO

I COULDN'T BELIEVE I was sitting across from Nadira. The girl I'd been thinking of every day for the last month.

But something felt off. She'd seemed confused when she saw me, and I wasn't sure why. Was she disappointed by what she saw? My chest tightened at the thought, and I had to take a deep breath just to focus on the road.

"Where are we going?" she asked. Her voice was higher pitched in person.

"I thought you wanted to walk at the trails?" I said, looking over at her and smiling. "But we can do whatever you want, babe." God, just being able to call her babe was like a dream come true. My chest lifted again at the realization that we were *finally* meeting.

"Ew. Dirt? No thank you," she said. "How about a coffee? I'm in major need of a caffeine pick-me-up."

I smiled slightly. I thought she was joking with the attitude, but then she looked at me and said, "What's funny?" She flipped down the visor to look at her teeth. "Did I miss a piece of salad?"

"Nothing," I said, sobering. "Where's a good coffee shop?"

"I'll show you." She told me to take a right at the next light and sat back in her seat, looking at her phone.

That tight feeling was back in my chest, and for the first time, conversation didn't come easily with Nadira. "How was school?" I tried.

She pointed her finger at her open mouth, then looked back at her phone.

"I remember those days," I said.

"Oh, left here!" She pointed, and I had to slam on my brakes to catch the turn. But when I looked up, I saw a tiny coffee drive-thru.

"You don't want to go in and sit somewhere?" I asked.

She pouted out her full lips. "Sorry, I have tons

of homework to do. I thought we could talk on the way back to the school?"

"Oh." It was the worst insult she could have given me. She'd met me and didn't want to spend any time with me. She wasn't even holding the flowers I'd gotten her, having set them haphazardly in the back seat. What had I done wrong?

"Oh no," she said. "I disappointed you. I'm sorry, Paul, it's just—"

Disbelief made my mouth fall open, and I was about to correct her when someone on the speaker said, "What can I get you?"

I rolled my window down, and Nadira said quietly, "Can you get me a non-fat latte with two pumps of sugar-free vanilla, an extra shot of espresso, and a sugar-free caramel drizzle? Make sure it's gluten free. Iced, please."

At least she'd said please... I cleared my throat and attempted to repeat her order. Nadira had to correct me twice, and finally she leaned her slender body across me so she could yell into the microphone.

She smelled like something sweet that reminded me of the yearly county fair back home. Not quite cotton candy, but something sugary. Maybe cherry?

I hadn't yet guessed when she sat back in her seat and chuckled. "Boys are so helpless."

I tried not to cringe. Instead, I pulled forward and paid the seven dollars for her coffee. SEVEN DOLLARS. For a coffee. I could have grabbed two drinks from Seaton Bakery for half the price. But the school she went to did look upscale. The amount of money sitting in the parking lot alone could have paid my future salary for decades to come.

In the back of my mind, I wondered if she would ever be satisfied on a military income. Then I kicked myself for thinking it. We'd only been talking for a month, but I'd felt a connection with Nadira on the phone. The kind that didn't just fade away. Would it exist in person too?

At the window, someone about my age handed me the cup, and I passed it to Nadira. She held the straw with one hand and began drinking it. It reminded me of the time I went to Applebee's with my brother and his fiancée and she got white-girl wasted on pomegranate margs.

"What are you smiling about?" Nadira asked with a coy smile.

"Nothing," I said, pulling back onto the road. I'd paid attention to the signs, so I could get her back to the school. "What do you have to study for? I know it's not math."

She snorted. "I'm not—oh, you're right." She flipped her hair over her shoulder. "I have a test for health class coming up. Mrs. Hutton is the *worst*."

"Ah." I nodded. "We didn't have health class at my school. The parents never would have allowed it."

"Where are you from?"

My eyebrows drew together. "Texas, remember?"

"Right." She tapped her forehead. "Brain fart. Texas is like another planet."

"Sometimes it feels that way," I said, longing for home. I missed walking down the silent streets with my friends, shooting hoops in the park, making a bonfire in the pasture behind Tristan's house and pretending like we owned the world.

We reached the school, and I said, "Which one is yours?"

"That one." She pointed at a bright pink Hummer.

My eyes widened.

"It's beautiful, huh? Sixteenth birthday gift from my parents!"

I pulled next to it, looking it over. "It's just... not what I expected." To say the least.

She winked a long-lashed eye at me. "I'm full of surprises."

"I'll say." I put the car in park next to hers. I couldn't believe she was already going back home. There had been a million things I had wanted to say—and do—to Nadira when we met. Getting her coffee and dropping her off early hadn't been on the list. But maybe it should have been. Clearly, I'd misread the signs.

I reached for my handle, and she put her hand on my arm. "Wait."

"What?" I asked, looking at her.

Her eyes were wide, full of concern as she looked around. "I haven't told you this, but I found out today that someone's stalking me."

Every inch of me went on the defensive. My fists clenched in my lap at the idea of anyone hurting her. "What do you mean?"

"I can't say too much because of the investigation, but I had to delete all my accounts and change my number. They've even tried to impersonate me with fake IDs. If anyone calls you or emails you from them from now on, it's not me."

My lips parted, and I scrubbed my face with my

free hand. That was a lot to take in. No wonder she was acting off today. "You must be terrified."

She nodded slowly. "It's been awful. You have no idea." She hunched over, her shoulders shaking, and I pulled her into a hug. She melted into my chest, and I wished I could keep her there, protected. But instead, she pulled away.

"What can I do?" I asked, feeling helpless. "How can I help?"

"Block my old number and email," she said. "I can wait while you do."

I nodded. "Of course." I'd do anything to make my Nadira feel safe. I got out my phone and blocked both the email and phone number, being sure to save the messages and voicemails. "What are your new numbers?"

Instead of saying them, she took my phone and typed them in. She must have been really scared if she wouldn't even speak them aloud. When she finished, she handed me my phone back and said, "I'll see you later, okay?"

I nodded. "Be safe."

She gave me a small smile before getting in her car and driving away.

THIRTY-THREE

NADIRA

THE FOUR OF us got into Des's car, and she asked, "Do you think he took her to Emerson Trails?"

I shook my head slightly. "I don't know. That was the plan before he came here."

She put the car in gear. "Let's see if that's where they went. You'll have to get out and tell him who you are."

Faith let out a frustrated groan. "Tatiana is so evil. Why would she do something like this?"

As I blinked, fresh tears spilled over my eyes. "She's not the evil one. I am. How could I have lied to him like that?" He was a nice guy, just messaging me, and I got so wrapped up in my insecurities that

I'd rather lie about who I was than treat him the way he deserved to be treated.

Adriel reached forward from the back seat and squeezed my shoulder. "You learned from your mistake. You don't need to keep punishing yourself."

I looked out the window, watching the city pass by. "The second I see him, I'm telling him who I am. I should have shouted it earlier before she could whisk him away." I shuddered at the thought of him having a complete stranger in his car without even knowing it.

Des glanced over at me, a determined look on her face. "We'll get there. You'll have your chance."

The trails neared, and Des drove us to the north trailhead. I looked around, desperately trying to find the gray sedan Apollo and Tatiana had driven away in. But the only thing we saw in the parking lot was a motorcycle.

I sighed. "He's not here."

Des parked, rubbing her temples. "Can you call him?"

Why hadn't I thought of that?

I got out my phone and dialed his number, hoping he would answer. Praying I could tell him that the girl with him wasn't who he thought she was. It rang twice before going to voicemail, and I looked at the screen in horror.

"He ignored my call."

Des paled. "That's bad."

Adriel said, "What if Tatiana told him you got a new number?"

My stomach turned. "I'm going to be sick."

Faith asked, "What are we going to do?"

With a sigh, Des said, "We have to go to Tatiana's house. Wait for her, right? Unless you know where else he might take her?"

I shook my head slowly, trying to think of what Apollo might want to show her—want to show me. "He loves the beach, but it could take us all evening to find the right one..."

Des put her car in gear. "Then we have to go wait at the school—catch him dropping her off at her car."

We drove back to the academy, and the ride felt like it took hours. What were Tatiana and Apollo doing together? What had she told him? What had he told her? It should have been me on that date. Getting those flowers. Seeing his eyes with the beautiful golden flecks around the pupils.

We reached the parking lot, finding mostly cars of student athletes.

Tatiana's pink Hummer was nowhere to be seen.

I let out a groan. "She's not here."

"Then to her house," Des said, whipping around the parking lot. "We'll get her."

I gripped the seatbelt over my chest, trying not to combust as we drove toward Tatiana's house.

From the back seat, Adriel said, "You should text him. Maybe he ignored the call before he saw who it was."

I nodded, fumbling for my phone. I wasn't thinking clearly. My brain was a mess with everything that had happened, so opposite of how I'd planned it.

My fingers flew over the screen as I sent the text.

Nadira: Hey, Apollo. It's Nadira. Can you call me? I have something really important to tell you.

But within seconds, an error message appeared on the screen. *Message not sent. Tap to retry.*

I furrowed my eyebrows, looking at my signal. I had full coverage. I tapped retry but within seconds got the same message again. What was going on?

I twisted in my seat to show Faith and Adriel the screen. "It's saying the message's not delivered."

Adriel's mouth dropped open, and she covered it with her hand. "Did he block your number?"

My heart sank. "No. That's not possible."

I tried again, only to get the same message. I dropped my head back against the headrest, banging it harder than I needed to.

"Hey," Des said, reaching over to rub my thigh. "It's going to be okay. We're going to get there and show Tatiana she messed with the wrong girls."

The fierce way she said it gave me something akin to hope. I held on to that tiny flame until we approached the massive house within a gated community. I couldn't see the pink car out front, but that was probably because they had a five-car garage.

Des unbuckled. "Come on," she said, getting out of the car.

The three of us followed her as she marched to the front door and pressed the doorbell, then banged the ornate knocker on the twelve-foot door.

Within moments, the door swung open, revealing a woman in a uniform. A maid. "How can I help you?" she asked.

Des spoke up. "We're looking for Tatiana."

"Ah, friends of hers?" the woman asked, eyeing

us. We clearly didn't look like the kind of people Tatiana usually hung out with.

Catching the suspicion, Des said, "Class project. Can we come in?"

The woman nodded and stepped aside. "Miss Tatiana is upstairs in her room. Second door on the right."

We stepped inside, passing the maid and following her directions to walk up the elaborate stairway. Under her breath, Faith muttered, "This house is massive."

Adriel nodded. "No wonder Tatiana thinks she's better than everyone else."

We reached the door, and Des pressed her ear to the wood, then shoved it open.

Tatiana dropped her hands from her earlobe, where she'd been fiddling with an earring. Her fists went to her hips, and she said, "What are you doing here?"

Des opened her mouth to speak, but I stepped forward, demanding, "Why did you do that?"

"I could be asking you the same thing. Apollo said he recognized me from the picture 'I' sent in an email." Tatiana quirked an eyebrow. "Now, Nadira, why would you do something like that? Did you think that adorable soldier was out of your league?"

My lip curled into a sneer.

"Because you're right," Tatiana said, looking back in her mirror to remove her earrings. "He is way too cute for you. Me on the other hand?" She winked at me in the mirror and ran her tongue suggestively over her lips.

Des lunged forward, but Adriel held her back.

Tatiana only giggled, unphased. "Why are you mad at me?" she asked. "Your friend wanted him to believe that I was her. I'm just helping her along."

I glared at Tatiana. "I was going to tell him today."

She pouted her bottom lip in fake sympathy. "And he saw me first."

My eyes narrowed further. "What did you tell him?"

Gingerly, she set her earrings in a jewelry box and looked away from the mirror. "Only that I had to get my number—and email—changed because of a stalker. I made sure he blocked both of them. He was very sympathetic, actually. Concerned about my safety. Being wrapped in those big, strong arms?" She let out a happy sigh. "Perfection."

My stomach twisted, threatening to spill acid all over the marble floor.

Des said, "Tatiana, this is crazy. You need to tell him the truth."

"Oh, I will," Tatiana said leisurely.

"Today," I said.

She shook her head.

I narrowed my eyes at her.

"Don't get so up in arms yet." She leaned her hip against her vanity. "I think there's a way we could make this work for both of us."

Raising my eyebrows, I waited for her brilliant plan. One that was sure to benefit her way more than me.

"I have an annual fundraising event I need to attend for Emerson Dance on Thursday night." She smiled coyly at Adriel. "You might remember it."

Adriel's lips pressed into a line.

Tatiana casually picked up a brush and began working it through her relaxed hair. "I need to have a date, and I'm so *over* high school boys. Why don't we wait until Friday to tell him?"

"Are you kidding?" I said, hurting for me, Apollo, and now Terrell too. "What about my brother?"

She scoffed. "What about him?"

"He likes you." I gestured at her. "And you're just going to toss him away like yesterday's news?"

"Don't be silly." She batted her hand. "He knows there's nothing serious between us. Your brother has basketball practice anyway. He can't make it."

I cringed. "That's the plan, then? Let you *borrow* Apollo for a week and lie to him even longer while you break my brother's heart?"

She shrugged. "I'll get to know Apollo so I can put in a good word for you, and you can look more sympathetic to him when the week is over. You don't have much experience with boys, but I do know one thing: he's already protective over me. If you go up to him now and tell him you're the real Nadira, he won't believe you. And then I'll tell him you're the jealous stalker and pretending to me because of the way you look... and of course he'll believe me because of the way you look."

My heart sank at her words, knowing she was right. "But what about my voice? We've been talking on the phone. He'd recognize how I sound."

"People sound different on the phone," she said dismissively. "And that's *if* you even find him, which would include stalking him to find out his dorm number and ambushing him there. Not likely to help your case."

I shook my head, struggling to find a way to make this work.

"But if I take him aside on Friday and talk to him, with just you and me there, then maybe we can help him understand that you were just misguided and that you're really a nice person. You know, *way* deep down. That way, you two will get a chance to talk after your precious Mathlete competition, where I'm being forced to volunteer, and I'll have the hottest date at my event. Easy peasy."

Des sputtered, "You're insane, Tatiana. He's not just some puppet you can work over to make you look good. You both need to tell him the truth, today."

"Nadira can try." Tatiana shrugged, seeming bored. "See what happens."

My lips parted, an argument on the tip of my tongue, but Tatiana cut me off.

"Now, I've been charitable to have the four of you here, but I'm tired of you. I suggest you leave my house before I have to call the police. Or cattle ranchers." She tapped her chin. "Not sure which would be more appropriate."

Des made to fight Tatiana again, but Adriel gripped her hand and pulled her back.

"Come on," Adriel said. "She's not worth it."

She took my hand with her free one. "We'll figure this out. Let's go."

We turned away from Tatiana and left the lion's den, hearing the roars of her laughter at our backs.

My eyes were burning by the time we reached Des's car. I couldn't believe what an idiot I'd been. Or how willing Tatiana had been to be so cruel.

"It's not over," Adriel said, getting into her seat behind mine. "There's still a chance."

Des started the car, putting her hands on the steering wheel. "Right. Just tell us where to go."

Faith agreed. "We're here for you."

I shook my head, making tears spill down my cheeks. "This is such a mess."

Des said, "We can go to the college. Right? We have to be able to find him at one of the dining halls or something."

My eyebrows rose. "Did you hear Tatiana? She's already planted the seed that she's being stalked. He's blocked my number and my email address. He has a picture of Tatiana to prove she's the one he's been talking to."

"So what?" Adriel asked. "You're going to wait until Friday and *hope* Tatiana puts in a good word for you? That's insane!"

"What else is there to do?" I asked hopelessly.

"Go to his college unannounced and look even more like a stalker? Create a new email to message him and, yet again, look like a stalker? She's backed me into a corner, and I don't know how to get out!"

Des's eyebrows drew together. "What about Josh? Can't you text him and talk to Apollo that way?"

Faith shook her head sadly. "Then it will look like Nadira's stalking Apollo instead of Tatiana. He won't let her get anywhere near him after that."

Des banged her hand on the steering wheel. "I hate her!"

"She's evil," Adriel agreed.

I sighed. "She wouldn't have been able to pull this if I hadn't lied in the first place. It's my fault."

Des turned toward me. "So what are you going to do?"

"What else is there to do?" I asked. "I'm going to wait. And I'm going to hope to God he forgives me Friday."

THIRTY-FOUR

APOLLO

THE SECOND I walked into my dorm room, Josh took off his gaming headset and leaned forward on the futon, a smile on his face. "So, how was meeting email girl?"

I couldn't blame him for being excited. I'd been talking to—and about—Nadira for weeks. Every day, I made sure I was back in my dorm by eight so we could talk on the phone uninterrupted. Every morning, I checked my phone to see if I'd gotten an email or text from her.

It was easy to see I had it bad.

But today hadn't gone like I'd expected. She looked just like the picture she'd emailed me, but something felt...off. She wasn't as warm or funny as she was on the phone. Instead, she'd seemed almost cold. Laughing too loudly at my jokes. Batting her eyelashes at me like it was her looks I'd fallen for instead of her mind.

I couldn't bring myself to tell Josh that though. Saying I was disappointed out loud would make it too real. Make this sinking feeling in the hollow of my chest even harder to handle.

"It was good," I said shortly. "I saw your girl, too."

He raised his eyebrows. "Carrie?"

"No, the one you ditched me for at the basketball game?"

He nodded, trying to seem disinterested. Although, I knew he'd been really disappointed when she broke it off. He hadn't even told me her name, but he'd talked about her nonstop after coming home from that party.

I could see why too. She was beautiful, but not in the way Nadira was. Josh's girl had soft curves that contrasted the harder edges of her eyes and cheekbones. Her eyes had been bright, like there were a million thoughts hiding behind them. And the white patches on her skin only made her that much more interesting.

I couldn't tell Josh that, though. No, it was best

to let him forget her, even if that meant never knowing her name.

Josh eyed me for a moment. "You're not telling me something."

Like the fact that I'm more into the girl you dated for half a second than the person I've been emailing for weeks? I let out a sigh. "Things were just off tonight. She'd clearly forgotten half the things we'd talked about, and she got me worried. She said someone's been stalking her and trying to steal her identity. She had to change her number and her email address."

Josh lifted his eyebrows. "Damn."

I nodded, taking off my uniform hat, then draping my jacket over my desk chair and sitting on its hard surface. "Maybe that's why things felt wrong. She must be so stressed out."

"Yeah," Josh said. "And it's probably weird seeing someone in person after only talking on the phone for so long. I bet she was nervous."

"Yeah. Her voice even sounded different. Like all of her was constricted somehow." I rested my elbows on my desk and rubbed my temples.

"It'll be okay, man. Just give it time," Josh said. I heard the rustle of his headphones as he pulled them over his head and the tap of his controller as he began playing again.

Josh was probably right. Seeing her in person had made me so self-conscious in a way I had never been before. I was worried about where my hands were on the steering wheel. How my uniform hat set over my head. Trying to keep my face even as I prayed my credit card wouldn't be declined at the coffee shop.

"I'm going on a walk," I announced to Josh, who didn't respond. He probably hadn't even heard me, but my message would be clear enough when I left the room with my phone.

Instead of the elevator, I took the stairs all the way to the ground floor and stepped outside. It was warmer here than Texas ever was in February, but I couldn't appreciate the weather. Not with all these thoughts swirling in my head.

In high school, I might have asked one of the guys to go out and throw a football or gotten together to shoot hoops at the park, but now I felt lonely. I hardly knew anyone at BU except Josh and the ROTC guys, but we didn't really hang out outside of ROTC.

I lifted my phone, itching to call my mom. I had always talked to her about girl stuff, but she hadn't answered any of my calls last semester, and I'd told myself that the ball was in her court now. I wasn't calling her until she called me.

I wanted to talk to Nadira too. Now was usually the time we spoke, but the thought made me nervous. Had she been as disappointed by today as I had been? I hoped not. I realized I wanted a chance to get back to who we were together, to the easy conversations we had about everything and nothing.

We'd never get there if we didn't try.

I tapped on my screen until I got to her new contact information and hit call. After a few rings, she answered.

"Hello?" she said.

Her voice still didn't sound quite right, but just the fact that she'd answered put a smile on my face. "Hey, baby."

"What's up?" she asked. I couldn't hear a smile in her voice. In fact, she seemed preoccupied Maybe it was the stress.

"Just calling to talk... Are you free?"

"I'm a little busy... text me?"

"Sure," I said, hanging up and feeling worse than I had before.

THIRTY-FIVE

NADIRA

I LAY awake in my bed, thinking about Apollo and wishing I could just talk to him. I missed our nightly calls more than I cared to admit. I would have given away my memory of the quadratic equation just to email him. To go back in time and tell him the truth from the start. But it was too late.

Unable to go to sleep, I got up and found a notebook in my desk. Someday, if he forgave me, I'd tell him how hard this had been for me. And I'd have something to show for it.

I put pen to paper and wrote him a letter I hoped he'd have the chance to read someday.

Dear Apollo,

By now you know how truly and deeply I've messed things up. You know that I lied to you. That I pretended to be someone I wasn't. You know that Tatiana twisted my arm and rather than risk losing you or having you always think I was nothing more than a stalker, I went along with her plan.

It is one of the hardest things I've ever done.
When I started emailing you, I thought I was just doing my mom a favor so she could complete her research project and hopefully get some funding for out-of-state ROTC students. I never expected what I got in return.

I found a true friend. Someone who was there for me whether I was celebrating a Mathlete win or sobbing outside of a basketball game because my parents supported my brothers more than me. Someone who I looked forward to talking to every day, who I thought of as my head hit the pillow every night.

I know I'm not a good writer, and I'll never find the words to tell you how sorry I am. If you forgive me, it will be the greatest gift I ever receive. And if you don't, the last month will always be one of the best of my life.

I'm sorry for the lie our relationship started with, but I promise I was always myself with you. I hope I have the chance to do that again.

Love,
Nadira

I set my pen down in the notebook and closed it, saving the page for later. I hoped, prayed, I'd be able to use it.

"She can't do that," Cori said the next morning as we walked into the building together with Ryker at her side. Although she was usually late to school, she arrived early today just so I could tell her what happened. Saying all of it over the phone didn't feel right. Not last night when all of my energy had been zapped by Tatiana and wishing I could talk to Apollo just one more time.

Ryker's eyes were dark, dangerous. "I can talk to her. Make her tell him the truth."

I shook my head. "Making her mad will just make things worse for me. She'll say something to him I can't undo."

He and Cori frowned simultaneously, so in sync.

I wanted that kind of connection for myself. No matter how many times I'd said I didn't want love or it wasn't a priority, I couldn't make myself believe it. I longed for someone I could share my life with—the fun and the sad times. Someone who understood me like I thought Apollo had. Like I thought he would if he ever gave me another chance.

Cori laced her fingers through mine. "He's going to forgive you."

My eyes stung. "How do you know?"

"Because he'd be stupid if he didn't."

Ryker chuckled beside her. "Cori has a good point."

My heart melted just a little bit. Less than a year ago, Ryker would have been right alongside Tatiana, making my life miserable just for entertainment. But love had changed him. Maybe it had changed me too.

"Will you be there for me on Friday?" I asked them. "Tatiana said she would tell him the truth after state, put in a good word for me. I think I have about a one percent chance of getting him to forgive me—and that's being generous."

"There's our pessimist," Cori said.

Ryker looked ahead in the parking lot, toward

Tatiana and her crew, then toward me. "You know what? Sending the wrong picture was a blessing to you. You're going to find out whether he fell for who you *are* or how you look."

Cori nodded in agreement.

"All we have to do is wait," he said.

Unfortunately, waiting would be the hardest part.

THIRTY-SIX

APOLLO

I READJUSTED the tie around my neck, feeling uncomfortable, and then turned to Josh, who was gaming with his new girl. They'd just met last week, but she'd been in our room every day since I first met Nadira in person, battling it out with Josh on World of Warcraft.

"Do I look okay?" I asked.

"Huh?" he said. "Oh, sure."

I shook my head. "I was asking Carrie."

The girl sitting next to him turned toward me, her dark, pierced eyebrows raised high. "Do you have to wear a suit? You look a little stiff."

I let out a groan. "It's a formal event. She was very clear about that."

She shrugged. "You should wear jeans. Tell The Man you're not his puppet."

"You're worse than Josh," I muttered.

"See?" Josh said. "She's perfect."

Carrie giggled. "You'll see how perfect I am when I crush you." Her tongue jutted out the side of her mouth, and she erratically pushed buttons on her controller.

Josh let out a groan and fell back on the couch. "You killed me!"

She leaned over and kissed him. At first it was a peck, but soon I was turning around, my cheeks and neck and ears getting hot. I hated when they did that in front of me.

Again, I found myself wishing I could video call my mom and double check that I'd done my tie the right way. Instead, I went to my voicemails and listened to the last one she left me, nearly a year ago now.

"Hey, honey, stopping by the store. Wanted to see if you had a preference on taco shells for supper. Soft or hard. But you're not answering, so I guess I'm getting... salad! Bet you'll answer your phone next time. Love you! Bye!"

My eyes smarted, and I shook my head. Maybe

I'd call my siblings after I got home tonight. After seeing how it went.

Nadira had asked that I pick her up in a limo, and when I told her I could barely afford to put gas in my car, she had seemed disappointed. It was so strange. I never thought Nadira was that materialistic, but she'd simply waved me off and said she would come get me instead. I had about five minutes until she was supposed to arrive.

I sprayed on some cologne, tucked my wallet and phone in my pants, then said goodbye to the lovebirds, who were so enthralled in each other they didn't even notice me leave.

Nadira and I hadn't even kissed yet. The thought made my stomach burn as I rode down the elevator. I'd dreamed of kissing Nadira since the first time I heard her voice on the phone. I'd wondered what her mouth would look like as she spoke. How it would look as she smiled at something I'd said.

But kissing her hadn't felt right yet, and she hadn't made a move. Maybe tonight, I thought. Although, after our first meeting, I didn't know if kissing her was still something I wanted.

The elevator arrived at the ground floor, and I glanced at my wristwatch. I still had a few minutes left. I went outside and leaned against the railing that led up to the building, waiting to see the limo pull up.

But six o'clock came, and the limo didn't arrive.

Then five minutes passed. Then ten.

I got out my phone and texted her new number.

Apollo: Still on your way?

Nadira: Should be there in a few.

I tucked my phone back in my pocket and folded my arms across my chest as I settled in to wait. Hadn't Nadira and I joked on the phone about how punctual she was? She felt like being late was telling someone else their time was less important than hers, and she would never do that to anyone else.

When the black limo pulled in, it had been more than a "few." I'd been standing outside for more than half an hour.

I tried not to be irked as the driver got out and made to open my door.

"I got it," I said, reaching for the handle.

He smiled at me and said, "Thank you, sir," then went back to the driver side.

It was weird to be called sir. Weirder to see Nadira in her revealing dress, tapping away on her phone.

"He could have gotten it," she said, not looking up from the screen.

I frowned, settling in a foot or two down from her.

She looked beautiful—any red-blooded guy could see that, with her breasts swelling against the red silk fabric of her dress and her bronze legs crossed through the slit that went up her thigh.

But I couldn't appreciate the view. Not when her eyes wouldn't even meet mine.

I swallowed back my disappointment. Maybe she was just nervous. I wasn't comfortable in my suit, either.

"You look beautiful," I tried.

She looked up from her phone at last, pinning a smile at me, and said, "I know, right? My boobs look amazing."

My eyes widened. Had my Nadira just said that to me? Out loud?

For a split second, I was starting to understand why maybe those girls had been mean to her, but I shoved that thought down even further. It was never okay to pick on anyone. Even if they acted conceited when nervous.

Her eyes slid over my outfit, assessing. She gave

me a nod of approval, then looked back at her phone.

"So, any pointers for the party?" I asked. Clearly, she was worried about how I would present myself, and maybe I should be too. "It's been a while since I've been to one of my dad's work events." Though, to be fair, I usually slipped out the back of the building to hang out with other kids my age. There were typically at least a few there. Something kept me from telling her that, though.

"Just stay by my side," she said, barely looking at me. "Act like you're in love with me."

At this rate, that was going to be hard.

I sat back in my seat, trying to quell the disappointment racking me. Maybe I had read her wrong. All those messages, calls, had been an act. Maybe *this* was the real Nadira.

I wanted to get on my phone, to distract myself from this disaster of a night that was only just beginning, but I refused to get on my cell during a date. That wasn't how I was raised to treat a lady.

We eventually reached an elegant hotel with an elaborately decorated entrance. There were so many flowers, I was thankful it was winter or else there would probably be a bee problem to go along with a shallow date problem.

We walked inside, and a photographer carrying a massive camera took several shots of us. Nadira posed me, telling me where to put my hands, to smile with my lips closed. To tilt my head toward her. I felt more like a Ken doll than an actual human being by the time we walked into the ballroom.

Someone passed by with a tray of tiny food and I reached for some, but Nadira hit my hand. "Don't eat yet. You might get something in your teeth before we see Galina!"

I pulled my hand back, clenching it in my pocket. I didn't appreciate being treated like a child getting caught with a hand in the cookie jar.

Nadira led me up to an older woman in a flowing ball gown. She turned toward us, eyeing us both like she was grading our appearance.

"Galina, this is my date, Apollo," Nadira said nervously.

The woman eyed me even longer. "He's attractive. But can he dance?"

Nadira giggled. "Of course not."

She hadn't even asked. Years of ballroom dancing lessons, wasted. I'd been planning to surprise Nadira with a dance, maybe even ask her to her prom, but I could see now that wasn't going to happen.

Nadira steered me away from the woman and introduced me to her parents. Her mom looked so young she could have been Nadira's sister, and her dad simply looked bored.

I shook their hands like my dad had taught me, but her parents quickly dismissed us, and Nadira took me to a table where I was finally allowed to eat. Although, my stomach clenched so tight, just the thought of food made me sick.

"Why are we here?" I asked Nadira. I didn't know if I could make it through an entire night of this.

"I told you," she said, an annoyed lilt to her voice. "This is a benefit for the studio where I dance."

"You dance?" I asked, confused.

She gestured at her body. "Don't I look like I dance?"

"That's not it—I just—you never told me."

"Of course I did, silly." She batted my arm.

I couldn't take this anymore. "Nadira, I'm sorry, but I don't think... I don't think this is going to work. I can stay here with you as your date for the night, but I think it's best if we don't try to force this into being something it's not."

A flash of anger crossed her face, but she quickly disguised it with a sweet smile. It scared me a little.

"I'm so sorry," she said, taking my hand in both of hers. Her long nails stabbed me a little bit as she did. "I'm just so nervous, and you're so attractive. Will you give me another chance?"

I hesitated, wanting to believe she was different, but I was already so done with this night.

"The state Mathlete competition is tomorrow. It would mean the world if you came to watch me," she said, making her eyes wide and open, inviting, more like the Nadira I thought I knew.

My heart tugged at the offer. Nadira cared about Mathletes more than anything else. Maybe seeing her compete would give me a glimpse into the real her.

"Okay," I said. "I'll come."

Her teeth glinted as she smiled. "Perfect. I'll see you then."

THIRTY-SEVEN

NADIRA

FIVE DAYS without talking to Apollo. It felt like an eternity. How had I ever gone eighteen years without knowing him?

But today I would see him. Today, I'd beg Tatiana to tell him the truth and not damn me in the process. As soon as I was done competing, I'd plead for him to forgive me and to keep my heart intact.

I got out my outfit for the day and then set an extra aside for after the competition. Tatiana had agreed to have him meet us behind the school once the event was over and everyone had gone home. I didn't need an audience for what would surely be either the best or the worst day of my life.

I rubbed lotion over my legs, taking away the

ashen pallor of my dry skin and replacing it with a vibrant brown contrasting with white patches. Then I did the same for my arms and pulled on my uniform skirt. I buttoned up my light blue shirt and tucked it into the skirt, careful to pull it straight from under so it wouldn't bunch. To top it off, I wore my Mathlete jacket, straightening the lapels.

There would be no need to hide the jacket. Everyone at the school would either be there to compete or volunteer.

I got out a spare drawstring bag and put the extra outfit in there—a pair of leggings and a long blouse that nipped in around the narrow part of my waist and flowed over my hips, accentuating my curves.

Although I usually skipped makeup, today, I applied smoothing cream along with mascara (the waterproof kind) and even a tinted lip gloss. That went in the bag for touch-ups later.

I gave myself a look in the mirror that hung over my desk and wished I had more to offer Apollo in the way of looks. But that wasn't the way life worked. When I was little and my parents explained appearances to us, they said we were all made of something called DNA and that everyone's DNA was different. It said whether you had brown eyes or blue eyes. Black skin or pale skin. Whether you grew to be as tall as Dad or as small as Grandma.

My DNA was coded for so many different things. My tight curls, the way my nose lifted slightly at the end. My broad fingernails and the condition that mottled my skin. But it also had been coded for intellect and humor and sarcasm and all the things that made Apollo want to meet me in the first place.

Ryker was right. If he only liked me because he thought I looked like Tatiana, it would be good to know now.

I finished getting my things together and went downstairs. Mom was working from home so she'd be closer to school when it was time to come watch, and Dad was downstairs in the living room, watching game film from other teams.

As she heard my footsteps, Mom turned from her spot at the island and said, "Hey, sweetie."

"Morning." I smiled at her and set my bag on one of the stools. "Are Carver and Terrell still asleep?"

"They had early practice." She glanced at her computer screen. "They should be getting home in about half an hour."

I nodded, feeling a little guilty. I'd been so

wrapped up in my issues with Apollo that I hadn't even thought about what they'd do for practice today.

She poured a glass of orange juice from the pitcher on the counter and passed it to me. "I have a questionnaire for you to fill out about the pen pal program," she said. "It should be pretty simple. Do you think you can get it done this weekend?"

"Sure." I took a sip of the juice.

"I'm curious... Did you make a friend? Get some good advice on college?"

I nearly choked on my juice and sputtered, beating on my chest with a closed fist. "Sorry," I croaked, then took another drink of juice to even out my voice. "It was fine. Apollo was nice."

Mom looked at me curiously. "Apollo?"

I nodded. "Apollo Banks. That's who you paired me with."

Her eyes widened, going to her computer. She tapped, opening a different software. "I thought I paired you with a girl... A.banks@brentwoodu.edu." Her lips pursed. "A for Apollo."

My heart beat faster, and I felt like I'd gotten away with something illicit. "He said you're his advisor."

"I am," she said.

"Is there something wrong with him?"

She eyed me suspiciously, then said, "He's a very handsome young man."

My cheeks flushed. That, I knew.

"Kind," she added. "But not very social. As far as he's told me, no extracurriculars outside of ROTC."

She said it like not being in a bunch of clubs was a negative, and I wanted to defend him. "I'm sure ROTC and classes keep him busy."

She nodded, watching me skeptically. "What about that other boy? The one you met for coffee?"

I shook my head. "He's just a friend." Even that was exaggerating, but she seemed to accept the answer.

"And Apollo? Do you plan to keep talking to him, now that the study's over?" Despite how she tried to act like the answer didn't matter to her, I could tell by the stiffness of her spine she was dying to know.

"I think that's up to him," I answered honestly.

She nodded slowly. "What do *you* want?"

I pressed my lips together. As an academic, I'd known the scientific names for body parts and the ins and outs of intercourse (no pun intended) since I was young, but actual relationships, matters of the heart? I didn't have the words to explain how I felt. But I was tired of lying. I'd promised myself the truth from here on out, so that's what I spoke.

"I like him, but I'm not sure the feeling will be mutual."

"You don't know yet?"

"Not really."

She reached out and cupped my cheek with her hand. Her palm was soft against my skin, and I leaned into the warmth as she said, "You're an amazing young lady, no matter what he thinks."

"Thanks, Mom. That means a lot." It really did.

I went to Waldo's Diner to meet my friends for brunch before the competition, and true to form, I was there earlier than everyone else. Stepping into the diner was comforting in a way. It still had the same décor from when I was a little girl. Chester still sat in the third booth from the entrance, a newspaper spread before him, along with a cup of coffee. There were the toy and candy dispensers in the corner. And then the table my friends and I called our own.

It was empty and clean, so I slid over the

pleather seat and sat toward the back. The maroon cushions were showing their age with too much give to be truly comfortable, but I loved it nonetheless.

If Apollo ever forgave me, if he ever wanted to date me, I would take him here. Would tell him about the New Year's resolution I made with Faith and hope he helped make it come true.

A waitress I didn't normally see came to greet me. "Just you, sugar?"

I shook my head. "My friends are coming soon. There'll be five of us."

"Let me get some more menus and silverware. I'll be right back." She walked away, moving with a slight limp, and I looked out the window at the bright sky.

Much faster than I expected, Adriel came in, followed by Faith.

I gave them a wavering smile as they slid into the booth.

"How are you feeling?" Faith asked.

I let out a shaky breath. "I've been better."

Adriel nodded. "I'm nervous. I can't even imagine how you feel."

The waitress came back, setting a pile of napkins and silverware at the end of the table. "I'll come check on you when the other two get here."

I nodded, looking at the menu like I hadn't seen it a million times before. The last time it changed, everyone got so mad that they brought back the old one within the week.

Cori and Des came in next, rounding out our group of five.

Des smiled at me approvingly. "You look beautiful, Dir."

I thanked her, but the last thing I felt was beautiful. "I feel like I'm going to throw up."

Cori glanced at her menu. "Do you think cheese fries will help?" I glared at her, and she giggled. "You know you love me."

"I do," I said, looking at my friends. "I love all of you. What am I going to do without you when I'm in Cambridge next year?"

Des held up her cell, wiggling it. "It's called a phone. Ever heard of it?"

I laughed, and Adriel said. "New York's only a couple hours away by train. We'll be able to meet up on weekends!"

"True," I said, feeling a little better. But I knew a piece of my heart would always be here in Emerson. And another piece at Brentwood University.

"Exactly," Des said with a cheeky grin. "And

you'll be able to watch me on TV when I'm famous."

"With the way your YouTube channel's growing, it's only a matter of time before you get discovered," I said.

She held up her crossed fingers. "Here's to hoping I don't sign with a record label just to lose my sound." She pretended to cough. "Jude Santiago." She'd been complaining about him ever since he got famous and started producing more mainstream music.

Faith giggled and said, "Depending on where the Peace Corps sends me, I think I'll have some training on the East Coast before I go."

I smiled at her. "We'll make the most of it."

The waitress came and took our orders, then Cori said, "Nadira, I feel like I'm not doing enough with the Apollo situation... How can we help you?"

I reached across the table and took her hand. "You're already doing it." The rest was in Apollo's hands.

THIRTY-EIGHT

APOLLO

NADIRA TOLD me to meet her at Emerson Academy at one. She said she had to help set up for the competition, but she'd send me the schedule as soon as she had it.

Going to a high school by myself now that I was in college felt a little weird, though, so I asked Josh if he was up to tagging along. He'd quickly agreed, eager to skip his algebra class. I was pretty sure he'd only gone a few times so far. The outlook on his grades wasn't great.

We got in my car and began driving toward the school, and I murmured, "She still hasn't texted me the schedule."

Josh shrugged, adjusting his seat. "Maybe she

forgot. I'm sure we can ask someone when we get there."

I gripped the steering wheel a bit tighter and nodded, not replying. I was trying to give Nadira another chance, but my heart wasn't in it. Maybe the magic of our relationship had only existed in emails, which would be great for when she went to MIT or when I got deployed, but I needed more than that. The chemistry had to work in person too.

Part of me wondered if we'd see the girl from the basketball game when we got there, if Josh would be okay with introducing us, but I quickly tamped the thought down. First off, bro code. Second off, she'd told him she didn't want to start anything serious before college. Who was to say she wouldn't say the same to me?

And then I realized I was thinking about Tatiana again when I should have been thinking about Nadira. I was going to Emerson Academy to see her, after all.

The directions on my phone took us through a part of the neighboring town I'd only been to once before. It was nice, with brick streets and planters along the sidewalk with leafy trees and blooming flowers. Perks of living somewhere with no real winter, I guessed.

Josh stared open-mouthed at the massive school building. "*That's* where she goes to school?"

I nodded. "It's high pressure. Nadira said several California governors have graduated from here and a couple presidents too." My high school's only claim to fame was a country music star with two DUIs and a divorce under his belt. It was just a simple light brick building with a flat roof. Nothing like the enormous structure in front of us with artistic sculptures and engravings in Latin.

I found an empty spot in the parking lot and turned off the car.

Josh looked around us at all the expensive cars. "A pink Hummer? How much lamer can you get?"

My cheeks got hot.

"*No,*" Josh said.

I nodded, tightlipped.

"Oh man."

"Uh-huh."

"I thought there would be more people here," he said.

I raised my eyebrows. "You're not the only one who doesn't care about math."

He grumbled something about how going to a Mathlete competition should count for algebra attendance and got out of the car.

I slipped off my sunglasses and set them on the dash, then got out too. Still no text from Nadira. I let out a sigh, then followed Josh toward the school, locking the car behind me.

On the way in, I could feel the looks I was getting from people around me, but I kept my eyes ahead. As we walked up the stairs, I noticed Ad Meliora carved into the entrance. I reminded myself to ask Nadira what it meant later. If there was a later for the two of us.

Josh and I followed a small group of people into the building, and eventually they led us toward a cafeteria area. I looked around at the tables, thinking this is where Nadira ate lunch every day. Except for Thursdays when she and her friends got the AV room to themselves. I smiled softly, remembering the first time she had told me about it. By the end of the story, which included impersonations of her guidance counselor, she'd had me laughing out loud.

Why couldn't she be like that when we met in person?

Another pang of grief swept through me, but I shoved it down as I looked where the people ahead of us were going. There were a couple of guys sitting at a table. One wore a crown made of paper with the words "Nadira's brother" on it in thick black marker.

Josh turned away from the table and mumbled, "I'm finding a water fountain."

"Sure." I stepped forward, chuckling at the guy. "I like the hat."

He gave me a crooked grin. "My sis *is* the future state champion of the Mathletes. A nerd crown was in order."

I laughed. This must have been where Nadira got her humor from. Not her ice sculpturesque parents. Now that I thought about it, where were her brothers on the night of the event? Still at basketball practice?

I realized I was being awkward and stuck my hand out. "I'm Apollo."

"Carver," he said, shaking my hand. But his face didn't seem to register any understanding at all. Did he not know who I was? He picked up a green sheet of paper and handed it to me. "Here's a program."

I took it and said a dejected, "Thanks," before turning around. Josh loitered around a I kept my eyes trained on the paper and Josh looked over my shoulder. Nadira hadn't mentioned me before. All

I'd done was rail on about her to anyone who would listen.

My phone vibrated in my back pocket then, and I handed Josh the sheet so I could check my text. Right on late, Nadira had sent me a picture of the very program I just handed Josh. Nothing more.

No, "looking forward to seeing you." Or "thanks for coming."

Nothing.

I let out a sigh and put my phone back in my pocket.

Josh said, "Looks like we'll be in room 112 for the first round."

"It might be our only round," I muttered and glanced around, looking for the nearest classroom. We followed the numbers over the doors until we reached the right 112. The plastic sign beside the door said Advanced Math – Mr. Aris.

Nadira had mentioned him—her favorite teacher. I drank in the room, wondering if I could see it through her eyes. Just as she'd said, there were posters of famous mathematicians decorating the walls. My favorite quote was the one by Einstein.

Attendance in the room was pretty sparse, but I realized I saw a familiar face. My advisor, Dr.

Harris, sat with a man I assumed was her husband just a few chairs over.

"Hey, Dr. Harris," I said, lifting my hand.

Her lips spread into a grin that told me she was happy to see me. "Hi, Apollo. I'm so glad you came!"

Her excitement confused me. In the nicest way I could, I asked, "What are you doing here?"

"My daughter's competing. Did Nadira not mention I'm her mother?"

My eyebrows drew together. "Are there two Nadiras at the Academy?" She did not look like the cold, stick-thin woman I'd met the night before.

"I don't think so," she said, looking confused. "Not that I know of anyway."

"Oh," I said, sitting back, trying to register what was going on.

Josh whispered, "How do you know Nadira?"

I leaned closer to him. "Nadira's the girl I've been talking to. Haven't I told you her name?"

"Email girl is *Nadira*?" he asked. "Because Nadira was the girl *I* met at that party."

I checked his pupils for extra dilation. His head for a sign of injury. "Are you on something?" I asked. "Your girl's name is Tatiana. Nadira introduced her to me last Friday."

"Tatiana?" he said. "I've never heard that name in my life." He got out his phone and showed me a contact. Clearly, it said Nadira.

"That's not a common name..." I said slowly.

Josh said, "What's going on here?" At the same time, Nadira walked into the room and said, "Hi, sweetie!"

I pulled my head back slightly at the greeting. Nadira never called me sweetie on the phone. Or anything other than Apollo for that matter. I was about to ask her if she knew another Nadira at the school, but multiple students dressed in school uniforms filed in and sat at the tables in the front of the room.

Five people filled the table labeled with a tented piece of paper for the home team. Including Josh's girl.

My eyebrows drew together, and I whispered to Nadira, "Why aren't you up there?"

She brushed a finger over her lips. "I have a surprise."

Something didn't feel right. It made me want to get up and leave as fast as I could, but someone closed the door to the room, and I couldn't. I felt trapped like a rabbit in a cage.

The man who'd shut the door moved to a

podium between the two tables. "Hello Mathletes, teachers, students, and supporters. I'm Headmaster Bradford, and I'm so thankful you've come to Emerson Academy for this prestigious event. It is even more of a joy being able to open the first round with students from my school in the room." He smiled at the girl at the end of the table. Tatiana. Or Nadira. I couldn't tell.

I studied her carefully, looking for a name tag or anything that would tell us who she truly was. All I could see was the sign she sat behind that said Captain...

My vision blurred as I remembered the first email she'd ever sent me. She was captain of the Mathletes. A girl on her team wanted the position too. Then I remembered something else. Nadira had complained about being bullied for her weight.

I glanced at the thin girl next to me and had a feeling she was *not* the Nadira I knew.

When I looked back at the table, Tatiana's eyes were on me. Or Nadira's eyes. Whoever she was, her face was pale. Her full lips were parted. Her throat moved with her swallow.

The headmaster continued, "I'll announce our competitors. On my right, I have the home team,

Emerson Academy. Our captain, Nadira Harris. Regina Baldwin...."

My mouth was dry.

Nadira Harris.

I looked at the girl next to me, an evil smirk on her narrow face. She smiled between me and Nadira, clearly having the time of her life, but I felt sick. My stomach turned, and I knew I had to get out of here before I lost it on the floor. Before I passed out. Before what was clearly happening registered fully and I lost my mind.

I stood, my chair scraping so loudly over the tiled floor it stopped the headmaster's speech, and bolted toward the door.

My hand was on the cold steel handle when I heard her voice.

"Apollo, wait!"

I turned and looked at her. Not the girl who'd been sitting next to me, but the girl standing behind the table. Behind the captain sign.

Her mouth moved, but no words came out.

That was the Nadira I knew, but as it turned out, I hadn't known her at all.

THIRTY-NINE

NADIRA

I WATCHED Apollo as he left the room. Even though his back was to me, his expression was seared into my mind. One of the ultimate betrayal and deceit. My eyes flicked to Tatiana, who giggled silently in her seat, then to Josh, who followed Apollo out of the room.

Without thinking, I moved to chase after him, but Regina tugged on my hand. "Nadira," she hissed. "We have a match!"

I glanced at the opponents. Everyone knew they'd made it to state on a technicality. Donovan could defeat them handily on his own. "You'll beat them just fine without me," I whispered. "I'll be right back."

I pulled out of her grip and continued toward

the door. Behind me, I heard my parents' and Mr. Aris's voices, but I couldn't let Apollo leave. I'd never see him again if I didn't speak to him now.

I hurried down the hall—they were already almost to the exit. I'd lose them in the parking lot if I didn't catch up.

"Apollo!" I called.

As if he didn't hear me, he fled out the door, and I chased behind, desperate tears stinging my eyes and exertion making my lungs ache. I couldn't let him go. Not without a chance to explain.

I sprinted to the doors, ignoring the befuddled expressions of those I passed, and finally I reached the heavy double doors. After yanking them open, I took the steps down as fast as I dared, yelling, "Apollo, wait! Please!"

He stopped at the curb, and Josh almost bumped into him.

"What?" he asked, turning to face me with his arms spread at his sides. "What could you possibly say to me? And how would I even know if it's the truth?"

His words hit me in the chest, but I kept jogging toward him, desperately trying to catch my breath. "*Please.*"

He blinked at me, folding his arms across his chest.

Now that I was standing in front of him, Josh watching us, my parents and Mr. Aris sure to be close behind, I had no idea what to say.

"What's going on?" Apollo asked, looking at me sideways. As if I were a threat. It ripped the fabric of my heart.

I stepped closer, needing to make him understand. Needing to be close to him. "Apollo..." I rolled his name over my tongue, savoring it and aching on it because I knew it might be the last time he ever heard me say it. The last time I could ever say it to him. "I lied."

The two words hung between the three of us. Two words but a million feelings.

Apollo said, "What do you mean?"

Josh watched me, waiting.

Waiting.

I took a ragged breath. "That first day that we emailed? I sent you a picture of a girl from school because I was embarrassed about how I looked. I'm the real Nadira. The girl you sat next to today? Her name is Tatiana."

Apollo stumbled backward, shaking his head, until he fell onto the bench.

Josh spoke for him. "He's been dating the wrong girl?"

I nodded.

Apollo said, "She told me her number was changed. That someone was *stalking* her."

"She was trying to trick you because she wants to make me miserable," I breathed, watching every expression his face made, flashing from disbelief to hurt to shock and denial once again. "She said if I didn't go along with it, she would tell you I was the stalker, and I'd never get to talk to you again."

"No," Apollo said, shaking his head. "No. Nadira wouldn't do that to me. She wouldn't lie to me."

My heart ached at the words. Because he was right. The girl who'd gotten to know him, who cared for him so deeply, never would have hurt him like that. Would never have let someone like Tatiana come near him.

"I'm telling the truth," I said. I reached for my phone in my jacket pocket and navigated to my social media account. The same one where I'd lifted Tatiana's picture, wishing so much I could look like her. I went to her profile, finding the picture with her name underneath it and held it out to Apollo.

His hands shook as he took it, staring at the

screen. His eyes widened and narrowed. He rubbed his hand over his mouth. His chest rose and fell.

My heart didn't beat at all.

He looked from the picture to me, so many emotions shining in his gold-flecked eyes.

"You were talking to Josh," he said.

"I broke it off with him because I like you."

He stood, extending my phone to me. "You lied."

I fumbled for words, knowing I would fail but having to try anyway. "I didn't lie. I sent you the wrong picture because I didn't want you to see me"—I gestured at myself—"and not even give me a chance. I wanted you to think I was beautiful."

He stared at me, his lip curling in disgust. "I did," he said, extending the phone again. "But now I think you're the ugliest person in the world. Not because of the way you look, but because of the way you lied."

Giving up on me taking the phone, he pressed it into my hand. "I never want to see or hear from you again."

He turned and walked away, and Josh gave me a final glance before following him.

FORTY

APOLLO

MY FIRST ATTEMPT at putting my keys in the ignition, I missed. They fell to the floor, clanging loudly against each other on the rubber mat. With a curse, I reached down and picked them up, jabbing them in place.

I twisted so hard I felt the metal turn as the engine whirred to life. I wished I had my grandpa's old Ford pickup. The one with the engine that drowned out all other sounds—even your thoughts.

My car was too quiet. Quiet enough I could hear Josh's breathing next to me. Feel his apprehension and even his concern.

Ignoring him, I reversed out of the spot and peeled out of the parking lot as fast as I could.

I wasn't sure where I was going at first, but I

kept taking turns until my car was pointed toward the ocean. I'd find the water eventually.

The farther we got from the school, the more my ROTC training kicked in. I leveled my breathing. Focused my gaze. Shoved out everything except for the thoughts that would be helpful to me in combat.

Because I *was* in combat. My mind warred with itself, trying to make sense of what had happened. The way my body had reacted to the mere sight of the real Nadira saying my name. Her voice was everything. *Everything.* But now it had to be nothing, because that was how she'd treated me. Like I didn't matter at all. Like I was the kind of guy who wouldn't see beyond her looks and into her heart.

I beat the steering wheel, letting the pain in my hand take over the pain in my chest.

Josh flinched.

I needed to get away from him. From myself.

We approached a small beach, and I parked the car haphazardly over the parking lot's faded yellow lines. Leaving it on with Josh inside, I jumped out and started running. I pumped my arms and pushed my legs, letting the adrenaline in my body carry me. But no matter how far or fast I ran, I felt the pain. It was inside me. A part of me.

My feet slowed in the sand, and I stopped at the water's edge, my chest heaving. The ocean was a bright blue today, lapping at the brown sand and my feet. Almost like a mockery. Why wasn't the sky gray and stormy, the ocean waves high and threatening? That would have been more appropriate for a day like today.

I'd been such an idiot. I'd known something was off about Nad—Tatiana. I *knew* that wasn't the girl I'd fallen for. If I had asked a question of her—any of the important things—I would have known.

Nadira had said she was going to tell me about her lie, but she shouldn't have had anything to tell in the first place. She was *incredible*, like no one I'd ever seen before. Tatiana's bland form of beauty didn't hold a candle to the bonfire flame that was Nadira.

A small part of me felt sorry for Nadira. What had the world told her to make her think that she wasn't beautiful? That she wasn't worthy of being seen and loved *exactly as she was*?

That sympathy was dangerous. It would lead me to forgiveness, and I knew better than that. My heart had been dragged through the coals once. I wasn't doing it a second time.

I dropped to the ground, digging my fingers

through the coarse mixture of sand and crushed shells. Footsteps sounded nearby, and Josh sat quietly beside me. I glanced over at him. He squinted toward the bright horizon, his mouth twisted thoughtfully to the side.

I let out a sigh. "You're going to say something. Might as well go ahead."

He smiled wryly. "Just that I'm sorry. I knew you really liked her."

I raised my eyebrows. "That's it?"

With a shrug, he added, "If you forgave her, I'd understand."

"Not even a remote possibility," I muttered. And I meant it. My mom always said, "Fool me once, shame on you. Fool me twice, shame on me." I wasn't going to be made a fool more than I already had. The sting of tears hit my eyes, and I sniffed. I turned toward Josh again. "Is it bad that all I want to do is call my mom?"

He shook his head. "Not at all." He began pushing himself up from the sand. "Why don't you call her? I'll go wait in the car."

I nodded, not able to speak with the lump forming in my throat. I tried to swallow it down as I shifted to reach my phone in my pocket. Even though it had been months since we last spoke, my mom's number was still on speed dial.

I typed one and her number automatically came up. With a shaky breath, I pushed call.

It rang.

And rang.

And rang.

And then her voicemail played.

A tear slipped down my cheek, and I brushed it away before standing up and going back to the car.

FORTY-ONE

NADIRA

"NADIRA!"

I turned around to see my mom walking toward me, the crack of her heels sharp against the sidewalk. Behind me, I could hear a car revving, tires squealing out of the parking lot.

"What was that about?" she demanded, her eyebrows coming together. Dad was only a few steps behind her, giving me a quizzical look.

My lips parted to explain, but she already had her hand on my arm and was leading me back toward the stairs. My dad walked on my other side, just as silent as I was.

"You're going to miss this round!" she said, starting up the stairs. "You'll be lucky if Mr. Aris lets you compete at all today."

Lucky. A word I never would have used to describe myself.

"And what was that about Apollo? Did he not know who you were? Why was he sitting with Tatiana?"

Dad held the door open for us, and we walked into the school, which was much quieter than when I had left it. The first round must have been well underway. And I wasn't in there. Not only had I missed out on a chance with Apollo, I'd forfeited participating in one of my very last matches.

We reached the classroom and Mom reached for the door, but I took her hand. "Wait!"

"What?" she said.

"We can't go in," I whispered. "They don't let people inside once the round's in progress. It could get us disqualified."

"Why?"

"Because the answers have already been given on some problems," I explained. "It was a big issue a few years ago."

Mom let go of my knob, stepping back. "Then what do we do?"

"We have to wait." I let out a sigh and began walking toward the cafeteria.

The next half hour felt like the longest of my

life. Not only did I have the constant image of Apollo's hurt expression on my mind, but his voice echoed in my ears, saying he never wanted to see or hear from me ever again.

My parents continually gave each other looks. I could tell Mom wanted to talk to me, but as far as I could tell, Dad was staying way out of it. Normally, I'd be embarrassed, but the pain was too big for me to care.

Slowly, the lunchroom became more and more crowded as teams came to wait a few minutes between rounds.

The hairs rose on the back of my neck as my team and their supporters—parents, grandparents, and more—approached. I knew they'd likely handily beat our opponents, but I'd still run out on them. Of course, Tatiana was nowhere to be found.

I chanced a glimpse at Mr. Aris, but he wouldn't meet my eyes. Regina, however, did. She glared at me so harshly, her gaze could have singed ash.

Mr. Aris checked a green sheet of paper, then said, "This way."

We followed him silently down the hall, a heavy cloud over our group, until we reached the art room. He led us inside, but when I went to take my seat in the captain's chair, Mr. Aris said, "No, that's Regina's seat now."

I was too stunned to move as Regina slid past me and sat down with a haughty grin. My legs barely registered as they carried me to the next chair over. Donovan and the other two boys were completely silent. Not that I could have heard them over the rushing in my ears.

The captain's position may not have meant much, but it was a title of respect. It said you worked hard in math, that you were smart, dedicated. I hadn't had someone chosen over me. I'd been *demoted*, which was ineffably worse.

I blinked my stinging eyes as I situated my scrap paper and pencil. The judge, our art teacher, asked if our team was ready.

Regina said, "Yes."

I threw myself into the competition, using each question to distract myself from the torment I knew would come tonight when I lay in bed with nothing to divert my attention from the mistake I'd made. Between Regina attempting to prove she'd earned her spot as captain and my furious calculations, the team performed better than ever. We progressed further and further throughout the day until we were seated on the auditorium stage for the championship round against our school's biggest rival, Brentwood Academy.

Unlike other meets, there were plenty of people here. Despite the spotlights being on us, I could make out the faces of my friends. Of my parents. Of my brothers sitting with the rest of the basketball team and Carver wearing a paper crown with writing on the front.

Tatiana caught my eyes and wiggled her fingers at me with a triumphant grin.

Rage stronger than anything I'd ever felt consumed me, and I turned my eyes back toward the judge. If I couldn't best Tatiana in her games, I'd be the best in mine.

Brentwood Academy sat across the stage from us, and they'd come to play. I remembered facing them earlier in the season and losing by a hair. But this time, I was determined not to let it happen.

While my team competed the best we had all season, so did Brentwood Academy. We reached the final question of the round, ending... in a tie.

Headmaster Bradford spoke into the microphone attached to the podium in the middle of the stage. "The last time the state championship ended in a tie was in 1947, between Brentwood Academy and Emerson Academy, with Emerson Academy ultimately taking the victory. The rivalry between our two great schools was alive and well then and has continued through the years. Let's see who will be the victor today."

He reached into the podium, taking fresh sheets of paper. "We'll dispose of your scrap paper from earlier and put a fresh page before you. You may not converse between team members. If both captains answer incorrectly, the next in line will have a chance to answer and so on until we reach the end of the table. Coaches, you may come align your team in the desired order."

I looked up from my spot to see Mr. Aris walking our way. He had a grim set about his face, like a tie was the last thing he'd wanted. As soon as he reached our table, he said, "Regina, you're in the captain's chair. Then Donovan, Richard, Bryan, and Nadira, you'll sit at the end."

Regina's eyes widened. "Mr. Aris. We need to have our best up front."

Mr. Aris looked at her and then met my eyes. "Being the best isn't just about finding the right answers," he said. Then he turned and walked away.

My heart shattered then, knowing there was no chance the opportunity to answer would ever reach me. Our team was making history—the first tiebreaker in more than sixty years, and I'd counted myself out of the competition, all because of a lie. All because of my insecurities.

Headmaster Bradford read off the question, and with tears streaming down my cheeks and blurring my vision, I copied it down. The seconds ticked past as I drew closer to the answer. I solved it and set my pencil down, silently begging Regina to get the question right.

She slammed her palm on the buzzer, and Headmaster Bradford called on her, a proud smile on his face. "Yes, Regina?"

Her voice shook as she read the answer, and I didn't need to hear Headmaster Bradford's words or see his face to know she'd gotten it wrong. Because I had the right answer on my sheet, and what she'd said wasn't it.

The Brentwood Academy captain buzzed in and read his answer.

Headmaster Bradford's voice was solemn as he said, "The Mathlete State Championship goes to Brentwood Academy."

I'd lost, in more ways than one.

FORTY-TWO

NADIRA

I TEXTED MY FRIENDS, asking them to come, and sat against the bumper of my car, pulling my knees to my chest and hugging them tightly like somehow that could keep me from falling apart.

Within minutes, they hurried to me through the parking lot, concern on their faces.

Des dropped to her knees beside me. "Dir, what happened?"

"Tatiana tricked us both. She brought him to the meet, waited for Headmaster Bradford to announce my name. My parents were there. They saw it all." A fresh flood of tears gushed from my eyes as I said, "Apollo hates me. He found out the truth, and he hates me."

My shoulders shook with a fresh wave of tears,

and I folded over my knees, wishing this day could be over. Wishing that I'd never agreed to Mom's research study or put my heart on the line.

This was my last semester of high school, and I should have been enjoying my friends and Math-letes, but instead I'd gotten caught up in a guy and let everything fall by the wayside.

On the opposite side of me, Faith rubbed my back. "Are you sure he wasn't just hurt? Maybe he'll come around."

I shook my head. "You should have seen the way he looked at me. What he said..." My throat tightened, and I choked over the lump forming there along with the moisture dripping down my nose and the back of my throat. I repeated the words that sliced me to ribbons. "'I think you're the ugliest person in the world. Not because of the way you look, but because of the way you lied.'"

Cori let out a quiet gasp. "He said that to you?"

I nodded, crying so hard now I could barely get any air.

"Breathe," Des said firmly.

But I couldn't. It felt like I was deeper and underwater, and no matter how much I gasped or choked, nothing could bring me closer to air.

"Nadira, breathe!" Des ordered again, her voice rising higher.

As if through the depths of water, I heard Adriel said, "She's having a panic attack."

Faith said, "Bend her over. Get her arms behind her head."

They moved my body until my legs were butterflied out and my head folded toward my feet. They held my hands behind my head, rubbing my back, saying soft words I couldn't quite discern.

Slowly, my breath came.

Slowly, the tears stalled.

Slowly, my heartbeat leveled.

But what was left in the aftermath was a shell. I didn't feel happy or sad or regret.

I felt numb.

My friends helped me into the car, and I sat in the back seat, curled into Faith's lap while she stroked my hair and Des drove. When we got to my house, we sat in the driveway for a moment.

The only light was from the few street lamps panning a golden orange glow into the vehicle.

Des unbuckled and turned to face me, sadness in her dark and stormy eyes. "I'm so sorry, babe."

My lips twitched. "It was my fault." Even my voice sounded flat to my ears.

She frowned, not denying what I'd said. "Everyone makes mistakes, Dir. It's doesn't make us ugly. It makes us *human*."

"I never wanted to be human," I said, tears leaking from my eyes. "I wanted to be his."

FORTY-THREE

NADIRA

MY HOUSE LOOMED in front of me, and I wanted to be anywhere else other than looking up at the brick building. My parents and brothers were inside, all of them with successful relationships of their own. Even my brother had chosen Tatiana over me.

A soft sigh escaped my lips. Dad had taught me how I should expect to be treated, not how I should treat someone else. That was the problem.

I couldn't stop replaying Apollo's words in my mind. He'd said he hadn't thought I was ugly before. Did that mean he'd thought I was pretty? Beautiful even?

Behind me, Des said through the open window, "Go inside, girl. You can do it."

I looked over my shoulder at her and then faced the house again, forcing one leg in front of another until I reached the front door.

Feeling like my hands were made of lead, I twisted the door open, praying for the first miracle of the day. That my family would be occupied and I could enter the sanctuary of my room unnoticed.

What I found instead was every single one of them hanging out at the kitchen island near the entrance of the house. When I walked in, all of their heads swiveled toward me, and Dad's face quickly fell.

"Honey, I—" he began.

I shook my head. "I don't want to talk about it." My feet carried me quickly over the floor to the stairs, and I pounded up as quickly as I could go before getting to my room and locking the door behind me.

I dropped my bag on the floor and lay on my bed, closing my eyes. Dad would be coming up here soon. Or he'd send Mom up. It was only a matter of time.

My phone vibrated, and I reached for it, hoping it was Apollo, that he'd thought it through and changed his mind. Instead, I found a message from Cori.

Cori: We'll bring your car back and leave your keys under the mat. Let me know if you need ANYTHING, okay? We love you, no matter what.

My heart ached at her kind words.

What *did* I want?

In the movies, girls always made heartbreak better with frosting and ice cream and romantic movies, but I didn't feel like any of that would help. I'd had one chance at a real relationship, one chance at butterflies, and I'd ruined it.

I wished I would have just told him the truth about the picture over the phone, because the disappointed look on his face would forever be etched into my mind.

A knock sounded on my door, and when I didn't reply, Dad called, "Dira, are you okay?"

I put a pillow over my face and groaned.

"That doesn't answer the question," he said.

Letting out a sigh, I removed the pillow and said, "Why are you even here? You don't care." My voice cracked on the last three words, and my chest felt hollow, like it could cave in at any moment.

"Of course I care," he said.

"I don't believe you." My voice broke again, and I stifled a sob.

"Can I please come in and talk to you?"

"No," I said, half expecting him to try the handle or ask again.

Instead, he said, "What happened with that boy?"

"Why does it have to be about a boy?" I asked, hating that it was. "Can't it be about the fact that I got voted Most 'Unique' in the yearbook or that I'm fat or that my skin looks like a freaking Dalmatian's? Or how about the fact that you and Mom have made it to almost every single basketball game of the season but only two of my Mathlete competitions?"

Dad was quiet for a moment. "Is that what it is?"

I didn't answer.

"Nadira, I don't know what to do."

The words were almost worse than any other he could have offered. Because instead of denying anything that I'd told him, he'd agreed through omission.

"Just go away," I said. "Leave me alone."

I waited for a reply, for an argument, but none came. Instead, I heard the faint sound of his footsteps on the stairs as he walked away.

The next morning, a soft knock sounded on my door. I almost told them to leave me alone, thinking it was Mom or Dad, but instead a rustling sound hit my ears.

I looked at the door and saw paper sliding underneath.

I got up and went to look at it. As I drew closer, I could see what it was. A paper crown with the words *Nadira's Brother* written in thick black marker. And underneath, in Carver's messy scrawl, *Love you, sis*.

I smiled, my lips wavering, and held it to my chest.

Sometime in the afternoon, another knock on my door woke me from the half-sleep I'd been trying to numb myself in. I was quiet this time as the handle turned. I blinked against the strip of light coming from the hallway and saw Terrell standing there.

"Hey," he said quietly. He lifted a paper bag. "I went to that bakery you like and got you something."

"Thanks," I said, my voice raspy. My head felt heavy, my eyes raw, and I just wanted to keep sleeping until I forgot what a horrible thing I'd done.

He came and sat at the foot of my bed, handing me the bag.

Slowly, I pushed myself up into a sitting position and carefully pulled at the edges of the paper until the staple came loose. Inside, there was a sandwich wrapped in cellophane, a bag of chips and a cardboard container they used to store cupcakes. Any other day I would have torn into it, but just the sight of food made my stomach turn.

"I heard what happened," he said quietly.

I waited for him to start in with the usual comments and judgments. "Get on with it," I said. "Tell me how dumb I was for lying and that Apollo deserves better." I'd thought all of it at least a million times.

"No," he said, resolute. "Tatiana should never have put you in that position. That's why I ended things with her."

"What?" I asked, stunned. "I thought you really liked her."

Terrell gave me a wry smile. "You weren't the only one hiding who you really were."

It pained me to realize Tatiana and I weren't that different in certain ways.

"Ryker's got a silence order on everyone," Terrell continued. "And Carver and I got the basketball team in on it. If anyone says anything to or about you, they'll have us to deal with."

I looked up at him, surprised by the conviction in his voice. Terrell and Carver and I had never been what I'd consider close, but they'd been more there for me this weekend than my parents had.

"Where are Mom and Dad?" I asked.

"They went clothes shopping with Carver." He flipped the rubber bracelet on his wrist. "I overheard them say they're planning on talking to you tomorrow. After you've had some space to process."

"Thanks for the heads-up."

He nodded slowly then stood up, clearly feeling awkward. I wanted to reassure him that I was thankful, but he said, "Want me to turn the light on before I go? It's still early."

I shook my head.

With a sad look, he turned and left my room, shutting the door behind him. The last thing I remembered seeing before falling asleep again was the bag from Seaton Bakery sitting on my nightstand.

FORTY-FOUR

APOLLO

"HOW LONG HAS he been doing this?" Carrie whispered.

"At least an hour," Josh responded. "But he's been working out all weekend. He's still upset about Nadira."

I kept doing push-ups, pretending I hadn't heard them. The only way I knew to get my brain to give out was to make my body go first. I didn't feel like walking across campus to the gym though, so I'd looked up a bodyweight workout and kept repeating the rounds until my muscles hurt more than the gaping hole in my chest filled with betrayal and disappointment.

"He's going to tear something," Carrie

muttered. "I didn't even know people could do that many push-ups in a row."

I switched from push-ups to squats, keeping my back to them.

"I don't mind this view," Carrie muttered, making my cheeks heat.

"You know," Josh said. "I would be jealous, but I get it. He's got buns of steel."

"Hey!" I said, pulling out my headphones. "Can you stop talking about my butt for five seconds?"

Josh seemed embarrassed, but Carrie pointed at me. "Aha! I knew you could hear us."

I shook my head, dipping into another squat. My legs were shaking from the exertion.

"Can't you deal with this the normal way?" she asked. "I can get some ice cream, and we can watch *Dirty Dancing* and cry it out."

I raised my eyebrows. "That's healthier than working out?"

"You're going to get rhabdomyolysis," she said.

"How do you know about that?" I asked.

"Where else? The internet."

I shook my head, finishing up the round of squats and going into sit-ups. Crumbs pressed into the bare skin of my back as I went up and down as fast as I could. We really needed to sweep the floor better.

Carrie tried again. "You know, it's okay to be sad after a breakup."

"It's not a breakup," I huffed. "We would have had to be dating for a breakup to happen."

Josh and Carrie gave each other a look that I ignored, then Josh tried another tactic.

"You know next weekend is Parents' Weekend, right?"

I ignored him.

"The college sent out invites. Do you think yours will come?" he asked.

I pressed my lips into a line and switched to push-ups again. "I suggest you drop it."

They exchanged another look.

Carrie said, "We're about to go get supper. Do you want to join us?"

"No thanks." When they didn't go, I pushed myself to my knees on shaking arms and snapped, "I mean it. Stop looking at me like I'm some sort of lost puppy. I'm in the ROTC, for Christ's sake. I'll go to war someday. I can handle a lie from someone I've never even seen before."

Carrie stood up, getting her purse. "Fine. But

you're not going to feel better until you admit she actually meant something to you."

I began doing push-ups again. "I feel just fine."

Josh trailed behind her, pausing at the door. I could feel his eyes on me, but I kept my gaze forward, focused on form, knowing the burnout was only seconds away.

"You know," he said. "I agree with her. And you're a terrible liar." Then he closed the door and walked away.

The second the door latched, I let my arms give out like they'd been begging to and lay flat on the dirty floor. Shaking and weak, I hauled myself up and crawled to my bed until I could climb up the ladder and lie down.

My muscles were tired, my mind was calmer than before, but my heart still ached with every beat.

FORTY-FIVE

NADIRA

THE LIGHT WAS BLINDING against my eyes. "Turn it off," I groaned, rolling over under my blankets.

But they were being stripped away from my bed, leaving me bare in my pajamas, exposed to the air that felt so cold in contrast to the warmth I'd been under.

I jerked up to find the culprit, my mother, stuffing the blankets in my laundry hamper. "Mom!" I cried. "Give them back."

"We've let you wallow long enough," she said firmly. "Get up, take a shower, and come down to the table. Your father and I would like to speak with you."

Before I could argue, she left my room, closing the door behind her.

I glared at it, considering for a moment what would happen if I didn't get up. I didn't want to. Leaving this bed meant moving on from what happened, and I couldn't. But my mom was a determined woman. If I didn't do as she asked, she would be upstairs, watching me do it until I was finished.

Deciding to spare myself more humiliation than I'd already faced, I got up and began getting ready. Einstein may have thought time was relative, but my time was coming.

Freshly showered and dressed in sweats, I went downstairs to face my fate. I wasn't sure what my punishment would be for my behavior. I'd never really acted out before. But Mom and Dad were fond of grounding Terrell for missed curfews or taking away Carver's phone when he didn't get homework turned in.

Whatever fate they landed on, it couldn't make me feel worse than I already did. So they took my phone? It wasn't like I could talk to Apollo anymore anyway. And I would see my friends at school.

So they grounded me for a few weeks? I didn't feel like going out.

All that had really mattered to me were my friends and Mathletes and Apollo. Two of those had been taken away on Friday.

As promised, Mom and Dad waited at the island. My brothers were nowhere to be found.

"Where are Terrell and Carver?" I asked, hoping for a buffer.

"Went out with friends," Dad said. "It's just the three of us."

Feeling apprehensive, I slid into a chair as far from them as I could get. Nonetheless, Mom slid a plate of cheese and crackers toward me.

"You need to eat something," she said.

My stomach turned just looking at it, and she sighed.

"Hon," Dad warned. "Be gentle."

His words didn't hit their mark, though, because Mom said, "This moping around has got to end, Nadira. You've had a weekend, and that's plenty time enough."

I raised my eyebrows, incredulous. "So I get embarrassed at the biggest event of the year, demoted from captain, and have the only guy I've ever really liked tell me he never wants to talk to me and I'm supposed to just get over it? Like that?"

Dad gave Mom a look. "That's not what she's saying. You know, we watched our beautiful, smart, talented daughter be reduced to something we don't even recognize. I hate any guy who could cause that."

"Am I not allowed to be upset?" I asked, grabbing crackers and stuffing them in my face. "Am I just supposed to be your fat and happy baby forever?"

"Dira," Dad said.

But I kept going, brushing crumbs off my face. "That's what Mom wants. She wants me to have no feelings, just like her, so I can grow up and have a job. Because nothing else matters, right, Mom? Everything comes second to the career?"

I knew I was hitting where it hurt, but it was true. For all of high school, I'd been patient Nadira. Easygoing Nadira. Never-get-in-trouble Nadira. But my heart had never been on the line like this before. I'd been too scared to make myself vulnerable, even online.

My friends were the brave ones, risking their hearts on love. Taking chances in trusting someone else with all of who they are. I couldn't even do that. I gave Apollo half of who I was and expected it to be enough.

Mom leaned forward, resting her elbows on the granite countertop. "What do you want me to say? Apologize for loving my job?"

Dad rubbed his hands over his knees. "We're getting distracted here."

Mom looked at him harshly. "Then what?" she demanded. "You just want to let her be a shadow of who she is until she moves out?" Mom's voice cracked. "We only have a few months left with her, and I'm realizing I hardly know her." She swiveled on me, her eyes wide and shining. "Why didn't you ever tell me what Apollo meant to you?"

Each of her words tugged at my heart, but how could she *not* know why I'd never told her? All it would have taken was a few questions about me and my life to know everything. She'd never ever asked.

"Mom, you've hardly been interested in anything I've done. You and Dad both. You've come to two Mathlete meets, and that's only because we made it to state! My friends hardly ever hang out here because half the time in the winter, we're eating microwave dinners every night. I'm constantly helping *you* with research projects and coming to *your* games. When has it ever mattered what I've been interested in as long as I'm getting good grades?"

I looked between the two of them, but neither of them met my eyes. Dad rubbed his temples, and Mom's jaw clenched as she looked anywhere but at me.

"And this young man?" Dad asked. "What's so special about him?"

My eyes watered as I stood up from the table. "He cared. And I didn't deserve it." Then I turned around and went upstairs. My parents let me go.

FORTY-SIX

NADIRA

I'D NEVER skipped school before. Not after I had my tonsils removed in second grade. Not after we were in a car accident in sixth grade. Not when the school van had broken down after a Mathlete competition sophomore year and we had to wait until one in the morning for our parents to come and rescue us from the middle of nowhere.

But on Monday, I wanted to lie in bed. I wanted to hide under the covers and not face the embarrassment and devastation that was sure to come at school, whether at the hands of my own feelings or at Tatiana's inexplicable hatefulness.

My friends had a different idea, though. Cori and Faith arrived around the time I usually got up with a cup of creamy iced coffee and a box of chocolates.

I blinked at them, my eyes rough from all the crying. "What are you doing here?"

Cori smiled gently, sliding under the covers next to me. "Thought you might need some friends."

Faith sat on the other side of my bed, rubbing my hip through the comforter.

A gush of hot tears soothed my eyes, and I leaned into her shoulder. "I messed up so bad, Cor."

"You did," she agreed, taking me off guard. "But he did too. If I've learned anything from being with Ryker, it's that relationships are a give and take, and they require a whole lot of grace and forgiveness."

I raised my eyebrows, surprised. "I thought you two were perfect together."

"We are." She laughed, resting her cheek against the top of my head. "But that doesn't mean we don't fight or argue or mess up. We're only human, Dir."

"Well I don't feel human," I mumbled. "I feel like a piece of garbage that got ran over by a bus."

Faith said gently, "Maybe the coffee will help?"

Cori nodded. "I know you're disappointed, but I

can't let you wallow. There's nothing wrong with you." She turned sideways so she was lying facing me on the bed. "You are a beautiful girl like no one else. You're smart as hell, and you're going to run the world someday. Don't let one mistake make you act like any less than the gem you are."

"Gem," I breathed, wiping my eyes. "More like a diamond in the rough."

She smiled. "Where else would a diamond come from?" She shifted, getting up. "Sit up, Dir." She took the coffee from Faith and handed it to me. "You're going to face this day and your feelings and your doubts head-on. My best friend deserves the best."

I shifted to sit up and gave her a hug, then extended my arm to Faith. The three of us embraced for a moment, and I reveled in the feeling of having them support me.

Maybe, maybe if I had friends willing to do this for me, to support me even when I was at my worst, maybe I wasn't as bad as I'd thought I was.

I drank deeply from the coffee, feeling the bitter mocha and sweet cream rejuvenate me from the inside out.

Cori got up and went to my closet, picking out the pieces of my uniform for me. "Go take a quick shower and get dressed." She winked. "Wouldn't want you to be late for math."

I smiled softly and got up, grabbing the hangers from her and walking into the hall for the bathroom.

Terrell was just coming out, and we nearly bumped into each other. I kept my eyes down to pass him, but he gently took my arm. "Hey," he said, "Are you okay?"

I looked up at him, seeing concern in his eyes that looked so much like mine. "I'm going to be," I said. And I hoped it was true.

FORTY-SEVEN

NADIRA

I RODE to school with Cori and Faith, letting the boys take my car. When we arrived, I was more thankful than ever to have my friends at my side.

Ryker got there only seconds after us, as if he and Cori had planned it. He walked beside Cori, his eyes darting between me and the threat we all knew we were approaching.

Tatiana, Isabella, and their groupies hung out around Grant's pickup, and it was only a matter of seconds before they'd see us walking by.

As if smelling my fear, Isabella caught my eyes, then nudged Tatiana.

Tatiana's gaze landed on me, and her lips curled into a feral snarl. "I'm guessing lover boy found out you were catfishing him?" She looked around the parking lot. "I was half expecting cameras to show up and film how pathetic you are."

"Enough," Ryker snarled.

She raised her eyebrows at him. "Still playing for the fatties, I see?"

Ryker's lips thinned, and from here, he looked absolutely terrifying. I was glad he was on our side. He lowered his voice to a menacing growl, and he said, "Tatiana, you know your dad recently hired on at Dugan Industries, right? Would be a shame if he was let go."

Her eyes widened and then narrowed. "Is that a threat?" she asked.

Ryker gave her a cold smile. "Of course not. I don't make threats. I make promises. And I *promise*, you will regret messing with Nadira."

Goosebumps rose on my arms, and Tatiana's skin went ashen.

"That's what I thought," Ryker growled. "Come on, girls."

He led us away from the viper den, and the farther I got from them, the more I realized how shallowly I'd been breathing. I took in a deeper gulp of air and whispered, "Thank you."

His eyes were kind as he turned on me. "I know I've said it before, but I'm sorry, Nadira. I can't believe I ever treated you like they do." He reached across Cori and took my hand for a second. "You deserve so much better."

My eyes stung, but I blinked quickly and nodded. I didn't quite believe him about me deserving better, but I hoped I would soon.

I slid into my seat in calculus and tried to keep my expression neutral as Mr. Aris began passing out our graded exams.

He placed mine face down and said quietly, "Not your best work."

My heart sank as I flipped it over and found the C staring back at me. I placed it back down, rubbing my temples. How had I let myself get so far from who I was? I'd lied, kept secrets, dismissed responsibilities, all for a chance at being loved.

Next to me, Regina asked, "How'd you do, Harris?"

I glared at her, but that didn't stop her.

"I got an A minus." She leaned over, catching sight of my grade and winced. "Oof. Losing your touch?"

"Drop it, Regina," I said.

She feigned innocence. "So hostile for an *ex*-Mathlete captain."

"You won, okay? Can you just let it go and stop being jealous?" I demanded, my voice rising with each word. "I have one thing that I'm good at. One thing. Can you let me have it? Or do you want that too? Do you want me to just be a pathetic little black puddle on the floor? Huh? Would that make you happy?"

"Ladies," Mr. Aris cut in.

I shook my head, tears forming. "I'm sick of arguing with you, Regina! I'm sick of never being good enough anywhere in my life!" I grabbed my backpack and stormed toward the hall. I'd thought I could handle school surrounded in the warm, supportive blanket of my friendships. But the real world didn't treat me like that. No, it tried to tear me down every chance it got. I couldn't take it anymore.

I opened the door and left, but Mr. Aris was only a step behind me.

"Nadira, wait!" he said. I paused outside the door, turning to face him. Through the window to the classroom, I could see the people in the front row peering curiously at us, but I focused on his face.

"What?" I said, more harshly than I meant to.

Concern laced his features. "What's going on?"

I shook my head, wishing these tears would just stop. That I could cry them out and be done. "I made a mistake, okay? And I know you hate me for what happened."

"What?" he asked, confused. "I could never hate you, Nadira. I was disappointed by what happened, but you're in high school. No one expects you to behave perfectly all the time. I'm *worried* about you."

I blinked toward the ceiling, seconds from breaking. Maybe I already had. "I had a pen pal. And he was amazing. And I fell in love with him. But I lied and showed him a picture of Tatiana and told him it was me. And then he found out I was lying. He hated me because I lied. And now I'm doing bad at math and Regina's being Regina, and I just can't take it anymore!"

I walked in a circle and tugged at my hair, pulling my curls straight.

"Nadira, Nadira." He put his hand on my shoulder. I'd expected to see judgement in his eyes, but only found sympathy. "I know I focus on math, but I also understand that being in high school is hard. That's why I have those posters in the room.

To remind you all to take a breath. To get back up and try again. And to not take yourself so seriously. Remember, there's not a problem that can't be solved. If you can't find a solution, you need a new equation."

What equation could there possibly be for me? I looked away from him, seeing through the classroom window to the poster that hung over my desk.

"If I had more time, I'd write a shorter letter." - Blaise Pascal

---

My eyes focused in on the words, and they went straight to my heart.

I'd already written all the letters. Maybe it was time to try something new.

FORTY-EIGHT

APOLLO

SATURDAY KICKED OFF PARENTS' Weekend at the college, and I promised myself I would stay as far away from campus as possible. Dad had already told me he couldn't make it because of a convention he needed to attend, and Mom still hadn't called. All of Brentwood U would be crawling with students and parents, and no matter how much I hated to admit it, I was so jealous it was making me sick.

So, I got up early and drove to the Brentwood Senior Community to see Great-Aunt Tilly. This place had become somewhat of a second home since I moved to California for school. Even though studies and ROTC kept me busy, I always knew I could escape here, and Aunt Tilly would be a quiet shoulder to lean on.

I walked through the front glass door and typed in the entry code. Miss Rosie sat in her wheelchair near the door, and her face lit up when she saw me. She extended her arms for a hug, and I leaned in, giving her a squeeze.

"How are you doing, Miss Rosie?" I asked.

She smiled, her eyes cloudy. "Good, good."

"Good to hear," I said, and told her I'd see her in a bit. The hallway with all the rooms stretched before me, and I took in the familiar sights, sounds, and even smells of the nursing home. In the recreation area, old TV shows played at a decibel that could injure a younger child's hearing. Through an open door to a room, I could hear family members shouting at their loved one in order to be heard clearly. There was the whir of cards in the shuffling machine as a group played at a table in a little lobby area.

At the end of the hall, I reached Aunt Tilly's room. There were a few photocopied pictures of her on the door. One from Christmas when they'd put her in a Santa hat. Another of her denture-clad smile on bingo night. Then photos of her with each of her nieces and nephews who'd attended Brentwood U and come to visit over the years.

The door was cracked, and I could hear Miss Honey talking to Aunt Tilly. I knocked, not sure whether or not she'd be decent, and the nurse called, "Come in!"

I pushed the door open and slipped inside. Miss Honey, was adjusting a tray table in front of Aunt Tilly while the TV played the gameshow channel. That was Aunt Tilly's favorite. And mine, if I was being honest.

"Hi, Miss Honey," I said. "Hi, Aunt Tilly."

Aunt Tilly smiled at me, and Miss Honey said, "Tilly, tell me your secrets. How do you get these fine-looking boys to always come and visit you?"

Lifting a weathered hand, Aunt Tilly patted Miss Honey's hand, and Miss Honey turned toward me. "Can I get you anything from the caf?"

"If you wanted to slip me a tray, I wouldn't complain," I said, going to sit in the extra chair next to Aunt Tilly's recliner. She picked up a piece of toast and began chewing.

"Sure thing," Miss Honey said and excused herself from the room.

A commercial break started, and she hit the mute button on the remote.

358 CURVY GIRLS CAN'T DATE SOLDIERS

"You want to hear about my drama this week?" I asked.

She turned her head toward me for a moment before looking back to her food. An invitation.

I unloaded my story about Nadira and Tatiana and what a horrible time I'd been having with it. "My roommate's girlfriend thinks I need to grieve, and Josh thinks I need to forgive her, but I wouldn't even know where to begin." I let out a sigh and rubbed my hands through my hair. "I'm a real mess."

She reached over and patted my hand and then continued eating. My eyes stung because she knew. It was the best she could do, and it was still more than my mom had done for me in the last eight months.

The door pushed open, and I looked up to see what Miss Honey had brought me to eat, but it wasn't Miss Honey at the door.

My mom stepped in, gripping her purse. "That was quite a story."

Aunt Tilly's fork clattered to her plastic plate and my lips parted, both of us equally as surprised to see my mom standing there.

"Mom?" I breathed. I almost couldn't believe she was standing in front of me.

Her lips faltered into a smile before falling again. "Oh, honey."

I got out of my seat and ran to her arms, just like I would have when I was a kid needing some invisible hurt kissed better. She hugged me tight, breathing raggedly into my chest, and I cried into her shoulder.

A frustrated sigh sounded behind us, and I looked back to see Aunt Tilly staring at us, an about-time look in her eyes.

We spent the morning with Aunt Tilly, then Mom and I went to get lunch at Seaton Bakery. Josh had introduced me to it a few months back, and it had quickly become one of my favorite places in California.

Gayle, the woman who co-owned the bakery with her husband, set us up with plenty of great food and even a new lemonade recipe they were trying.

Mom sat across from me at the booth, looking around. "You've got quite the place here."

I smiled, looking around. But there was still an ache between us. We hadn't talked about our rift, not in front of Aunt Tilly, but I couldn't bring myself to approach the topic. Not now. Not when I had her so close.

So instead, we ate and caught up. She told me about her volunteer work with the local hospital. How my youngest sister Jane was doing in her vocal lessons and how Josh and Bette's wedding planning was going.

I drank in her words, all of the knowledge about my family. My sister and I texted sometimes. Dad called occasionally, but it wasn't the same as hearing from Mom. She noticed little details Dad never picked up and my siblings never thought to share.

By the time our food was cleared from our plates, I felt so much closer to home than I had since leaving.

She began piling her napkins and silverware on her plate—a carryover from her time as a waitress —and said, "Do you want to show me your dorm? I'd love to meet your roommate."

I nodded. "That would be great."

She followed me in her car to the college, and I kept glancing at my phone in the passenger seat. I'd imagined when my mom and I reconciled, I'd be introducing her to Nadira. Mom would have loved the story of the uncanny way Nadira and I met.

That was not happening today.

I wondered when the reminders of my heart-break would stop playing in my head. When I'd broken up with my high school sweetheart, it hadn't hurt this bad, and we'd been together for two years.

We circled the crowded parking lot until I found a couple of openings next to each other. As I got out and greeted my mom, I said, "Sorry, it's a bit of a walk from here."

"No worries." She smiled, extending her hand to loop her arm through mine. "Reminds me of when I went here."

We walked together toward the dorm, passing other students with their families, and I didn't feel jealous anymore. In fact, I was proud. Thankful that my mom, the woman who'd raised me, had come from Texas to see me, even with the awkward-ness that still lingered between us.

As we approached my room, I said, "Just a warning, Josh is an art student, and his girlfriend's a little over the top."

Mom batted her hand at me. "Do you remember the horror story about my first roommate?"

I snorted. "True. At least Josh hasn't started collecting my toenail clippings yet."

Mom shuddered.

I slipped my key into the knob and looked in to check if Josh was home. "It's just us," I told my mom, opening the door to our empty room. At least Josh had thought to spray Febreze before his parents got here. And he'd even used the Swiffer to clean the floor.

Mom scanned the room, nodding, a watery smile forming. She let out a strangled sob and covered her mouth.

"Mom," I said gently, but what was there to say?

"I've missed so much," she said, wiping at her eyes. "This is an amazing new home you've made for yourself."

My throat felt tight, hearing her praise. All I'd ever wanted to do was make my parents proud.

"I was scared I was going to lose you, so I made the choice my own." She shook her head, as if at herself. "I'm sorry." She looked up at me. "Can you ever forgive me?"

I smiled, pulling her into a hug. "I already have."

FORTY-NINE

NADIRA

I STOOD in front of my mirror, taking in my typical game-day outfit. I wore a dress-length Brentwood University jersey with the name HARRIS and the number 00 printed on the back, along with a pair of leggings. It was so comfortable, I couldn't wait to get to MIT, where I could forego wearing a blazer and pantyhose every single day.

A knock sounded on my door, and I glanced to the crack to see Mom stepping in. She wore a similar outfit, except she had on dark jeans and a button-up shirt under her jersey. It was like dressing professionally was a part of her DNA.

She took me in with surprise. "Hey, I wasn't sure if you'd be coming today."

"Why wouldn't I? We go to all Dad's home

games," I said simply, but an edge of bitterness crept into my voice.

"You're right," Mom said. "Families are supposed to be there for each other. No matter what, no matter when."

I watched her, curiously, as she moved to sit on my bed.

"Will you sit with me for a moment?" she asked.

Reluctantly, I walked to the opposite side of the bed and sat. I didn't understand what she was doing here—what she could possibly have to say.

"What you said last week really threw me for a loop," she began. "I've been a feminist all my life, and I love my career and my students—you know I do—but I've been letting a lot of balls drop at home that never even should have come close to the floor."

My heart stalled, aching to believe what she was hinting at.

"The reason your dad and I go to your brothers' games in the evenings isn't because we care about them more than you. It's because we're free and we can, so there's no reason we shouldn't. But Mathletes happens during business hours, so we let it slide. It was never about you or how much you matter to us." She scooted a little closer on the bed, placing her hand atop mine.

I didn't move my fingers to grip her hand back, but I didn't shy away either.

"But that's not what you saw," she said with a sigh and shook her head. "All these years, we've gone to a meet here or there as we could get away. Why didn't you tell us it was eating you up inside?"

The curiosity in her voice hurt almost as much as the fact that I'd kept all that hurt to myself. Why hadn't I told them that I really wanted them there? "Maybe... Maybe I was afraid if I told you and then you didn't come that it would feel like an even bigger rejection. And I've had enough of that to last a lifetime."

Mom's forehead creased. "Honey. We want to be there for you whenever we can and however we can. I know it will look different now that MIT's just a few months away, but Daddy and I love you." She brushed back a flyaway hair on my head. "And to be honest, I don't get the boys like your dad does. We girls have to stick together."

The corner of my lips lifted as my eyes burned. I'd always wanted to have a close relationship with my mom, but I never felt good enough for her before. Now, we were running out of time. I'd messed up so many things.

"Did I ever tell you how your father and I met?" she asked, taking me off guard.

I hadn't expected her to bring it up, but I remembered the story. "Dad was on the basketball team, and you were his math tutor."

She nodded. "He was the most pigheaded person I'd ever met. So full of himself. And God forbid he ever walked a piece of paper to the trash can. No, every piece had to become a basketball."

The thought made me laugh. I'd seen him do it about a million times by now. "Not much has changed, huh?"

"Nope," she said, chuckling. "But I didn't tell you the part about how I almost ruined it all."

"What do you mean?" I asked. As far as I knew, Dad proposed after college, and the rest was history.

"A few months before graduation, I got offered a great job at a college in Kentucky. Well, your father got recruited to play for an international team in Latvia. But he said he wouldn't take it if I wanted to marry him. He'd follow me wherever I went and coach at the YMCA if he had to." She shook her head. "I knew how passionate he felt about basketball, and what an incredible opportunity it would be for him to see the world. So of course, I told him I didn't love him and that he should go. I couldn't stand the idea of love coming before a job."

My eyebrows drew together. "You never told me about that..."

"It was the longest year of my life, being away from him. Because I couldn't tell him how I felt." She pressed her lips together and let them loose, then turned to look at me. "Instead of letting him decide what he wanted from his future, I lied to him, Nadira, and that lie changed the course of his life. *Our* lives."

My heart sank at the three-letter word. "What did you do?" I asked, desperate for a cure for the mess I was in.

"I quit my job," she said. "And I spent all my money on a plane ticket, and I flew to Latvia with just what I could carry."

My eyes widened. Of all the things I'd expected my mother to say, that was the very last. "You quit your job for a guy?"

She nodded. "I did. But when I got there, he was still upset with me. He said if I wanted to be with him, I needed to do better than show up unannounced and ask him back."

My mouth fell open. "What?" My brain was spinning with all the information.

"Mhmm." With a shake of her head, she said, "I was so stubborn, I said, 'That's fine. I have three months on my travel visa, and I'll go to all of your games until you realize I'm the one you're supposed to be with.'"

"You're kidding," I said, already knowing she wasn't. My mother didn't give up on the things that mattered to her.

"I went to every single game. I rode busses, hitchhiked, took taxis. At the end of every game, I would tell him good job, he'd say thank you, and his coach would have him get on the bus. And even though he never told me he wanted me back, he didn't ask me to leave either."

"I can't believe you flew all that way and he didn't forgive you," I said, imagining her following him around the country with a broken heart and a spark of hope.

She nodded slowly. "Well, it was the day before my visa expired, and he still hadn't said he was ready to come home. So I thought I'd make it to one last game. I decided I'd given it my all, and if he didn't come around, then maybe it just wasn't meant to be."

My heart hurt thinking of Mom following Dad around a foreign country. Of the pain he must have had to be rejected by her.

"So after the game, I didn't even wait. I watched him play, thinking it might very well be the last time I ever saw him again. And then I left."

My eyes flew open. "You left!"

She nodded, but then a sly smile grew on her face. "And he came after me. Slid into the cab seat beside me and said, 'I'll make you a deal.' Of course I was pissed. I'd followed this man around the damn country, and he was trying to make deals with me? I let him know how mad I was about it, but then he said, 'I don't want to leave Latvia without a wife. And I want her to be you.'"

My jaw went slack. "What?"

She nodded. "So we went to a chapel nearby and had a ceremony. A couple of his teammates came. I was wearing a sundress, and he had on a suit he wore traveling between games."

"But you guys got married in Albany. In Grandma and Grandpa's backyard." That photo smiled at us from the mantle every day.

"We had a *wedding* in Albany," she said, reaching

for her phone. "But we got *married* in Latvia." She swiped to her album. She'd taken a picture of her and Dad. Just as promised, she wore a blue sundress; Dad had on a black suit with a red tie. They smiled at each other outside of a restaurant I couldn't read the words on, holding their hands toward the camera, showing the wedding bands I saw every day.

My lips parted. "You got married in Latvia."

She nodded, pulling the phone away.

"Why are you telling me this?" I asked.

She smiled, putting her arms around me. "Because you know better than anyone how much telling a lie can hurt. But I want you to know that making it right can lead you to the most beautiful adventure of a lifetime."

FIFTY

APOLLO

MOM and I had supper in the dining hall and sat with Josh and his parents. For the first time, the world I grew up in and the life I'd created collided, and it felt...right. Like I was exactly where I was meant to be.

Almost.

I missed Nadira like I'd miss my right hand if it disappeared. I couldn't stop thinking that my mom would have liked her, had they had a chance to meet.

When we finished eating, I showed Mom the ice cream machine that had an unlimited supply of soft serve and cones.

She chuckled. "Hello, my old friend. This is how I gained my freshman fifteen."

Of course she was familiar with the dining hall, having gone here. I put a sugar cone under the twist dispenser and twirled it high, and then she got her own, smaller version.

"Want to walk around campus?" I asked, wanting the day to last forever.

"Sure." She took a lick of her ice cream and followed me toward the exit. We stepped into the warm evening air and began walking the sidewalks that wound about campus. She had a nostalgic look in her eyes. "Dad and I used to sit under that tree and study." She nodded toward a tall sycamore, and I could almost picture the two of them, huddled with their books and a blanket.

"What else did you do for dates?" I asked.

"Since we didn't have much money, we'd go do whatever was free with a student ID. Your dad's favorite was basketball games. I always packed snacks in my purse." She chuckled. "Life has certainly changed since then."

"There's a game tonight," I said, then instantly regretted it, remembering that Nadira's dad was the coach.

Mom's face lit up, and it was clear she wanted to watch. "Can we go?" she asked. "Are you up for it?"

I hesitated for a moment before nodding, but Mom didn't miss my reluctance.

"You don't want to. Is it about that girl? Nadira?"

Hearing the name on Mom's lips seemed so right and wrong at the same time. "Her dad's the coach," I explained. "We might see her there, but we can go. I'll live." I wasn't going to let one person ruin an entire event for me. I still had three years left at this school.

"Are you sure?" She turned at the fork in the sidewalk, shifting direction toward the sports arena. "Do you want to talk about it?"

I shrugged, eating the rest of my cone. "I don't know what there is to be said that you didn't hear me say to Aunt Tilly."

With a frown, she replied, "So this girl sent you the wrong picture and then let someone else pretend to be her? Why would she do something like that?"

"She's insecure," I said.

"Why?"

I bit my lip. "Because she's different."

Mom's eyebrows rose. "What do you mean?"

"She has this skin condition, vitiligo, and it

makes some of her skin lose color. And then she's bigger than other girls."

"Ah," Mom said.

I nodded.

"Can you blame her for wanting to be someone different, though?" Mom asked, surprising me. I thought she was supposed to be on my side.

"I can blame her for lying. Absolutely."

"No." She put her hand on my arm for a moment before letting it fall. "You've never really been girl crazy, so you haven't noticed the way girls look at you, honey."

I raised my eyebrows. "What's that supposed to mean?"

She chuckled softly. "You're an attractive young man with a good head on your shoulders. I could see how a girl would be intimidated by that, especially if she's grown up being called less-than because of her size or her skin."

A muscle in my jaw twitched. "So you're on her side."

"I'm on the side of a girl who would call me to tell me what an idiot I've been for ignoring my son."

"What?" I stopped, unable to move any farther. Some people behind us walked around us, but I just kept staring at my mom, trying to comprehend what she'd just said.

Mom looked at me with gentle eyes. "She found your dad's office number online and asked him how to contact me." She chuckled softly, shaking her head. "I suppose he was sympathetic to her cause, because I got a call from a very determined young woman telling me how amazing you are and how stupid it was to waste what time I had to be your mom."

Each beat of my heart came more painfully than the one before it, and my throat got tight. I swallowed, trying to shove the lump down, but after trying to control my emotions for so long, I couldn't. They were bubbling to the surface, so strong they were undeniable now.

I let out a curse word and stepped off the sidewalk into the grass. "How could she do something like that? She acts like I'm just some paper figure on the other side of the computer screen and then..." gives me everything I've been longing for. I couldn't even say the words with the lump growing in my throat and my eyes stinging like they were. "*Damn it.*" I raked my hands through my hair, then turned to my mom. "You're a girl. Explain."

She laughed now, but this wasn't funny.

"Mom!" I half yelled, half begged.

"Oh, honey." She stepped onto the grass with me, cupping my cheek with her hand. "She loves you. And I can tell you love her too. What else is there to understand?"

FIFTY-ONE

MOM GAVE Terrell and Carver money so they could get us snacks before going off to talk to their friends in the college. We walked together up the bleachers to the family seating section, finding seats near the front.

She glanced around the gym, checking the student section. "Is he here?"

Knowing who she meant, I followed her gaze, hoping to see Apollo with his mom. She hadn't told me if my words had gotten through to her, only thanked me for my concern and hung up with a "bless your heart." It was so southern it hurt.

But even if she was here, there was no guarantee they'd spend their time at the basketball game. Maybe they were playing bingo with Aunt Tilly or checking out the place where ROTC students learned and trained.

Still, the gym was packed for Parents' Weekend. There were thousands of faces to sift through. "I don't see him," I said, trying to hide the weird mix of disappointment and relief that flooded my body.

She put an arm around me. "Well, now that I know you're into college boys, maybe Dad can introduce you to someone on the team."

I rolled my eyes. "Dad would *never* introduce me to one of his players like that."

"True." She winked. "Wouldn't want you distracting them before the playoffs."

I shook my head, glancing back to see if Terrell and Carver were heading our way yet. I could really use some food right now. Stress-eating was calling my name.

Of course, my brothers were still nowhere to be found. They'd probably been intercepted by some of their friends or gotten sidetracked by a pretty girl.

I looked back at the court to see the teams finishing their warmup. The announcer came on, talking about family weekend and asking the parents of all the players to stand up to be honored. We clapped loudly for those who stood all around us.

They were so proud of their children—I could see it on their faces, in the way their shoulders straightened and their smiles lifted. I wondered if someday my brothers would be getting the same treatment playing college ball. If my parents would have a chance to celebrate me like that too.

The game started, and the familiar sounds of basketball enveloped us. Sneakers squeaked on the floor, blending with referee whistles, cheers, and the jolt of buzzers.

Next to me, Carver's voice jerked me out of the game. "Hey, I got you something."

I turned toward him, expecting to see a tray of nachos, but found something completely different.

Apollo stood behind him, and a woman who had to be his mom followed behind.

My eyes widened, taking him in, but my mouth didn't move. It was as if his mere presence had captivated me. As though the T-shirt clinging to his muscled arms had wrapped itself around my mouth, blocking any words.

Mom leaned around me and said, "Hi, Apollo."

She extended her hand. "You must be Mrs. Banks. Join us!"

Apollo's mom walked past, sitting by my mom, but Apollo still stood. People were beginning to grumble in the row behind him, but he kept his eyes on me. "Nadira, can we talk?"

My heart froze at the sound of my name on his lips. What was he going to tell me? That I'd crossed a line? That he really wanted me to stay out of his business? I couldn't stand another look of disappointment. Any more dismissive words. My heart had taken all it could handle and then some.

Mom nudged my arm. "Go, honey."

Her words had me standing. Had my feet moving after Apollo, down the bleacher row and then down the aisle steps.

He looked over his shoulder periodically, as if to make sure I was coming, but said nothing. Just seeing the way his shoulders moved, the stiff set of them, made me fear bad news. I silently begged that he would make it quick and that I would be able to escape to a bathroom, outside, anywhere he wouldn't see me cry.

There was an indoor track behind the bleachers, and Apollo led me to an outcropping of space outside the track. It was an emergency exit, away from the concession stands or bathrooms. If I left, the doors would buzz, but at least I could flee if I needed to.

He reached the corner and turned toward me, taking me in. I wondered what he thought of me up close. The real me. In my Brentwood U jersey that showed the fat on my arms where they pressed against my sides or the line of my stomach where it bulged against my leggings. But I didn't move to hide it by putting my hands on my hips or sucking in. No, I'd hidden enough. Apollo had said he wanted the real me, not an ugly lie.

Here I was.

I stared at him, daring him to flinch. To look away. To show he was repulsed by me and that I'd been right to be afraid.

He opened his mouth to speak but then closed it. His eyes shut too, forming a dark fringe of lashes.

What was he holding back?

He opened them up and looked at me again. "I wanted to say thank you."

"What?" I breathed. That was the last thing I had expected.

"Thank you," he repeated, "for calling my mom

and getting her to come here. She said you reached out to her." He paused for a moment. "But it doesn't change the fact that you hurt me."

My heart ached, but I nodded. I knew this could happen. "I would love another chance with you, Apollo. I would. But that's not the only reason I called your mom. I did it because I care about you, and you care about her."

His mouth opened and closed, but that was fine because I had plenty to say that I hadn't been able to in the Emerson Academy parking lot.

"This isn't a game to me. You and me." I gestured between us. "I know I treated it like one, but I cared about you—care about you. And I know some grand gesture isn't going to change what I did or the fact that I hurt you."

He looked away, shielding the hurt in his eyes, but I pressed on.

"I know I don't deserve a second chance, and maybe you shouldn't give me one. I'm going to be three thousand miles away in August. The idea that two kids who met online could ever be anything more is ridiculous. Almost as impossible as a guy like you falling for a girl like me. Logically, I know that. My heart will catch up eventually."

I looked him over for a moment. Trying to

memorize his face. The scar on his ear and the arch of his eyebrows and the hard line of his jaw. But then I said, "It's been nice getting to know you. I hope your life is the most beautiful adventure."

And I walked away.

FIFTY-TWO

APOLLO

SHE TURNED her back to me and started walking away, and such a feeling of loss overwhelmed me, it almost brought me to my knees.

I couldn't let her go.

Couldn't let her leave thinking that we could never have made it work.

Because I still wanted to.

"Wait," I said, reaching to take her hand.

It slipped into mine for what I realized was the first time. Her skin was soft. Supple. And it sent a shot of lightning straight to my gut—just that contact with her fingertips.

She turned toward me, her black eyes guarded, and I hated that I had been one of the people to make her feel like she needed to protect herself.

"Why?" I asked. "Why did you lie to me for so long?" I needed to know as much as I needed air.

She didn't pull her hand away from mine, something I was consciously aware of as her lips came together to form a word, then gave up. She relaxed them and tried again. "Because I knew I would never have a chance with you."

"Why?" I repeated, anger tightening the muscles in my jaw. How could she decide our fate without even giving me a chance?

"Wh-what do you mean?"

"Why would a guy like me never fall for a girl like you? Why would it never work?"

Her chest heaved with a derisive laugh. "Are you delirious?" She took her hand from mine, and the absence nearly took me down. My hand was cold now, without hers, and I realized if I never held her hand again, something would always be missing.

She gestured at me, waving her hands wildly. "Look at you! You're practically the poster boy for hot soldier, and I'm..." She blinked quickly, shaking her head. "*Unique.*" She spat it like it was something dirty. Something to be ashamed of.

And I recognized the word. From what those mean girls said about her in yearbook.

"You say that like it's a bad thing," I said, stepping forward.

She stepped backward, bumping against the wall, but I stayed close. Her breath caught; I saw it in the hitch of her full chest.

Her eyes flitted from mine to my mouth, her breathing shallow. "It is a bad thing."

I shook my head, putting my hand on the wall by her shoulder. "It's the best damn thing there is, Nadira." My muscles tightened like my body wanted to defend her from even the memory of her bullies. From the mean voice inside her head that lied to her daily. "There is no one like you. You're beautiful."

Her lips parted, her eyes searching mine, full of disbelief.

"I'll say it again if you don't believe me," I growled. I was tired of people acting like Nadira was less-than because of her size. Especially her. Since when did a number on a scale or clothing tag take away from someone's value. From their worth? As far as I was concerned, Nadira's curves were one of the sexiest things about her. And standing this close, there were plenty of reasons I was attracted to her. "You deserve to know how beautiful you are."

She lifted her chin, defiant, stubborn as always. "Tell me then. What's so beautiful about me? Is it the way my thighs rub together when I walk? Or how about the fact I could fit a whole extra tooth between my front two teeth? Or how about my skin? Huh? I have to get two colors of foundation like a damn clown."

I lifted my fingers to her mouth, silencing her. "Can you be quiet for one second? You're the most stubborn person I know!"

Her lips pursed together under my fingers, making the muscles in my stomach tighten, but I kept my focus on her. On the way she both infuriated and intrigued me more than anyone else I knew.

"You don't like your thighs?" I asked, dropping my fingers to her chin, lifting it up so I could see her eyes more clearly.

She shook her head.

I trailed my finger to her hips and felt her suppress a shiver under my touch. "I love your thighs," I breathed.

She closed her eyes, blinking slowly.

"And your hair?" I said. "Do you like that?"

"No," she breathed.

I reached to the base of her neck, working my

fingers through the tangle of curls. "I want to get my fingers caught in here when I kiss you."

Her breath came in a gasp, but my brave girl looked up at me defiantly. "And my skin?" she demanded.

I brought my fingers from her hair, tracing my thumb over the spots on her cheek and bringing it to her lip, peeling it free of her teeth. "Is incredible."

She let out a shaky breath.

I could practically feel her defenses crumbling. "So tell me again why we can't be together?"

"Because we're going to live too far away," she said, as if reminding herself. "Why would you want to date someone you'd only get to see twice a year?"

"Why would you want to date someone who might get deployed for an entire year and not come back?"

She didn't have an answer. But I did.

"I'd date you because I like you, Nadira. Not the person you thought I wanted you to be. Can't you see that?"

She nodded, tears brimming in her eyes.

"Then stop counting yourself out of something before it even has a chance to start."

Her lips trembled, and I just wanted to kiss them, to still them and make the tears go away.

"Nadira," I breathed.

She closed her eyes at the sound of her name and asked, "What about the lie? You said it made me ugly."

My chest physically ached at the reminder of what she'd done to me. I'd always been my real self with her, telling her things I hardly told anyone else. "I said that because I was hurt," I admitted, waiting until she opened those beautiful black orbs to me. "But watching you walk away again, would hurt even more."

She bit her lip, and when she spoke, her voice broke. "I don't know what to do."

My eyes flicked from hers to her perfectly full lips. "I have an idea."

FIFTY-THREE

NADIRA

MY BREATH HITCHED, and my voice came out a whisper as I asked, "What is that?"

In response, he closed the gap between us and covered my mouth with his own. His hand gripped the nape of my neck, his fingers tangling into the curls at the base of my head like he had before.

My entire body responded, leaning into the hardness of his chest, the softness of his kiss. His mouth tasted sweet, but his touch sent shivers through me. Breathing didn't seem necessary now, like all my life I'd been settling for oxygen instead of Apollo.

Tilting his head to the side, he deepened our kiss, and my hands moved of their own accord, circling around the breadth of his muscular shoulders. His broad hand flattened on my hip and moved to my thigh, which he hooked behind my knee to pull us closer together.

My heart stumbled and my stomach heated and feelings in me awakened that I'd never felt before. Kissing Apollo was a frenzy, a battle of want and need, savoring and consumption. I could have spent hours, days, in his embrace and still not have enough.

"Nadira," he breathed my name, pulling apart and resting his forehead on mine. "Date me."

His words caught me so off guard, I would have taken a step back if I weren't already against the wall. If my thigh wasn't in his hand. But his body enveloped mine, kept us in our own space. In this world where his touch sent shivers down my spine and his words commanded my heart.

"What?" I asked, my breath still coming in short gasps.

His jaw ticked as he nodded. "I want to know *you*. The real you, not the one you always try to hide."

"What if..." I took a breath, biting my swollen bottom lip. "What if you don't like what you find?"

A small smirk formed on his perfect lips. "What if I do?"

I couldn't help a smile of my own. Or the heat creeping up my neck.

His lips pressed against my grin, and he said, "Is that a yes?"

I kissed him back and said, "That's a definitely."

FIFTY-FOUR

APOLLO

MOM and I sat in the hotel dining room, eating our breakfasts surrounded by other guests. Some ready for the day with their newspapers, others in pajamas, and even more trying to get their children to eat more than just syrup-soaked waffles.

She smiled across the table at me. "Will you come home for spring break?"

I nodded. Although Nadira and I hadn't even had our first date yet, I knew she'd be gone to Cambridge with her math teacher and Regina for a research convention. Plus, going home would be better than staying in the dorms like I had over Christmas break. That place was practically a ghost town over the holidays.

"Good." She tucked her napkin in her lap. "You *should* come home. And the summer?"

Cutting my sausage with a fork, I said, "We have basic training for six weeks. But after that I can."

She nodded, her eyes falling slightly at the mention of military training.

I set my fork down, knowing I needed to say this. The military was the one thing Mom and I hadn't broached the entire time we'd been together. "Mom, I know you don't want me to join the Air Force, but you don't understand. I *have* to."

Her eyebrows drew together, and her hand stilled over her plate. "You have to? Why?"

"It's hard to explain."

"Try me."

I looked over my shoulder at the coffee pots. One had a slow drip that seemed to echo in my ears. "It's the one place I've felt at home since I left."

Setting her silverware down, she wrapped her arms around herself.

"I know that my life may eventually be put at risk, Mom, but my life's at risk every time I get in the car. Every time I walk on campus. I don't know if you've seen, but terrorists don't just live overseas.

I want to choose how I spend my life—and give it a meaningful way to end if it comes to that."

Her breath came shakily, but she slowly nodded and met my eyes. "Sometimes it's hard to admit you're a man and not my baby boy."

"Sometimes it's hard for me too," I admitted. "There's been more than one time this year I've wished I could just pick up the phone and call you."

Reaching across the table, she put her hand on mine and said, "I promise, I will always be here when you need me from here on out. No matter what."

I smiled at her, feeling the weight of a year slowly lifting off my shoulders.

FIFTY-FIVE

NADIRA

MY PHONE WAS PROPPED on my dresser in a video call with my friends while I finished getting ready for my very first date with Apollo. My hands were shaking as I worked the mascara wand through my eyelashes. I capped it and shook out my wrists, breathing deeply.

Des said, "Remember, you have nothing to be worried about. He fell in love with you. And he forgave you."

Cori nodded emphatically. "I can't believe he was making out with you where anyone could have walked by!"

Adriel smirked. "I can."

Faith nodded. "Tonight's going to go great. Do you know what he has planned?"

I shook my head. "I texted him to ask, but I'm still completely in the dark. I'm going to wear sneakers just in case we're going to be doing something more active."

Des waggled her eyebrows. "You won't need sneakers for that."

My cheeks instantly heated. "Stop it!" The girls cracked up laughing, and I said, "Ha ha. Laugh at the girl who barely got her first kiss."

Des rested her chin in her hand. "I wish my first kiss would have been like that. Mine was so... sloppy."

"Ew," Faith said.

"His tongue was like..." She gestured at her entire face. "Everywhere. Like an eager little puppy."

"Okay, I'm vomiting in my mouth now," I muttered.

Des smirked. "Don't worry, I've gotten better guys since then."

Cori snorted. "When is he coming anyway? You're still getting ready, so... another hour?"

I glared Cori, who was still chuckling at her own joke. "I'll have you know, he's supposed to be here in thirty minutes, but since he values punctuality like I do, he'll probably arrive in twenty."

Adriel giggled. "Sounds like a match made in heaven."

I crossed my fingers, holding them in front of the camera. "Here's to hoping."

Faith said, "Promise you'll text us right after and tell us how it goes?"

"Girl, you know the group chat's going to be blowing up the second I get home." I smiled and shook my head. A notification slid down my phone. "That's him."

Apollo: Can't wait to see you.

I grinned and read them the text.

Cori raised her eyebrows. "Texting you thirty minutes early? He's a keeper."

I grinned. "I think so too." I waved at the camera before ending the call and taking a few deep breaths. Not hyperventilating was a full-time endeavor at the moment.

FIFTY-SIX

APOLLO

I SET my phone down and checked my appearance in the mirror over my desk while Josh and Carrie battled it out on Call of Duty.

I had to look perfect for my first real date with Nadira. I hadn't been sure what to wear, so I took a few options to the retirement home and had Aunt Tilly help me pick. She'd smiled especially big at the dark green button-up, so I paired that with a white T-shirt and khakis. I hoped Nadira would like it too.

Josh crooned, "It's his first date with my sloppy seconds."

Both Carrie and I glared at him. Carrie whacked his shoulder with the back of her hand.

He lifted his hands, leaving his controller in his lap. "Only joking."

"Uh huh," Carrie said. Took the words right out of my mouth.

I looked back in the mirror, swiping my fingers through the extra growth at the top of my head.

"You look great," Josh said.

That was my sign to stop fidgeting. I turned toward them. "This is it."

Carrie shook her head, grinning. "This is only the beginning."

FIFTY-SEVEN

NADIRA

CARVER YELLED UP THE STAIRS, "Dira! Ya boy's here!"

I shook my head with a small smile on my lips. I liked the sound of that.

I started down the stairs, straining my ears to hear what my family was saying to Apollo. They'd been almost as excited to see him as I was.

Dad was asking him something about intramural basketball—a pretty safe topic—when I reached the living room.

Mom looked toward me, and Apollo followed her gaze. The second he saw me, he stood from the chair. I drank him in, a thirsty woman longing for every sip. He had on these khaki pants that hugged his thighs without being too tight and a mossy-green shirt rolled around his taut forearms. His hair was a little darker with a slick of gel, but it was his eyes that captivated me.

He looked at me like I was incredible. Like I was *beautiful*.

"Hi," I breathed.

"Hey, Dir." His lips spread into a grin, showing his straight white teeth. This was the guy picking me up for a date? I could hardly believe it. But he walked toward me, extending his hand. "Ready to go?"

"Definitely." I easily slipped my fingers through his, feeling both a tingle of excitement and comfort like I'd never known.

I could feel my family's eyes on us, so I waved at them, and Dad said in a British accent, "Remember, Dir." He tapped his forehead.

I gave him a wink. I remembered our father-daughter "date," but I didn't think he had anything to be worried about. Apollo had never been anything but kind to me.

"Have her home by nine," Dad said.

Mom chuckled, shaking her head. "Eleven."

Dad rolled his eyes. "Nine, eleven, whatever. Just *be safe*."

I shuddered at the words. Any time a parent

said "be safe" in regard to a date, it was super cringey.

"We will," Apollo promised, then began leading me toward the door. I couldn't wait to see what we'd do.

FIFTY-EIGHT

APOLLO

MY HEART BEAT fast as she walked with me down the sidewalk. I couldn't believe I was holding Nadira's hand. That I was getting to take her on a real date.

She'd worn this adorable dress that I knew would be soft under my fingertips and leggings that clung to all the curves of her legs. They should be outlawed, the way she wore them. And then her shoes—white sneakers—added sass to her outfit that was so her it made me want to burst.

I reached for the handle on the passenger side of the car and opened it for her.

She smiled up at me, saying, "Thanks," before getting in.

God, her smile made my insides melt. The fact

that I'd been the one to put it there made it even better.

"Are you in?" I asked.

She nodded, and I shut the door before walking to my side of the car. I could feel her eyes on me. It made me feel bolder, braver than I'd felt before, and I got in my side of the car.

"So are you going to tell me what we're doing?" she asked.

I chuckled. "What if I want it to be a surprise?"

"I can be surprised now," she argued, making me laugh more.

"First, I'm hungry," I said. "Can I take you to dinner?"

"Sure?" She shifted in her seat, seeming uncomfortable.

My hand fell from the gear shift. "You don't want to eat?"

"That's not it. It's just—" She shook her head, clearly warring with herself. "Eating is fine. Where are we going?"

I turned toward her in the seat, not giving up. "What is it?"

She looked up as if rolling her eyes at herself. "It's going to sound pathetic."

"Try me," I argued.

"Fine." She let out a sigh. "I don't like eating in front of people. It makes me feel fat."

"You are fat," I said.

Her mouth fell open, and she reached for the handle. "Seriously? All this effort just to insult me?"

"Wait! Wait, I just... you say 'fat' like it's a bad thing?"

She slowed, her hand still on the handle. "It is, according to ninety-nine percent of the human population." She stared petulantly at me, ready for a fight. But I wasn't backing down.

"Why?" I demanded. "I love your curves. Why be ashamed of them?"

Her mouth opened and closed.

"Exactly," I said. "There's no reason."

She glanced at her lap, unconvinced.

I reached for her hand, wanting her to understand how serious I was. "I understand why you kept the secret—but if we want our relationship to work, we have to be the real us, always."

She bit her lip, nodding, then squeezed my hand. "I want you to know. I was always myself with you."

My eyebrows drew together, my body rebelling against what seemed like a lie. "How?"

"It was like the photo gave me the courage to

show you who I was underneath it all. I didn't have to compensate for my looks or make up for my brains." Her words were quiet. "In some ways, it's the most me I've ever been."

At her admission, I found myself wanting to protect her all over again. I reached out and cupped her cheek with my hand. She leaned into it slightly, closing her eyes.

I smiled softly at her. "No more hiding."

Blinking her big eyes open at me, she said, "I promise."

"Good." I shifted the car into gear. "We're eating."

She snorted. "And here I thought I was the stubborn one."

I glanced over at her, grinning. "Maybe you've met your match."

She smiled at that, another win for me, and I took off down the road, heading toward my favorite restaurant in the area, Seaton Bakery. I'd even talked to Gayle and Chris, and they agreed to decorate a table with a votive candle and a flower just for us.

It was a little cheesy and over the top, but when you meet a girl like Nadira, you pull out all the stops.

Sitting this close to her in the car was hard, because all I wanted to do was recreate our kiss from yesterday, but I held her hand instead. Our intertwined fingers rested in her full lap. I loved how the softness of her body met the firmness of mine. Loved how her shape molded to mine.

"How was Parents' Weekend?" she asked.

"It was great." I smiled over at her. "Thanks for that, by the way." Just another thing to love about her—how she'd brought my mom and me back together. Who knew how long it would have taken without Nadira. I rubbed my thumb over the back of her hand, facing the road again. "We got a good visit in with Aunt Tilly, I got to take her to my favorite restaurants, and we had breakfast this morning before she had to get to the airport."

"That's awesome," she said happily. "Will your dad get to come visit sometime?"

I shrugged. "Maybe. He has a business retreat later in the year a few hours away from here. You should meet him—I think he'd like you."

Her small smile warmed my heart from the inside out. "That sounds fun."

"I hope your parents liked me," I said. I couldn't imagine how difficult dating Nadira would be if her mom and dad didn't approve.

"Of course they did," she said. "Did you see the way my mom was grinning at you? And if my dad saw you open the door for me, he's already head over heels."

I chuckled. "I didn't do it to impress him. I did it because that's what you deserve."

"Oh, stop it," she said, rolling her head toward me.

"Stop what?" I asked.

Her smile was soft as she said, "Being so perfect."

"For you?" I smiled back at her. "I'll never stop."

FIFTY-NINE

NADIRA

THE STROKE of his thumb was sending the butterflies in my stomach wild, not to mention the way he smiled at me like I was the beautiful girl I'd always dreamed of being. I tried to keep my eyes on the road ahead of us, but my gaze kept sneaking over to Apollo.

His profile was just as beautiful as seeing him straight on, with his angular nose, full lips, and the chiseled edges of his jaw.

He glanced my way, catching me staring, but only smiled slightly and squeezed my hand.

Was this what dating felt like? Was this what being in love did to people? It was like the first time I'd jumped from a high dive, standing on the edge of the board, both nervous and excited, knowing once I jumped, I could never go back.

The farther we drove, the closer we got to Seaton, and I wondered where he could be taking me. I only knew of one restaurant there, Seaton Bakery. I loved the place, but as someone from out of town, he'd probably never heard of it.

But the roads became familiar, and soon we pulled into the bakery's parking lot.

My mouth fell open. "No way."

"What?" he asked nervously. "You don't like this place?"

"Are you kidding?" I said. "I love it!" I reached for my door, but he held on to my hand.

"Let me get it."

"You don't have to. My dad isn't watching anymore."

His lips quirked into a crooked smile. "Just one of the benefits of dating a southern boy." He let go of my hand and got out of the car, and man, if I had trouble not staring before...

The way Apollo walked was full of purpose and power. Even under the button up and white T-shirt, I could see the flow of his muscles. The strength of his stance.

Too soon, he reached my door and opened it. (I

could have watched him walk all day.) Taking my hand, he helped me out of the car and didn't let go even as we walked into the bakery. But instead of going toward the counter where we were supposed to order, he walked toward the dining area.

"Wait," I said, tugging him gently toward the cash register. "They don't have servers here."

With a coy smile, he shook his head. "I have something better planned."

It was then I saw the corner booth, covered in a white tablecloth, a vase of flowers and a flickering candle on top. It was so different from the rest of the casual seating, but so special I covered my heart with my hand. "This is for me?"

He nodded, leading me that way. "Of course."

I slid into a chair, and he sat across from me. Thank goodness, because this way I had a better view of his gorgeous face without twisting my neck throughout dinner.

"How are we going to order though?" I asked.

He grinned and lifted his chin toward the guy in an apron walking toward us. I recognized him as Gayle's husband. But he always stayed in the kitchen, hardly ever handling customers. Gayle did that. How had Apollo gotten him out of the kitchen?

"Hi, you two," he said, grinning. "What can I get you?"

Apollo smiled back and gave him his order. I watched the interaction, in awe. What had he done to convince them to do all of this? I needed answers. But I wouldn't get them until I ordered, so I got my usual and sat back.

"I'm impressed," I said.

For the first time, I noticed a dimple in Apollo's right cheek. It was shallow, but there, and oh-so endearing. "What can I say?" he said. "I've got friends in low places."

"Quoting country songs?" I teased. "How very Texan of you."

"It comes out from time to time." He leaned in, elbows on the table, and despite having a dozen people in the bakery, it felt like we were the only two there in our own special world. (Now, that was an aeronautical phenomenon that should be studied.)

I put my hand above my eyes, pretending to look for something.

"What?" Apollo asked.

"Oh, you know, just looking for the sky-writing plane or a dozen roses to appear out of thin air. You know, the usual from Mr. Perfect."

He chuckled. "I don't want to be Mr. Perfect."

I raised my eyebrows. "Why not?"

He reached across the table and took my hands. "I just want to be Mr. Good Enough for a girl like you."

SIXTY

APOLLO

I LOVED the white patches on Nadira's skin that showed color when she blushed. It was one of my favorite things about her. That and the way she smiled at me like I personally hung the moon.

Eating supper with her felt just as natural as breathing, and I could hardly believe there had been a time when we didn't know each other. When we didn't talk or laugh or joke or simply sit together to pass the time.

The flame of the candle was low to the melted wax when we finished eating, and I asked, "Are you ready for destination number two?"

"There's more?" She perked up. "What could be better than cupcakes and iced coffee though?"

I smiled, thinking about what I had planned next. "I have a few ideas."

"Let's see them" she said.

I got up, leaving money on the table for the food and then led her out of the bakery. The sun had already set, leaving the sky full of shades of indigo. Glancing up, I could see a few pinpricks of stars, even with the light pollution in town.

I let Nadira into the passenger side and then got in, reaching for her hand. She laced her fingers through mine like that was exactly where they belonged. If all we ever did was hold hands, I swear, I'd die a happy man.

She settled into her seat, shimmying her shoulders into the seat back, and it was the most adorable thing I'd ever seen. Each second I spent with her, I discovered more things to love.

We reached the small parking lot I'd discovered on what was one of the absolute worst days of my life. Today, I was changing that memory for good.

I got out of the car, opening her door for her. Then I went to the trunk and pulled out a couple of massive blankets and a body pillow.

Taking all the items in, she said, "We're stargazing?"

"I want to see it through your eyes."

Her smile was brighter than the moonlight bouncing off the ocean, and I instantly knew this had been a good idea. I hoped she would like the surprise that came next...

We walked toward the shore, tracing the same steps I had taken that day when everything went wrong. But coming here with her was like therapy—erasing the old memories and replacing them with something better. Something purer.

In the sand, she kicked off her tennis shoes and peeled her socks away from her feet. I did the same, then we walked hand in hand until we found a space where we were close to the water but far enough away we wouldn't get caught in an extra strong wave.

I breathed deeply, inhaling the salty air and a hint of her perfume. She smelled like heaven—with a hint of coconut and springtime flowers.

"It's peaceful here," she said, following my gaze over the shore.

I flicked my eyes back to her. She was a million times better to look at, with her shining eyes and the hopeful smile on her lips. I spread out the first blanket and carefully placed the pillow where our heads would be. She squatted down, lying atop the spread, and I hurried to be next to her, eager to feel the heat coming off her body against the cool night air.

I covered us with the other blanket, creating our own cocoon against the cold, against the world.

Nadira reached up, pointing. "The Little Dipper."

I followed her finger with my eyes. "That was fast."

"I've had practice," she said, swinging her hand farther to the right. "That's Cassiopeia."

"All I see is Orion's Belt," I admitted.

"Newb." She chuckled. "I'll teach you."

I rolled to my side, facing her. "I'm looking forward to it."

With a smile on her face, she turned to me too. "Thank you...for the best date ever."

My heart lurched. "I'm only giving you what you deserve, baby. Surely you know that."

She blinked, shielding her emotions, but I reached out and brushed her cheek with my fingertips. "Why are you hiding?"

Her eyes were vulnerable as she turned them on me. "I just never would have thought that anything like this was possible. Between you and me."

I drew my fingers from her cheek to her shoulder and down to her hand where I laced our fingers together. "Me neither," I admitted. "Not because of the picture you sent me, but because from the first email, I felt like we clicked. I've never had this kind of connection with anyone else. Can you feel it?"

Her words came out a whisper. "I do."

I leaned in and kissed her lips, softly, for just a moment. "I know we did what we could to mess it up, but I feel like I'm exactly where I'm meant to be, out here with you."

Her eyes searched mine, seeking the truth I felt with every breath.

I rolled to my back and pointed to the spot in the sky I'd memorized. At the twinkling light I'd purchased and specially named. "Do you see that star?"

She scooted close to me and looked up my arm to the point of my finger. "The one that's a little blue?"

"That's the one," I said. I reached into my pocket and got out my phone, went to the certificate of ownership, and passed it to her.

SIXTY-ONE

NADIRA

I SQUINTED at the brightness of his screen, at the words I read there.

This star belongs to Apollo Banks and Nadira Harris. It's official name is:

Nadira.

There were signatures at the bottom and a website to look up for more information. But I couldn't help staring at the name.

He'd put me in the sky, right next to the moon.

"Look at the stars," he said softly. "They don't worry about which one is brighter. All they do is shine."

No one had ever gotten me a gift like this— something so thoughtful and meaningful. "Apollo," I breathed. Moisture pooled in my eyes and slid down my cheeks, but instead of the devastated tears I'd been shedding the last several weeks, these were tears of joy.

He brushed away a tear. "You, Nadira, are just like that star. You've always been shining, and now, in case you ever doubt yourself, you can see it in the sky."

Overwhelmed with emotion, I pressed my tear-soaked lips to his. "I love it." But those words weren't enough. "It might be crazy to say, but I love *you*." I did. Apollo was right. Something about the two of us felt right in a way I'd never felt before. Like we were the answer to an equation that always existed but had only just been discovered.

The grin that grew on his face was genuine, just like everything about him. "I love you, too, baby."

Blanketed by the stars and warm under our covers, I closed the small distance between us and pressed my lips to his. His breath spread across my cheeks, enveloping me in him and him in me.

His tongue teased the edges of my lips and tangled with mine, sending shivers down my spine and heat pooling in my stomach. When his lips broke from mine, they found a new home on my cheeks, the sensitive shell of my ear, my neck, my collarbone.

Our bodies moved under the blankets, gripping, holding, pulling, trying harder and harder to get closer than we already were.

My breath came in pants, blending with the husky moans coming from deep in his throat.

I felt him through his pants, pressing into my waist, awakening sensations I didn't know I could feel, and I realized I wanted it all with Apollo. Cuddling on the couch for movies. Talking on the phone and sending goodnight texts. The physical things that made my stomach swoop and my heart beat faster.

Apollo was mine, and in that moment, and every moment after, I was his.

SIXTY-TWO

NADIRA

I HELD my phone to my ear as I drove to school with my brothers in the back seat. "Are you sure you can't skip going to MIT over spring break?" Apollo teased, airport sounds in the background. His own flight was leaving this morning, and mine was set to depart after school.

"Only if you agree not to go to Texas," I retorted. "I'm going to miss you."

In the back seat, Carver muttered, "You two are worse than Terrell and his new girlfriend."

Terrell and I both told him to shush.

On the phone, Apollo said, "Are you sure your parents are okay with me picking you up from the airport?"

"Yes," I said, "But...."

"Oh no... but what?" he said.

"My friends demanded they also greet me at the airport. They said it should be a new Curvy Girl Club tradition to see each other after flights away."

"And you're sure guys aren't allowed in that club?" he asked suggestively.

I laughed out loud. "For the millionth time, it's girls only."

"Uh huh." The academy approached in my windshield, and I turned into the parking lot. "We just got to school."

"That's okay. I should be boarding here soon."

But neither of us hung up as I parked and my brothers got out of the car. In the privacy of my vehicle, I said, "Text me when you get there?"

"Absolutely. And I'll call you tonight, okay?"

"Are you sure?" I asked. "Your family's going to want to catch up."

"And? I've had nineteen years with them and a month of being your boyfriend. They can miss me for twenty minutes."

I smiled at his words, at the way he made butterflies take flight. In the background, I heard someone on speakers make the call for his flight.

"I love you," I said.

"I love you, too." The emotion was clear in his

voice. He meant what he said, and I'd never stop being grateful for that. "Talk to you soon, baby."

"Talk to you soon."

I hung up and looked at my phone in my hand. Was it bad that I already wanted to text him? That I missed his voice only seconds after hearing it?

A knock sounded on my window, and I looked over to see Adriel and Faith. They made kissing faces at me, and I rolled my eyes, getting out of the car. "You two are ridiculous."

"And you're in love," Adriel sang.

Faith laughed. "Looks like you won our New Year's resolution."

"Your turn's next," I reminded her, hitching my bag over my shoulder. "You only have to get kissed before the end of the year, not before me."

"True," she agreed.

We walked toward the building. As we approached the courtyard, I saw Regina getting out of her mom's car, struggling with the extra duffel bag that was clearly meant for tonight.

I glanced at my friends and said, "I'll catch up with you later."

"Sure," Faith said.

"See you at lunch," Adriel added.

I waved and hurried to help Regina, who was at

risk of dropping all the contents in her half-zipped backpack. "Let me get this," I said, reaching for the duffel bag.

"Thanks," she said, then realizing it was me, she stiffened. "I can get it."

"I know." I picked up the bag anyway, almost staggering under its weight. I lifted the strap across my body for extra support and continued walking toward the school.

"Thanks," she muttered.

"No problem."

We reached the steps, and I took them quietly beside her. Well, as quietly as I could while huffing for breath. (Did I mention her bag was heavy?)

At the top of the stairs, I paused for a rest, and Regina turned toward me. "Why are you being nice to me?" she hissed so the students walking by couldn't overhear.

I shrugged, looking toward the sky, but that just made the strap of her bag dig even deeper into my shoulder. "Why do I need to have a motive? Can't I just help one of my classmates?"

She gave me a skeptical look.

I set down the bag, knowing this was going to take a little while. "Look," I said. "I don't want to be your enemy." At her look of surprise, I explained, "Don't worry, I'm not all that keen on being your friend either. But I don't want to waste my time on worrying what you think about me or trying to be better than you. I just want to be me."

She studied me for a moment. "So you're calling a truce?"

I shrugged. "Something like that."

Seeming satisfied, she walked toward the front doors, and I picked up her bag, doing the same.

"For the record though," I said, a teasing lilt to my voice, "I would have won that sudden death."

"Oh shut up," she sighed but let out a quiet laugh. "You're the worst."

"I'll take that as a compliment."

Math class passed quickly, and then it was time for yearbook class. I made my way to my seat in Mrs. Johnston's room and fired up the computer, logging in so I'd be ready when the bell rang.

At the front of the room, Mrs. Johnston gave us a status update on the pages we had completed and then asked the editors, Isabella and Tatiana, to make the rounds and check our progress on unfinished pages.

I worked on my spread for the Mathletes, typing captions and filling in empty picture slots. Not two minutes in, I felt a presence looking over my shoulder.

I glanced up to see Tatiana peering at my screen.

"You need to be working on the 'Best of' page," she said. "I still haven't seen it, and I need to get edits in the week after spring break. Think you can finish it today?"

I closed my eyes, not wanting a fight. So, I simply said, "Okay," and opened a different tab.

Satisfied, she walked away.

The "Best of" spread stared at me from the screen. I'd put in all the photos except my own, which was in a prominent wild card position every year.

The words "Most Unique" were bold and bright, drawing my eye instantly. I'd worried over them for far too long. Why had those two words held so much power over me? I thought about Apollo and how he'd told me I was like no one else. That my uniqueness was a good thing.

I knew Tatiana and Isabella intended it as an insult, but what did the opinion of people I didn't care for matter? I'd meant what I said to Regina earlier. I was tired of worrying about what people thought of me. My friends were there for me. My family loved me. And my boyfriend had put me in the sky next to the moon.

What more could I ask for?

I went to the folder of candid photos, searching for one of me. When I didn't see one, I got out my phone and swiped through the images. I found the one I'd been looking for. It was from that day on the beach by Des's house. I grinned at the camera, gap tooth on full display, hair wild in the wind, skin contrasting black and white, and finally, I saw what Des had always wanted me to.

I saw someone beautiful. Someone unique.

Someone I *loved*.

It was about damn time.

EPILOGUE

FAITH

GREETING NADIRA at the airport after her trip to visit MIT was the most exciting thing I'd done all spring break.

Headmaster Bradford had asked my family to take in a foreign exchange student who was, as far as I could tell, a big deal. My parents had agreed to keep her information confidential, but why did it matter who they were anyway? Who cared if she was the heiress of a massive fortune or the princess of some unheard-of country? She would be in our home for nine weeks and then gone for the rest of my life.

Regardless, I'd have to greet her at the airport today like I was happy to have her here the last quarter of my senior year. I supposed I was used to being overshadowed by my four brothers. What was one more person thrown into the mix?

I walked past the empty luggage claims with Des, Cori, and Adriel, wondering when Nadira would get here to make our Curvy Girl Club complete.

I glanced around, wondering if I would see Nadira or Apollo first. He was coming to pick her up and take her on a welcome-home date.

The two of them were the cutest thing I'd ever seen, and that was saying something because all of my friends—except me, big surprise—were now in relationships. Even my friend Des, who was more committed to dating around more than any guy, had a man of the moment. It wouldn't be long before she caught some rock star's eye and lived happily ever after.

Me on the other hand? The odds of that were lower than the floor walked on.

Cori pointed up ahead where a group of people were congregating around a baggage claim. "That must be her flight."

I searched for Nadira's curly hair and quickly found it toward the back of the crowd.

Shamelessly, Des yelled, "Nadira!" at the top of her lungs.

I blushed as almost every head in the airport turned toward us, but it did the trick because Nadira saw us too. She lifted her arm in a big wave and came running toward us, wheeling a bag behind her.

"Hey!" she said, then wrapped us in a hug as wide as her arms would go. "I told Apollo to come in half an hour so we could have some girl time. I'm dying for a smoothie."

"Yay!" I said. I definitely needed some time with my girls.

"I love that idea." Des grinned. "My treat."

Cori took Nadira's bag, and I held her purse as we walked toward the smoothie stand on the opposite side of the terminal.

"How was MIT?" I asked. "As amazing as you remembered it?"

"Better." She breathed a happy sigh. "I even got to meet some of my future professors and ask them questions about their research and how it's being applied. I feel like I'm really going to be able to make a difference there."

"Awesome!" Cori said. "And what about Regina? Was she okay?"

"Actually..." Nadira shrugged. "We had some time to talk, actually I think Mr. Aris sent us off together on purpose, and I think she doesn't totally hate my guts anymore. I'm just sad we didn't make amends earlier. Would have made Mathletes a lot more comfortable this year for sure."

I nodded, but I didn't really know how that felt. I didn't have any enemies, and before the Curvy Girl Club 2.0, I didn't really have any friends either. Unless you counted my grandma. She was the best, but she couldn't exactly put on a uniform and come to school with me either.

A few girls walked by us, rolling their suitcases behind them, talking about Boston, and I couldn't help but be jealous. I'd lived in California my whole life and hardly traveled anywhere else. My dad said he didn't see the point since we had mountains and beaches and desert within a day's drive, but I longed to see the world. For now, I could settle on asking my friends what they'd seen.

"Tell me about the flight," I said to Nadira. "How was it?"

"It was great," Nadira said. "A little turbulence over the Rockies, but other than that, all good."

"What does turbulence feel like?" I asked.

Nadira shuddered. "Like the plane is falling out of the sky."

My stomach turned. "But it's not, right?"

"Nope." She tilted her head. "Tell me about your spring break. All of you. What did I miss?"

I nodded toward Des. "She's dating a DJ who played at Spike this week."

Des winked. "And he is just as hot as his tracks."

Cori snorted. "The cruise with Ryker's family was great. You know, aside from family dinners with his parents. I don't think it could get any more awkward than it was."

Nadira frowned. "Is his dad still mad at him for the football game?"

I cringed, remembering Ryker's dad fighting to get into the announcer's stand when Ryker took the mic at homecoming and apologized to Cori in front of the entire town.

"Oh yeah." Cori shook her head. "He says that I make Ryker do things he wouldn't normally do. Not to my face, of course."

"Um..." Adriel said. "Ryker was a bully. That's kind of a good thing that he's behaving differently."

I agreed, but Cori just shrugged.

Adriel said, "Cancun was great. Mom and Ted made plans to go back for their five-year anniversary and have a vow renewal. And Carter and his grandma *loved* it."

I smiled at the thought of Carter's grandma on

the beach, wearing a fabulous red bathing suit and large sunglasses.

"And you?" Nadira asked.

I groaned. "Grandma and I finished a needlepoint, and the floors in my house are clean for the mystery guest."

"Still no word?" Nadira asked.

"Nope." I glanced at my watch. "I should know in about two hours."

"Text us," she said.

I promised I would.

We finally reached the smoothie stand and put in our orders. As we stood around one of the tall tables, taking sips and catching up, I couldn't help but feel a sense of despair. We had nine weeks left of our senior year.

Nine weeks with my best friends.

Nine weeks before I joined the Peace Corps and went to a faraway destination.

Nine weeks before I graduated high school without ever having a boyfriend or any romantic interest to speak of.

Nadira looked at a spot over my shoulder and broke into one of the biggest smiles I'd ever seen her have. "Apollo!" she cried. She moved around Des and ran to him.

He jogged toward her and caught her, spinning her around in a hug and kissing her slowly.

The love between them was so real, so raw, I looked away.

Adriel let out a dreamy sigh. "They're so adorable together."

I agreed. "Beyond cute."

Des gripped my hand, a plotting grin on her face and a dangerous spark in her eyes. "You're next."

Want to see the special gift Apollo gives Nadira before she leaves for MIT? Check out the bonus story today!

Read Faith's story in Curvy Girls Can't Date Princes! You'll love sing Faith get her very own fairytale ending!

EPILOGUE

FAITH

Greeting Nadira at the airport after her trip to visit MIT was the most exciting thing I'd done all spring break.

Headmaster Bradford had asked my family to take in a foreign exchange student who was, as far as I could tell, a big deal. My parents had agreed to keep her information confidential, but why did it matter who they were anyway? Who cared if she was the heiress of a massive fortune or the princess of some unheard-of country? She would be in our home for nine weeks and then gone for the rest of my life.

Regardless, I'd have to greet her at the airport today like I was happy to have her here the last quarter of my senior year. I supposed I was used to being overshadowed by my four brothers. What was one more person thrown into the mix?

I walked past the empty luggage claims with Des, Cori, and Adriel, wondering when Nadira would get here to make our Curvy Girl Club complete.

I glanced around, wondering if I would see Nadira or Apollo first. He was coming to pick her up and take her on a welcome-home date.

The two of them were the cutest thing I'd ever seen, and that was saying something because all of my friends—except me, big surprise—were now in relationships. Even my friend Des, who was more committed to dating around more than any guy, had a man of the moment. It wouldn't be long before she caught some rock star's eye and lived happily ever after.

Me on the other hand? The odds of that were lower than the floor walked on.

Cori pointed up ahead where a group of people were congregating around a baggage claim. "That must be her flight."

I searched for Nadira's curly hair and quickly found it toward the back of the crowd.

Shamelessly, Des yelled, "Nadira!" at the top of her lungs.

I blushed as almost every head in the airport turned toward us, but it did the trick because Nadira saw us too. She lifted her arm in a big wave and came running toward us, wheeling a bag behind her.

"Hey!" she said, then wrapped us in a hug as wide as her arms would go. "I told Apollo to come in half an hour so we could have some girl time. I'm dying for a smoothie."

"Yay!" I said. I definitely needed some time with my girls.

"I love that idea." Des grinned. "My treat."

Cori took Nadira's bag, and I held her purse as we walked toward the smoothie stand on the opposite side of the terminal.

"How was MIT?" I asked. "As amazing as you remembered it?"

"Better." She breathed a happy sigh. "I even got to meet some of my future professors and ask them questions about their research and how it's being applied. I feel like I'm really going to be able to make a difference there."

"Awesome!" Cori said. "And what about Regina? Was she okay?"

"Actually..." Nadira shrugged. "We had some time to talk, actually I think Mr. Aris sent us off together on purpose, and I think she doesn't totally hate my guts anymore. I'm just sad we didn't make amends earlier. Would have made Mathletes a lot more comfortable this year for sure."

I nodded, but I didn't really know how that felt. I didn't have any enemies, and before the Curvy Girl Club 2.0, I didn't really have any friends either. Unless you counted my grandma. She was the best, but she couldn't exactly put on a uniform and come to school with me either.

A few girls walked by us, rolling their suitcases behind them, talking about Boston, and I couldn't help but be jealous. I'd lived in California my whole life and hardly traveled anywhere else. My dad said he didn't see the point since we had mountains and beaches and desert within a day's drive, but I longed to see the world. For now, I could settle on asking my friends what they'd seen.

"Tell me about the flight," I said to Nadira. "How was it?"

"It was great," Nadira said. "A little turbulence over the Rockies, but other than that, all good."

"What does turbulence feel like?" I asked.

Nadira shuddered. "Like the plane is falling out of the sky."

My stomach turned. "But it's not, right?"

"Nope." She tilted her head. "Tell me about your spring break. All of you. What did I miss?"

I nodded toward Des. "She's dating a DJ who played at Spike this week."

Des winked. "And he is just as hot as his tracks."

Cori snorted. "The cruise with Ryker's family was great. You know, aside from family dinners with his parents. I don't think it could get any more awkward than it was."

Nadira frowned. "Is his dad still mad at him for the football game?"

I cringed, remembering Ryker's dad fighting to get into the announcer's stand when Ryker took the mic at homecoming and apologized to Cori in front of the entire town.

"Oh yeah." Cori shook her head. "He says that I make Ryker do things he wouldn't normally do. Not to my face, of course."

"Um..." Adriel said. "Ryker was a bully. That's kind of a good thing that he's behaving differently."

I agreed, but Cori just shrugged.

Adriel said, "Cancun was great. Mom and Ted

made plans to go back for their five-year anniversary and have a vow renewal. And Carter and his grandma *loved* it."

I smiled at the thought of Carter's grandma on the beach, wearing a fabulous red bathing suit and large sunglasses.

"And you?" Nadira asked.

I groaned. "Grandma and I finished a needlepoint, and the floors in my house are clean for the mystery guest."

"Still no word?" Nadira asked.

"Nope." I glanced at my watch. "I should know in about two hours."

"Text us," she said.

I promised I would.

We finally reached the smoothie stand and put in our orders. As we stood around one of the tall tables, taking sips and catching up, I couldn't help but feel a sense of despair. We had nine weeks left of our senior year.

Nine weeks with my best friends.

Nine weeks before I joined the Peace Corps and went to a faraway destination.

Nine weeks before I graduated high school without ever having a boyfriend or any romantic interest to speak of.

Nadira looked at a spot over my shoulder and broke into one of the biggest smiles I'd ever seen her have. "Apollo!" she cried. She moved around Des and ran to him.

He jogged toward her and caught her, spinning her around in a hug and kissing her slowly.

The love between them was so real, so raw, I looked away.

Adriel let out a dreamy sigh. "They're so adorable together."

I agreed. "Beyond cute."

Des gripped my hand, a plotting grin on her face and a dangerous spark in her eyes. "You're next."

Want to see the special gift Apollo gives Nadira before she leaves for MIT? Check out the bonus story today!

Read Faith's story in Curvy Girls Can't Date Princes! You'll love sing Faith get her very own fairytale ending!

I can't believe this story is over. In many ways, it's been the most difficult book I've written in the Curvy Girl Club. As you know, Nadira really struggled with self-esteem, more so than the other curvy girls I've written. I know everyone loves to read about a strong, confident plus-sized woman, but the truth is that's not always reality. In a society that values thinness above many other attributes, it is hard to be a self-loving curvy girl.

Not only does Nadira contend with her size, she also has a skin condition that makes her stand out more, along with being a major math genius. Although I never had vitiligo, I related to Nadira more than is truly comfortable to admit.

In my hometown, athletes were treated like

royalty. Although I played sports, I was never the best, and I was always more academically inclined. No matter how well I did in school, it always felt like I was "less-than" others. Boys would teasingly tell me to use smaller words so they could understand.

Nadira struggled with being compared to her brothers' athletic success and the conventional beauty of other girls in school like Isabella and Tatiana. However, one of the people who judged Nadira the most was herself.

She had a mean voice in her head that said she wasn't beautiful, wasn't worthy of love. So anytime someone echoed those thoughts, it completely destroyed her. The problem is, falling in love with a nice guy doesn't take away that voice.

This isn't the story of Nadira getting a boyfriend and suddenly loving herself. It's the story of a young woman realizing how much damage that self-deprecating voice had done and working to treat herself with so much more kindness than she ever had before.

Loving yourself isn't a decision you make one day and that's it. No, loving yourself is a constant battle against the voice in your head formed from years of mean words and societal pressures. It's a commitment to choosing the way you speak to yourself and gently setting yourself on the right path when a course correction is needed.

No matter where you are on your journey, I hope you know you deserve to speak to yourself as you would your own best friend. I know you can get there, and I'll walk the journey with you.

ACKNOWLEDGMENTS

I have so many people to be thankful for! Of course, I want to thank my husband for being a partner in my home and constantly working with me in this balancing act of marriage, parenthood, business ownership, and life!

My children are huge supporters for me. They will always be my biggest priority and greatest blessing. Our nanny, Michelle, has been the best blessing over the last six months. Knowing my children are cared for and loved while I work toward my dream is the best feeling ever.

Thank you to my dear friend Sally Henson. In addition to being an incredible novelist, she's become the best sounding board and friend a girl could ask for!

Speaking of friends, thank you Annie for welcoming me to my new home state and sharing a vacation with me! I finished a draft of this story alongside the pool on vacation with her and visiting the beach with ice cream dripping down our arms was the perfect way to celebrate!

Thank you to my family, who never fails to tell a friend (or stranger) about my stories. I love you all dearly!

To my sweet Cupcakes in the readers club, you are so cherished! I love hanging out with you during our ice cream chats and seeing you all share such uplifting, body positive messages. The Curvy Girl Club has brought together so many incredible women, and I'll never be thankful enough for that.

Special thanks to Tricia Harden, who's edited more than fifteen novels for me! Working with you is such a joy, every single time. You are such a light in my life, and I hope I can meet you in person soon to give you a big hug!

Dear reader, so many people have come together to put this novel in your hands, and I hope you know how absolutely loved you are. Thank you for sharing this story with me. I hope you enjoyed every single second.

GLOSSARY

Latin Phrases

Ad Meliora: School motto meaning "toward better things."

Audentes fortuna iuvat: Motto of *Dulce Periculum* meaning "Fortune favors the bold."

Dulce Periculum: means "danger is sweet" - local secret club that performs stunts

Multum in Parvo: means "much in little"

Locations

Town Name: Emerson

Location: Halfway between Los Angeles and San Francisco

Surrounding towns: Brentwood, Seaton, Heywood

Emerson Academy: Private school Rory and Beckett attend

Brentwood Academy: Rival private school

Walden Island: Tourism island off the coast, only accessible by helicopter or ferry

Main Hangouts

Emerson Elementary Library: Where Rory tutors Anna, open to students K-7

Emerson Field: Massive park in the center of Emerson

Emerson Memorial: Local hospital

Emerson Shoppes: Shopping mall

Emerson Trails: Hiking trails in Emerson, near Emerson Field

Halfway Café: Expensive dining option in Emerson, frequented by celebrities

La La Pictures: Movie theater in Emerson

Ripe: Major health food store serving the tri-city area

Roasted: Popular coffee shop in Emerson

JJ Cleaning: Cleaning service owned by Jordan's mom

Seaton Bakery: Delicious dining and drink option in Seaton where Beckett works

Seaton Beach: Beach near Seaton – rougher than the beach near Brentwood

Seaton Pier: Fishing pier near Seaton

Spike's: Local 18-and-under club

Waldo's Diner: local diner, especially popular after sporting events

APPS

Rush+: Game app designed by Kai Rush and his father

Sermo: chat app used by private school students

IMPORTANT ENTITIES

Bhatta Productions: Production company owned by Zara's father

Brentwood Badgers: Professional football team

Heywood Market: Big ranch/distributor where everyone can purchase their meat locally

Invisible Mountains: Local major nonprofit - Callie's dad is the CEO

Dugan Industries: Owns and manages Brentwood Marina, along with other entities. Owned by Ryker Dugan's father, Trent Dugan.

ALSO BY KELSIE STELTING

The Curvy Girl Club

Curvy Girls Can't Date Quarterbacks

Curvy Girls Can't Date Billionaires

Curvy Girls Can't Date Cowboys

Curvy Girls Can't Date Bad Boys

Curvy Girls Can't Date Best Friends

Curvy Girls Can't Date Bullies

Curvy Girls Can't Dance

Curvy Girls Can't Date Soldiers

Curvy Girls Can't Date Princes

The Texas High Series

Chasing Skye: Book One

Becoming Skye: Book Two

Loving Skye: Book Three

Anika Writes Her Soldier

Abi and the Boy Next Door: Book One

Abi and the Boy Who Lied: Book Two

Abi and the Boy She Loves: Book Three

Abi: The Complete Collection

The Pen Pal Romance Series

Dear Adam

Fabio Vs. the Friend Zone

Sincerely Cinderella

The Sweet Water High Series: A Multi-Author Collaboration

Road Trip with the Enemy: A Sweet Standalone Romance

YA Contemporary Romance Anthology

The Art of Taking Chances

Nonfiction

Raising the West

ABOUT THE AUTHOR

Kelsie Stelting is a body positive romance author who writes love stories with strong characters, deep feelings, and happy endings.

She currently lives in Colorado with her high school sweetheart and three sweet boys. You can often find her writing, spending time with family, and soaking up too much sun wherever she can find it.

Visit www.kelsiestelting.com to get a free story and sign up for her readers' group!

facebook.com/kelsiesteltingcreative

twitter.com/kelsiestelting

instagram.com/kelsiestelting